The Reaping
Immortalibus Bella 2

SL Figuhr

This is a SL Figuhr Book

Published by SL Figuhr Publishing

www.slfiguhr.com
Email: info@slfiguhr.com

Follow SL Figuhr on Twitter:
https://twitter.com/SLFiguhr

Like SL Figuhr on Facebook
www.facebook.com/SLFiguhr.Author

ISBN-13: 978-0-9911498-3-4 (SL Figuhr Publishing)
ISBN-10: 0991149831
Library of Congress Control Number: 2013919780

Book / E-book cover design:
www.celairen.com
https://www.facebook.com/celairen1

Manufactured in the United States of America

Acknowledgements

Edited by:
Josephine Henke

Design by Celairen, using stock from
YorkBerlin/Shutterstock.com conrado/Shutterstock.com.

DEDICATION

To everyone who takes a chance on Indie Authors.
Thank you for reading and making it to the second book in the series.

CONTENTS

CHAPTER ONE

The little hut lay in darkness; out of the night came the snorts of the pigs and the grunts and moans of his mother and father. Nicky could hear the soft puffing breaths of his brothers and sisters as they slept beside him. He, however, lay wide awake. He waited for his parents to finish, and soon was rewarded by the snores of his father.

Nicky eased up, so as not to disturb those beside him. He scrambled into his clothes and peered over the edge of the loft to where his parents slept in their corner of the hut. Gradually, the boy eased himself down the ladder onto the dirt floor. The night was dark, the moon barely a sliver in the sky. Fine with him, he didn't have far to go.

The boy, absorbed in his work, didn't see the darker shadow slide across the entrance to hide in the blackest area in the back of the cave. Why couldn't he keep the bunnies alive long enough to discover the spark which brought them life? He had found a way to keep them calm, but they always died after he skinned them alive.

He threw the body out of the cave in frustration. Was it his choice of animal? Rabbits were jumpy, nervous creatures. He needed something bigger, a fox perhaps? It took him until nearly daybreak to complete his preparations.

Even though he was tired, Nicky raced back home. He slipped inside the hut and began his daily chores by the time the sun peeked over the horizon. His father was the first to stir, and as always was impressed with his little boy.

"You'll be a fine farmer one day, son." He ruffled the boy's hair, missing the hateful glower.

* * *

The little boy moved restlessly, his eyeballs pinging back and forth beneath his closed lids. He barely remembered the early years of his life, and this was not a memory he cared to revisit. Why should he dream of those times now? Why was he dreaming at all? He had been in the middle of something. What was it? He moved again, dream memories jumping ahead a year.

"You little freak!" His older brother burst from the bushes to grab him by the arm. "You wait'll Da hears of this! His perfect younger son!"

Terror gripped Nicky. All his plans would be messed up! They would call the village priest in to pray over him, perhaps force him to become a part of the church. "Let go!" Nicky hollered.

"Move it, freak! I knew your good-little-boy bit was fake!" His brother wrestled Nicky to the ground and tied him up with vines. "Get up!" He demanded of his little brother.

Nicky sat on the ground, winded, aching from the beating, "No. You'll be sorry! I'll make you sorry! You better let me go!"

"The only one'll be sorry is you. I knew you been hanging in the forest too much. It be forbidden for a reason; you had your head turned by the evil spirits in here. I know what to do to help."

Nicky clung to the ground, but his brother was older, bigger, and stronger. He picked the little boy up and slung him over his shoulders until Nicky tried to bite him. Then he dropped his little brother on the ground and dragged him, not caring if the little boy banged off rocks, roots, or bushes. The little boy was a scratched, filthy mess when he was hauled into the farm yard. His Ma collapsed, wailing she always knew something was wrong with her youngest. His Da refused to believe his perfect son was capable of such unspeakable things. Nicky gloated inwardly, and began to cry.

"He's always hated me, Da! He hates me 'cause I get up earlier than he do and do me chores so well." He fanned the flames, listing all the things he did so much better than his siblings. How his traps caught more game, how he tickled fish out of the creeks and ponds when others couldn't.

"He's bewitched is why, Da! The evil tempter in the forest put a spell on him! Remember just last week Widow May was found wandering around with her wits addled, talking about her lover the forest demon!"

Nicky's Ma continued to cry and yell, on her knees in the dust, rocking back and forth and pouring dirt over her hair in shame.

"For the love of the creator, woman! Cease your wailing! I need to think!" Nicky's father shouted. "We'll take him to the village priest. Will, pick out one of the shoats to give in payment, and tell Marcus he be in charge until we get back."

"No!" Nicky shrieked, "I don't need a priest! Will lies! He just wants to get rid of me!" He struggled futilely against his bonds.

It took half a day of walking to reach the outskirts of the village, and the priest's house. Nicky was a silent, seething mass by the time the three arrived. The priest listened gravely to the father's and brother's tale, and then asked the boy be stripped to search for demon marks. Will had to wrestle Nicky's clothes off as his Da was too shocked to be of much help.

He endured the priest's inspection, humiliated beyond words, vowing he would have revenge on them all. Nicky tugged his clothes back on under the all too watchful eyes of his brother

"I could find no demon mark on him," the priest said. "It is possible you have intervened in time. Still, it is a grave matter, grave indeed. Just the other week, the Widow May, was found addled in the woods, praising the dark lord, under similar circumstances."

"But can nothing be done?" Nicky's father groaned out in despair. "His Ma is beside herself with grief and worry."

"Leave him here with me. I will pray over him as I do for all those who have been brought in with this affliction. The arch-bishop is coming down to inquire into the matter. It affects more than just us; I have heard this unknown evil has spread to all the towns ringing the forest."

"How long will it be? How will we survive the coming winter if we can't harvest wood and nuts?" his Da asked.

The priest stroked his chin. "I will send word if I can when the arch-bishop comes. In the meantime, I shall give you these blessed crosses to wear when you must venture into the forest. Mind me now, do not go in too far; everything I have heard says the evil lurks in the very heart of the forest, extending its influence as the darkness spreads and retreating in the brightness of the dawn. The fringes are safe only when the sun is high."

The farmer nodded wearily, as beside him, his other son, Will, snorted in annoyance. They hung the crosses around their necks. Nicky's father's face seemed to have aged. He laid a work-rough hand on the boy's head and flinched when his son jerked his head out from underneath the touch. "May God have mercy on you, and restore you to the loving, bright boy I remember you as."

Will spat on the ground, just missing his brother's bare toes. "You little freak, I hope they beat it out of you."

It was the last Nicky saw of his family for a long time.

* * *

Betrayal floated through the mind of the dreamer. That was all people had ever done to him. But who had done it this time? Why could he not see or think?

* * *

Blackness and a searing pain, Nicky could barely open his eyes. The archbishop had been zealous in his search for any sign the little boy was infected with evil.

He had been stripped again, and even more thoroughly examined. When the second search proved futile, the older man said there were other signs, but first he had to prepare.

The archbishop stretched the little boy's arms and legs wide and chained him between two posts. He lit incense, and praying, walked around the boy. He took oils, anointed the boy all over.

"Get off me, you old goat!" Nicky cursed the man. "I told you I'm innocent! My brother hates me! He lied! He's the evil one!"

The priest only kept up his chanting and praying; it seemed to go on for endless hours. The little boy fell asleep in his chains and woke slowly to realize he barely could feel his hands or feet. Pain shot through all four of his limbs when he tried to move. Nicky gritted his teeth and moved each arm and leg at a time. They were burning now from strain and fatigue, and sweat poured off him from the effort. He passed out.

When next the boy woke, he was laying on a hard wooden bed, covered by a frayed blanket that smelled of mouse and moth and mold. Moving his limbs caused lancing bolts of needle-like pain. He was starving, and his mouth felt like desert sand in dry season.

It took the boy a long time before he could roll over and slip off the bed onto the rough stone floor. It took an equal amount of time for him to half-crawl, half-slither to the stool. The porridge was cold: a lumpy, gray congealed mess. Nicky didn't care, he scooped it up with his fingers and crammed it into his mouth. The mug of well-water helped to get the food down.

After eating, the little boy drooped to the floor, still exhausted enough to sleep. He fought against the sensation, instead trying to work his arms and legs. He managed to make them stop hurting when he heard a key in the lock. The door swung open, and the archbishop entered.

"Ah, you have eaten. We mustn't let you lose too much strength, not until I have decided whether you are pure."

"I told you my brother lies!" Nicky shouted, struggling to sit.

He yelped as a burning pain scoured his right side, dimly aware the man had struck him with a whip.

"Children must not talk unless they are answering questions! I see your parents never taught you manners. Maybe we should learn that lesson before moving forward?" The voice held cold anger.

I hate you! Nicky thought, but didn't want to know what the whip could do, so he bowed his head, shaking it.

"Excellent. I would hate to have to interrupt my search." The archbishop hauled the boy up.

Nicky struggled, trying to punch and kick but the bishop was too strong despite being an older man. Soon the boy was chained back up between the same pillars. The priest brought a stool over and placed it before the boy, arranged his robes before sitting down. The little boy felt an itch between his shoulder blades; he didn't like the man's head so close to his waist.

"I have had reports you are considered intelligent, more than others your age. I must determine to which areas this extends, for often those born of demons or demon-marked show urges beyond their years."The archbishop ignored Nicky's squalls and continued his explorations. When he was done, he dumped the little boy back in his cell.

There the boy vomited repeatedly, his whole body shaking with the pain and humiliation of being so intimately violated. He curled up into a fetal ball, vowing to find a way to kill the man. He refused to sob, though the tears leaked out all the same. He tried to stay awake so he wouldn't be surprised by the arch-bishop coming into his cell. Eventually his eyes grew heavy and he fell asleep.

* * *

Lord Nicky woke suddenly. How long had he been out? He could hear screams, shouting and pounding from behind him, so it couldn't have been long. He sat up in a rage. *They will all pay for this! Especially Rablias! Damn him!*

Where had he received the knowledge to set off something of that nature? Not from him, the boy knew; he looked down at himself and felt a cold terror. His clothes hung off his frame, his boots too big for his feet. He was a little boy again!

No, no, no! He should have had months left on the spell! Damn his acolyte! Nicky couldn't let anyone see him in this state or risk all his carefully created plans. The Advisor cast a look behind him as the door to the garden shuddered under the blows from outside. The young man who was now a little boy scrambled up, hampered by his garments. Quickly he took off the boots, rolled the pant legs and shirt sleeves up so he could move.

How dare DiJinn teach Rablias the spell...NO! Don't think it. That kind of betrayal could not be borne. If his slave had turned against his master, he wouldn't have left the little boy lying there. But when he tried to call his pet to him, there was no answer. Nicky didn't realize he was panting, gasping, feeling a compound of fear and terror, so long had it been since he experienced either.

"Get ahold of yourself! Get the hell out of here, get to the grove and become big again. There is still the army, when they get here, you can take the throne. You can't be found here like this, they'll imprison you."

He hated to be chained for any length of time. It was too forceful a reminder of the damn archbishop. He had been held for months by the religious man, forced to perform shameful acts. The man became too complaisant, and Nicky was able to free himself;

he knocked the man out with a thick piece of wood, then slaughtered him. When he left, the archbishop was scattered throughout his own dungeons in unrecognizable shreds. No servants were about, having been given the night off.

The little boy stole what jewels and coins he could find, stuffing them into a sack. He found some clothes belonging to a page and yanked them on, then finished filling the sack with food and whatever else caught his fancy. Nicky thought better of taking the arch-bishop's horse. Instead, he riled the remaining mounts up to cover his escape on a mule into the forest surrounding his home.

Nicky's bare feet slapped against the cold stone as he ran toward his chambers and the passageways that let him move about unseen. His thigh was charred where his protection from the demon was tattooed, but the protection was still there. Who had tried to remove it? Surely not DiJinn, he couldn't. It had to be Rablias, damn the man! Nicky would teach the cur the meaning of revenge. Nicky's head ached abominably, and flashbacks kept popping up and engulfing him.

* * *

The little boy shivered in his cave. At winter's onset, he'd had to sell the mule he'd stolen months ago from the arch-bishop. He had tried to eavesdrop to rumors about his former jailer while in the market, but the news was all about how the forest was becoming increasingly hazardous. There was even talk of asking the king to send troops to deal with the problem.

A draft of icy wind swirled outside the cave, making the boy's feeble fire flicker and shrink. He hissed in annoyance and laid another branch in the flames. Though he had an ax, he wasn't big or strong enough to do more than chop small limbs; deadfall proved the majority of his firewood.

Nicky crawled into the back of the cave and inspected his dwindling store of food. A few vegetables remained, and a hard heel of bread but that was all until he stole more. Even his traps hadn't netted him much game.

The next morning dawned cold and bright. It had stormed overnight, so the world looked coated in glass. Nicky was shivering uncontrollably by now. His small fire had gone out, and his fingers were so stiff and frozen he barely was able to move them. He realized dimly he was close to dying out here, but he refused to return to town.

Slowly, painfully, the boy put on every piece of clothing he had, becoming aware of steady movement in the forest outside his cave. He crawled to the entrance, glad his fire was out, so the smoke would not betray him. Nicky heard singing; he didn't understand the words, but guessed it to be Latin as it sounded churchy.

In a moment, a lean man in a woolen robe and cowl, his feet and legs wrapped in cloth, slogged through the snow mere feet from the little boy's hiding place. The man had a staff, and a rope over his shoulder tied to a deer he dragged behind him. Nicky didn't know of any monks nearby, for that's what the man reminded him of. But the man or monk had food and was therefore worth following, if only to see if he led to a better spot to hide. Nicky crept out of the cave, his sack with what remained of the archbishop's treasures over his shoulder. The monk walked for quite a while, further into the forest itself, until he came to a clearing. The monk's abode, hard to see, was built into the hillside, as was a small stable. Smoke rose from the top of the hill, and a stream ran through the clearing. Crude boards bridged the icy though unfrozen rivulet.

Nicky watched the man go about his work all morning and partially into the afternoon. He appeared to be alone as no other monks showed themselves. When it grew dark, the man disappeared inside. Nicky waited, to be sure he would not emerge. He crept closer to the hut, staying on the edges of the forest.

There was a small chicken coop; eggs, even raw, tasted like ambrosia to him now after so prolonged a span of scant rations. A goat ate hay in the stable, and though she bleated grumpily, the boy extracted a little milk from the doe. The boy stole an armful of wood from the wood pile and scurried back to his cave. In the morning, the boy returned to hide in the forest by the hut, and again he shadowed the lone monk about his daily chores. At night, Nicky crept out and stole milk and eggs.

The following day, however, the monk straightened up and

called out, “There's no need to keep hiding. You’re welcome to come in out of the cold. I won’t hurt you.”

Nicky stayed away for several days until cold and hunger drove him back. He was half-starved, but still ready to bash the monk’s head in with a thick branch if he tried anything funny. Instead, he found in the stable a wooden bowl holding fresh bread, dried meat, and a few shriveled apples. Next to it was a mug full of goats’ milk. The boy fell on the meal ravenously. He suffered for it too; his stomach, unused to so much food, cramped and he threw it all up.

It was while the boy was bent over, sick, that the monk found him. Nicky was too weak to fight, and the man had no problem hauling the boy and his sack into his hut. When Nicky got better, he decided to stay as, unlike the others, the monk neither hurt him nor tried to convert him. He left the boy in peace, asking only that he do a few chores in return for food and lodging.

* * *

The little boy nearly slammed face-first on the floor as the memories retreated. Damn it! He had to get to his hunting lodge; there was no telling how long it would take before the king sent men for him. Nicky couldn’t afford to let anyone else take over his position. He needed to find out why he couldn’t call DiJinn to him, and fix the problem. He needed his servant to bring him the proper sacrifice so he could make himself big again.

As he contemplated events in the hall, it seemed more and more likely Rablias had tried to steal DiJinn from him. What had the asshole promised his demon? He would free him from Nicky’s bondage if he taught the Head Questioner how to do magic? Laughable, but at least he could rest assured the damn duchess hadn’t been a part of it. He should have stopped to see if she were still alive. Oh well, if she lived, perhaps she would come to fear him as she ought.

* * *

Nicky lay on the ground, bruised, bloody and bound with rope.

He was able to turn his head and see the monk, tied to a beam of the stable. Both had been beaten badly. Their attacker was inside the hut, ransacking it. Nicky concentrated; he had not used his unique gift since the day his Da turned him over to the priest.

He was not about to become a slave again to some twisted freak of a man, and used as the archbishop had done, but he was hog-tied. The boy closed his eyes and rested the side of his face against the ground. He envisioned how the knots on the rope would have to undo for him to be able to slip out.

Nicky felt them loosen, and after a few more minutes of work, was able to free his hands. He rolled over and worked on the knots around his ankles. So engrossed was he, he forgot to keep watch on the hut. He felt a sharp pain. The world blacked out.

The boy awoke, once more in a cell, but unchained. A pallet of linen-covered straw made a bed of sorts in a corner. A stool and a small table. A chamber pot. The cell was dimly lit, with smooth glowing orbs. He had never seen anything like them. The boy rose, making his painful way to stand underneath, staring up and concentrating. The orbs seemed to sing, or hum.

It was a haunting melody, something he felt he should know. He hummed under his breath, trying to match the tune coming from the orbs. He managed to make them brighter, then duller, but couldn't extinguish them.

Nicky was bored. He was left alone in his cell; no one came to threaten him, or even speak to him. But someone entered when he slept. Every day when he woke, there was food, and water to wash with, and the chamber pot emptied. He had figured out how to make the globes go on and off. It seemed with that little victory, a whole new world opened.

Everything hummed with the energy; it all wanted to speak with him. Sometimes taunting, sometimes tantalizing, but Nicky was determined to master the songs, as he had nothing better to do. Eventually, the boy undid the locks on his cell, and could wander around the larger room at will.

Nicky didn't know how long he took to work his way out of the room, much less if he had done it of his own volition or been released by his captor. One night, the boy found himself walking up a long staircase, free of the dungeon. At the top was a single door, which opened to the boy's touch. He came face to face with the man who had captured him. The man he was soon to call master.

* * *

The boy stumbled into his suite, glad once again he had cut out the tongues of his slaves so they couldn't betray him by speaking of what they saw. The one slave left able to speak was blind.

"Lord Nicky?" the blind slave inquired at the sound of the door slamming shut.

"Rainton, should the king send slaves looking for me, you will make them understand I am hunting down those who created the disturbance tonight. I will send word to him when I can, and I was only nominally injured."

"Yes my lord. Was it assassins?"

"Yes, if he wishes to know." He could feel the memories overtaking him as he stumbled to his bed chamber. He tried to force the images away as he gave a few more orders, before being swamped by exhaustion.

* * *

"Why are you doing this to me?" Selene begged, "I cared for you, loved you, protected you!"

"You betrayed me! You told Mica about me! Now he wants to kill me!"

"I didn't know he hated you! Please don't do this! I can make it up!"

"Your death will serve a greater purpose. You think I like the life I live? That I enjoy being stuck a child?! The pitying looks I get? Or the ones who think just because I look like a kid, I can be used however they want?" Nicky yelled at her.

Selene was crying, curled up on the dirty brick floor, "I never, never..."

"You never do!" he screamed in rage. "No one ever does! You just look at me and think *Oh, what a cute, poor little boy! Let me mother him, let him be the child I lost, or never had!*"

The boy's chest heaved as he sucked in air. "You never treat me like an adult!"

The woman looked up, tears streaming down her face, eyes red. The boy darted in to punch her. Chains clanked as she flinched back, one hand going to her cheek, the other held up in an effort to ward off any more blows.

"I'm sorry. Please, I'll do better, I can do better. Just let me go, and I promise, I'll treat you like an adult."

Nicky sneered at her, "Would you?"

"Yes!" she exclaimed, crawling as far as her chains would allow toward the boy's feet. "What would you like to do first? Get a place of your own? Have a bank account?"

He savored the look of hope and eager anticipation; it would be so much sweeter when she was crushed by learning what he wanted. "So you can use it against me later? Take it away when I do something you don't like?"

Confusion briefly clouded her face. "No, no, never. We can...We can put it all under your name." She sat like a puppy looking for its master's approval.

"A good start, but not what I really, truly want." He played it out.

"I, I don''t know what else I can give, what I can do. What do you truly want? Tell me, I'll do anything I can to help you get it."

"Anything? Would you really?"

"Yes!" Her face creased in a frown, "It's not illegal, is it? I mean, I haven't led a clean life but, I won't murder anyone," she added, fearfully yet defiantly.

"I want someone to love me," Nicky said.

"But, but I did. Do," she hastily corrected. "I've loved you since I saw you."

Nicky looked at her in contempt, knowing she still thought of him as nothing more than a child. "Prove it."

"But I just..."

"Prove it by kissing me," Nicky interrupted her.

Selene hesitated a moment, rose up onto her knees and kissed him on the cheek. She sat back onto her haunches, looking at him for approval, surprised when his face crumpled in rage.

"I knew you still think of me as a child!" Nicky screamed, his hands balling into fists.

The bewilderment on her face at this outburst changed to one of horror as she realized what he meant. "I..."

The rejection was too much for the little boy; he wasn't waiting for the look of disgust soon to follow. He struck her with a fist, and danced back out of her lunge. She was no longer so compliant, or eager to treat him as an adult.

"I knew it!" Nicky screamed in rage and picking up a loose brick, darted behind her and smashed it against her head.

She gave a brief cry of pain, toppling over, fighting to stay awake. The back of her head bled. "I..." she began weakly. "I'm sorry, but I, I just can't. Not, not that."

Nicky bashed her again until her head was a caved-in mess, brains and blood leaking out onto the floor. He let the brick drop and walked away, shaking in anger. She would join all the other women who had refused to love him.

Chapter Two

The bar was dimly lit. Eron sat at a small table toying with a glass of whiskey, listening to the jazz band. He was contemplating drinking the bar out of business, although his fast metabolism made intoxication almost impossible. The waitress stopped by, asked if he wanted another, which he declined. He could see his friend onstage squinting at him and shaking his head.

After a few more songs, the band took a break, and his friend came over. Well, not really his friend, more a friend of Mica's, though the man was good company. Steve was working the crowd as he made his way over. The waitress appeared again, and Steve ordered water, with a bottle of beer.

"She likes you, why don't you ask her out?" Steve rasped as he lit a cigarette.

Eron shrugged, continued playing with his glass. What was the use? Everyone he loved died eventually.

"Come on!" Steve replied in aggrieved tones. "She's nice, she's *single*. Not like that other one."

Eron lifted his head briefly to glare at the man. "Is that what you think? That I'm mooning over some...some unattainable woman?"

Steve took a sip of his water, then the beer. "Well, it sure looks like it! I mean, what do you really know about her? Hell, she doesn't always seem to be on the up and up."

"Mica told you that?" Eron asked.

"Look, for someone so old, who's supposed to be all wise 'n shit, you certainly can pick 'em, can't you?" Steve asked in disgust. "Donnie's just a street kid what don't always know better. He gets sucked in too much by shiny things, easy money."

"He'll learn, Steve; time will give him experience."

He missed the look of disgust tossed his way before his friend took another gulp of beer and acknowledged a patron. "If he makes it that far. I don't like that woman, and you know why? 'Cause she's fake; there's something not right about her. My guys? They can't find any real mention of her, it's like she never existed."

"Steve, there are lots of people you don't have complete information on."

"Speaking from experience?" his friend razzed him as he finished the last of his beer. "Look, all I'm saying is, Missy is interested; what would it hurt to ask her out on one date? You might find you have more in common than you think."

Steve left his empty on the table, and taking the water with him, joined his bandmates back onstage as they started the last half of their set. Eron continued scowling at his glass. Movement nearby had him looking up. Missy was picking the empty up. She leaned over to look him in the face.

"You still OK? Ready for another?"

"I'm fine, thanks." It came out a little sharper than he intended.

She compressed her lips, nodded once, tightly, "OK." And turned to the table next to him.

"She likes you." The silky voice near his ear startled him so he jerked and spilled what was left of his drink on the table top. He caught a whiff of some expensive, seductive perfume.

Eron looked to his side, but the speaker had already walked around the table and was now seated across from him. He inhaled, and smoothed his face out, so nothing showed; inside he felt happier. "Not you, too." He mopped up the liquid with the useless paper coaster and his coat sleeve.

He watched as she settled back into the seat, her black camel-hair coat falling open to reveal a cream cashmere sweater, slender gold link chain belt snug around her slim waist. He just saw the top of her skirt, a red and black tartan. She wasn't dressed much different from the other patrons, but the cut and material always made her look better turned out.

"She is cute, would you like me to make you reservations at L'Canard Blu?"

"I don't need help asking a girl out, especially from you."

Her eyebrow winged up. "What about asking out a woman?" She turned her head to evaluate the waitress. "She is older than a mere girl."

Eron scowled and, forgetting he had spilled the last of the whiskey, went to drink another mouthful.

"You do not look happy, ma chèrie, is it really so bad? You are alive, no one is trying to kill you, and a pretty woman is interested in you. What more do you want?" She reached a hand out and laid it over the back of his. She must have fed at some point, for her hand was warm and not her usual icy cold. The silken feel of her skin against his sent frissons of pleasure through him. *As if she cares, if I were to tell her, I would only be giving her power over me.* He yanked his hand out from under hers.

He noticed it was a while before Missy came back over to ask coolly, "What can I get you?"

"Espresso." Missy turned her back to the woman at his table in dismissal and went to answer another table.

"I'll have another, thanks," Eron called after her, not sure if she heard him. "Why are you here? I didn't think you liked jazz."

"I don't. I find it snooze inducing."

Eron spread his hands. "So, again, what are you doing here?"

"Waiting."

He looked at her, expecting her to elaborate, but she didn't, merely turned her head to watch the band onstage. Missy came back with her espresso, and another whiskey for him. Illyria held up a Euro toward the waitress, not really paying attention. Eron noticed how Missy took it in two fingertips, with a slight sneer for the other woman before walking off. He glanced briefly toward the stage, saw Steve was now giving "what the hell?" looks.

"Is that not your friend on the sax?" Illyria asked. "He is unhappy with you."

Eron hunched his shoulders. "Yeah, he is. Besides, he's really more Mica's friend." *Why the hell is everyone so concerned with my love life all of a sudden?* He noticed she wrapped her hands around the tiny cup but didn't drink any of it.

"I thought you couldn't eat or drink?"

Illyria was watching the people in the bar. He idly wondered if she was mentally tallying up which ones could be considered food, and which ones to leave alone.

"We do not. But the warmth," her voice sunk a note with longing, "we crave it." She gave a small shudder, her eyes closing briefly and reopening and her tone taking on a brisker note. "We are in a bar, it is what people do when they are in one, is it not? Order a drink?"

He did not respond, did not know what to say.

She turned back to him, her eyes drifting past his head and he watched as they lit up with happiness. *Why won't they do that for me?* he thought churlishly and felt another presence behind him.

"Darling," Illyria gave a dazzling smile to the person.

In a moment, the man was bending over, and they briefly brushed their lips together before he sat down in the chair facing the bar, with his back to the band. Steve's eyes narrowed again at Eron, cut his gaze to the man and gave a chin jerk. Eron ignored him. He wanted to sit in peace and think, and now he felt like a fifth wheel. Missy came over with change, and another espresso was ordered. The drink came back quickly, and Phillip smiled most dazzlingly at Missy. She blushed, almost dropped the money he gave her, and fled, her cheeks crimson.

"Please tell me you two don't intend to spend all night here."

"Don't worry, we have a dinner date later," she laughed.

As the words sank in, he grimaced and downed half the contents of his glass as the male leaned in to whisper in Illyria's ear. He could have stepped from the pages of a men's magazine. Charcoal gray slacks sharply creased, a snowy-white immaculately pressed linen shirt complete with studs at collar and cuff. A subtly patterned red vest. When he shifted, there was glimpses of an expensive men's watch under the sleeve of his coat. His hair didn't fall in its customary waves to his shoulder, but was a mess of curls precisely styled to look like it hadn't been. His black cashmere topcoat lay tossed artlessly over an adjacent chair, and there was the faint scent of some expensive and subtle cologne. Eron was aware the two of them received admiring looks from both sexes. It made him feel scroungy, sitting as he was in his comfortable jeans, burst-elbow cotton sweater of no particular color or all of them, salt-stained navy blue peacoat, and beat-up boots.

Missy made another appearance, checking to make sure they were all right. Eron noticed she had trouble tearing her gaze from Phillip's face. Even though Eron had not given her any encouragement, it still rankled. After she had left, he risked a glance to the stage. Steve was ignoring him, concentrating on the music.

"I believe that is he now," Phillip remarked.

Eron didn't want to know, but it was like a train wreck—he couldn't help but look. All he saw was a large man in a sharp Armani business suit with two men at his back who screamed personal protection. The man made his way to the bar and, by the look on the faces of the waitstaff, was not wanted.

"But that's..." He trailed off and looked back at the two vamps.

"Every rumor about him is true," Illyria breathed hungrily. "Slippery, and cannot be tied directly to anything."

"He will make a lovely feast, shall I? Or would you like the honors?" Phillip murmured.

"You, I got the last one," she replied. "Besides, I like to watch you work." She trailed a glossy red nail down his coat sleeve.

He gave his devastating smile, emerald-green eyes lightening with promises of things to come. "As you wish." He seemed to slip through the crowd like butter, engaged the man in conversation, and soon Illyria was rising.

"You should ask her out, Eron; she might even be willing to spend the night." The vamp squeezed his shoulder gently and bent her head near his ear to whisper, "You need something to put you in a better mood." and was soon leaving the bar with the other men.

Eron wanted to hurl his glass against the wall. He downed the last of his whiskey instead, wondering how they planned to keep the man's demise out of the news

Missy came over, collected the now-cold cups of espresso, his empty. "Another one?"

"Yeah, sure, thanks." He was back to staring at the table top.

When she brought his refill back, she tried to engage him in conversation. "Your friends didn't stay long."

Eron glanced up. "They only stopped in for a bit, to say hello, this...this isn't really their thing."

She smiled at him, a sweet smile that was a little rueful as she admitted, "They did look a little too boardroom for here, as if they should have been at some function making millions."

He had to admit she had a nice laugh; it brought a smile to his face, lightened his mood a bit, so they managed to chat some before she had to go back to work. It was a while before Eron realized Steve's set was over, and the band had put away their instruments. The bar was a lot emptier when Steve came over with a beer in each hand and sat down.

"God, what a night." He took a long pull. "Saw that woman come in, and that man. You nearly blew it with Missy, pal; you still might have." Steve gave Eron a look of disgust. "Look, you wanna be alone the rest of your life, chasing after screwy women..."

"There's nothing screwy with those two," Eron hotly replied. *At least not in the sense you mean.*

Steve shook his head again, taking another long pull, finishing off the bottle. "Whatever." He lit another smoke, blowing out a stream, jabbed the end toward his friend. "And another thing, they looked like a couple. What the hell you doing running after her if she's in a relationship? What kind of man are you?"

Eron motioned for Missy and held up the empty. "Steve, you're as bad as some old woman."

"Look, pal, you may be older than me by several thousand years, only you look 30, so lemme tell ya something I've learned and which you haven't. Or maybe you've forgotten," he added after taking another pull of beer and another hit. "Guys looking like that one don't like poaching on their territory when they're still with the woman. And that's another thing: why would you want a woman like her anyway if you know she cheats?"

"Steve, your attitude is puritan. Some people are in open relationships."

"Hey, it's called having morals," He shook his head and took another slug and hit. "All's I know, she screams danger, and the businessman her and her friend were with? Not the kind of people you hang around with voluntarily if you get my drift. But hey," he lifted a hand and let it fall, "it ain't none of my business."

Missy came over with two more bottles and a double shot of whiskey, "Last call, guys. Here ya go." Eron was all set to refuse the drink when she said, "On the house. Laphroaig."

Steve looked at him, a smirk pulling up one side of his face, and took another drink of beer. "I'm telling you, ask her out." He called out before Eron could stop him, "Hey Missy, my friend here's a little shy. Would you be interested in going out with him sometime?"

"I curse you, and those, not of my kind that stand here, perpetrators of crimes against our people. I curse you!"

The short phrase resounded and reverberated inside Eron's head. He was dissolving into a sea of burning whiteness as the blonde woman's curse thundered through his being.

"Missy, that was her name." Eron had not realized he spoke aloud until he saw it wasn't the steady white electrical illumination of the bar's fluorescents he was seeing, but the flickering fluctuating flame-orange of torches. He was lying on a cold stone floor. Behind him, a door shuddered as people outside tried to break it open.

"What the hell?" He couldn't think, couldn't remember what he was doing here.

How long has it been? It was a great effort, but he sat up, a fading ache at the back of his head reminding him of the blow which had taken him out. He had been at the Harvest Ball. The young man who looked like a grown-up version of Nicky had staged a coup. Some weirdo with a staff had set off a firework which burned bright as the sun.

He realized a veil had just been torn from his eyes. Stray memories locked away for centuries crashed down on him intensely. They left him momentarily crippled with emotion. *What else am I not remembering because of her? I think Steve was right; I've been chasing shadows.*

Just thinking of the long-dead man, the innocent woman, made his blood boil in anger and frustration almost as great as his anger at Illyria. *We were cursed, she got us all cursed.*

Why now? Why had it broken now? What or who had caused

it to break? Was it from those two men and their strange bomb? One thing Eron had learned in his very long life: the older he got, the faster he healed. As he sat up, he dislodged Illyria's body.

He had only time to gasp out "Oh shit!" before her eyes flew open, her fangs sank in his neck, and there was nothing he could do as he fell back against the shuddering wood door to the garden.

* * *

I looked up at the webbing of metal catwalks and stairs ringing the room. There had to be other doors leading out, but everything had been painted black, so the foreground blended into the background and made finding the doors a pain. I thought I saw the glint of glass near the middle top, and metal tracks near the ceiling. A large open platform hung from the tracks directly centered in the cavernous room. I could see people inside cages dangling from the cross-bars.

"Son-of-a-bitch," I muttered, low-voiced. I wasn't going to play this game. I wasn't. But I knew if I wanted to save them, I had to play anyway. "Fine, asshole."

I had already figured out from the taunts of our enemy that the building was wired for audio and video. I didn't know if he were still watching, so I took the long route up all four flights before making my way to the metal tracks, the platform and its burden hanging down to my right. I could see Alric and his queen, the head of his army, and another man not of their clan but a great warrior in his own right. They looked up at me, able to track my movements. Each one was gagged; chains ran from their wrists and ankles to the cage floor. The Queen looked at me calmly enough, but it didn't mean anything. She could be in a towering rage and a person wouldn't know until it was too late.

"I told you not to split up; now look at the mess you're all in."

The blond was rattling his chains again to get my attention as I studied the setup. He jerked his chin in an odd motion and I followed to see he was indicating the wheels. There was a brick of explosive at each support, so the whole contraption would fall.

"There's no way I can support such a weight, I'm not that damn good," I informed him as he gave me The Look. Our enemy loved using explosives. I figured there was more I couldn't see. I wasn't sure if the setup had been pre-wired, or even if the people before me had been conscious when they were put in the cages.

"Are the cage locks wired?" He nodded yes.

"The floor where it's welded to the sides?"

He hesitated, a puzzled look in his eyes I took it to mean he wasn't sure. I didn't want to step on the top, for fear it would set off the wheel charges.

I could see the glass from here, dark tinted and opaque. Drat, I couldn't read my enemy's mind; it had to do with his kind. However, they did register as blank spots on my mental map. I tried scanning and was fairly sure the control booth was empty, so he was elsewhere in the huge old building.

I looked at the chains holding each corner of the cage, and saw a lumpish gray mass wrapped around the links: some type of moldable explosive. I had no way of knowing if it constituted a small charge, or a large one.

"So, falling the equivalent of four floors constitutes massive damage for you, doesn't it?" I asked conversationally.

I got an angry rattle of chains and muffled noises as he glared at me. I took the answer as a curse in his native tongue. "Just a question, chill, I'm not going to let you fall when there's still explosives undetonated."

I continued my inspection, concluded there was only three significant points set to blow. But I had no idea whether the others would detonate if I tampered with one. I hadn't come equipped for a problem like it. I wondered if things were rigged to blow if he died. I knew that the charges had to be primed prior to the detonation. I approached their queen and crouched close.

"I don't have the equipment with me to defuse the charges, and I can't get it, so I'm going to ask you a rather personal question, and believe me, Majesty, when I say that all your lives depend on a truthful answer." I waited for her to acknowledge me. Blondie was banging the chains again.

"Shut it, Blondie, this isn't the time for ceremony or niceties." I looked his way in case it was a warning, but no, he was pissed with the way I addressed their queen.

I would have to leave them dangling, try to find our enemy,

whom I had nicknamed Dead-Man. He had many control centers; each one held redundant systems so he could log in and blow stuff up throughout the building. I wished for the dozenth time the complex had blast doors to seal off sections of the structure.

"I have to leave you here temporarily. I have to get inside the control booth." I saw the queen close her eyes, not liking my idea. I continued to explain in detail why I needed to do so.

All of them remained silent, dazed horror in their eyes. I needed to locate the rest of the crew; my earpiece had been silent for a very long while. I made my way off the tracks over to the catwalk. Stairs led up to the outside of the booth. "All units report your location, copy, out."

I waited but heard nothing, so I repeated the call signal again and fumed.

At great length, I heard, "Raptor, Ducat here, copy."

"Copy, Ducat, what's your location? Out." I replied.

"I'm not sure, Crusader One got cut off a while back. Out."

I felt my irritation grow by leaps and bounds, wondering why neither one hadn't told me this when it happened, and knew it wouldn't help to yell at the kid. "Situation, Ducat, out."

"Whole lotta nothin', out"

"Can you make your way to base, out."

"I hope so, out."

I was not sure where I was, or how to guide the kid to me so we could get the captives out. The earpieces had been a last-minute thought. I knew Crusader One could take care of himself, but he would never forgive me if I let something happen to his friend.

"Any sign of the enemy, out."

"Negative, out."

"Return to base Ducat, Raptor out."

"What about Crusader One, and the packages? Out."

"Crusader One will call when ready, you're ordered back to base. Out."

"I think I should look for Crusader One, out."

"Negative on all counts, Ducat. Return to base, copy."

I was inside the booth now and could see the controls and a door leading further into the structure. There was also a table set up with some monitors, a mike, and a rack of computers. A chair sat in the middle of the space, empty drink cans and junk food wrappers strewn about the cabling which ran everywhere. A box of half-eaten still-warm pizza sat on the chair. This room was active, so whoever was running it would be back soon.

I waited for a reply; if the kid had turned me off, I was going to smack both him and Crusader One next I saw them. I heard a new voice in my ear.

"Raptor," followed by amused laughter, "Oh I like it. I'd tell the kid to say hello, but he can't talk right now, literally." I received more laughter before the piece fell silent.

"You're a dead man, copy." I threatened in menacing tones. The plan had gone to hell in a hand basket.

"I've got a surprise for you." I heard crackling noises and thought he had smashed the earpiece, but no, it was him making those sounds and they reminded me of something.

"Then come and give it to me," I taunted. I heard locks click and ducked behind the door as it opened. Perfect.

* * *

Fire shot up in columns, metal screamed as the room shook, huge chunks of glass from the ceiling shattering into deadly shards. The blasts nearly ruined my hearing. Alric had grabbed onto the bottom of the chain, and we were pulling him up when the catwalk he had been on collapsed in a roar of metal. We had just gotten him onto the roof when a particularly lethal cloud of jagged metal rolled up and out the opening. We jumped back in panic.

I motioned the Fae to follow me, and we sprinted across the rooftop. Alric and his court could run almost as fast as I, and we fairly flew across the tops. They found the way down first, and I waited for the two immortal men to catch up. Just as I looked back at Alric, another explosion rumbled from inside and the roof disintegrated. I saw him being thrown free from the blast, engulfed by a rolling cloud of smoke and debris.

I found the queen and her court first. She was keening, wailing a song in her native tongue beside the remains of Alric, which hardly looked like they had once been a man.

Blondie looked up sharply at my approach; he was tall, slim

and muscular with long shining blond hair and green eyes. He spoke harshly in the same language as the queen and drew his swords. I stopped several paces away.

The other blond-haired, green-eyed warrior had drawn his long sword and stood in a protective stance, rage making his beautiful, fine-featured face into something frightening and ugly.

I waited. I could hear the calls of concerned humans on the mental ether, and knew emergency personnel were on their way. I heard shouting as Jester, called Eron, came up. He and Crusader One, known as Mica, had cuts, black with dirt and smoke. Their young friend had been blown to bits from what I could make out of their shouting. We did not know what became of the one I had called Dead-Man.

Mica was the first to yell we all had to go. The remains of Alric's people resisted. The two immortals insisted. The queen turned to me, her anger more terrible than the warriors'.

"It is because of you, night-walker, that my mate is dead. It is because of you our nation shall be cleaved in two and made weak so our enemies may pick us apart. Our time will come to an end because of you," she excoriated me.

I'm Sorry seemed an inadequate apology.

"It will be dealt with by our kind." A new voice spoke from the darkness and out of it stepped Phillip. "The box for you."

I misliked the promise and prepared to battle when the queen replied, "The murder of our kind calls for justice from our kind."

Her tone made me afraid for my un-life. She raised her arms, palms out toward me, "Illyria Sasha Nicolette Caladonea of the Maison du Corbeau. I curse you!"

She was beginning to glow, incandescent, as unseen winds blew her ankle-length hair back. I tried to step back but felt rooted to the spot. "I curse those not of my kind who stand here, perpetrators of crimes against our people. I curse you!"

The short phrase reverberated inside my head: "I curse you! I curse you! I curse you!" I was dissolving into a sea of burning whiteness as her words thundered through my being.

* * *

My eyes flew open in the dark. I was already sitting up, my hands wrapped around the throat and shoulder of someone who had disturbed me. My fangs buried in their neck. I swallowed, the taste of cinnamon, vanilla, and ambrosia flooded my being. There were only a few people I knew who tasted that way. I thrust the person away from me, and Eron slammed into the door.

* * *

Eron and Illyria stared at each other for several heartbeats as they sat on the floor. Behind them, the door shuddered from blows. The commingled voices of slaves, townspeople, and guards filtered through. The memories which had been locked away by the curse a storm in their heads. The strongest, which came to the forefront, over and over, was the night it all happened. They were back there in the parking lot of the abandoned factory. The intervening years, the here and now, retreated before the urgency of the now-ancient night. The bitterness he never knew he harbored against her welled up and slid into place as if it had never left.

"You bitch! You heartless, soulless, cruel bitch!" His hands curled into fists as he struggled to contain his rage, breath coming in ragged gulps. "How long have you remembered that we knew each other then? Did it give you pleasure? Satisfaction to play your games with us unawares? Did you enjoy ordering me about like one of your slaves? Did you have fun planning Mica's kidnapping with his enemy? Heartless bitch! Answer me!"

He didn't realize he had gotten to his knees and then his feet and loomed over her, reaching down, hauling her up by her arms. He shook her.

"Answer me, you bitch!"

"I was as ignorant as you. I woke to the truth; woke to it with the words of the Fae ringing in my ears amid the dead and dying."

"You suckered us into your games back then, your schemes, same as now. You got the boy killed, blown to bits, and the rest of us cursed for eternity!" The veins stood out on his face and neck as he accused her. "If it hadn't been for that damn...whatever it was, we'd still be cursed, stupid to the truth, blind to your treachery and perfidy. And now, it's Mica who will pay the price!"

The door was starting to splinter and crack under the repeated poundings, and running feet could be heard along with shouting, as palace guards poured down the hall with Saizar behind.

"They're here!"

"Stay where you are! Don't move!"

"Hands, let me see your hands!"

It took a few moments for the men to understand we had been caught in the attack. The garden door burst open and more guards poured in. As soon as it was understood the perpetrators had fled, the king entered. He stopped short at sight of the blackened hall and gaped, swinging toward the man and woman.

"Duchess! What is the meaning of this?"

"My servant and I were attacked by robed and hooded men, one of whom Lord Nicky seemed to recognize. I am not sure what they used," she gestured to the smoke-streaked hall, "but it blinded us and knocked us out. When I came to, Lord Nicky was gone with those men."

"They have dared to kidnap my advisor? They were not assassins?" Maceanas demanded.

Only Eron heard her muttered, "As if we could be so lucky," She said louder, "I do not know what or who they were, or what their plans were."

"How dare you tell such lies about my advisor, Madame!? I weary of your attempts to make him the villain just because you two don't see eye-to-eye!" the king thundered as behind him, the townspeople whispered about events to each other.

"If I may, Sire," Saizar stepped forward and bowed, "We should mount a search for the attackers. They can't have got far. It wasn't too long ago the blast rang out."

"Yes, guards! Fan out and search every inch of this place! No one leaves until you are done!" The men hurried to obey; all but a select few remained behind to see no harm came to the king. "How dare you spread lies about my friend!? The truth, or I'll toss you in the dungeon!"

"I speak truth, Sire," she said. "Lord Nicky and I were conversing when two robed men attacked. Your advisor called one of them by name before they detonated their strange weapon."

"That does not mean he was a part of the attack!" Maceanas angrily replied.

"What would you name it if he called out *DiJinn*? Is that not his slave's name?" she demanded.

The hall fell silent, even those whispering outside. The King's face turned purple before he exploded, "WHAT? WHAT! Where is my advisor? Have his rooms searched at once!"

Saizar knew rumors would be running rampant, and fear as well. It behooved him to get to the bottom of the matter before His Majesty became further unhinged with thoughts of plots and assassins.

"If I may, Majesty, let me question them now on all the events which took place after they left me to see Lord Jenabram home," Saizar offered.

The sheriff took them through the evening, information which the duchess and the earl could corroborate. The fact of her servant walking in at the start of the attack attested to her lack of involvement. The guards came back, to report they could find no evidence of which way the interlopers had gone, though they did find the bodies of three men. This news did not sit well with the king, nor did the news Lord Nicky was not in his rooms and that all but one of his slaves were mute and that one able to speak being blind.

"We must recall the army, Sire," Saizar said as respectfully as he could manage.

"No, this is inconceivable! Why would Lord Nicky be a part of this plot? You must have mistaken what you heard; he would not dare protect traitors! The ball is over. Get people out."

The palace guard scrambled to see their monarch's orders were swiftly followed. "As for you, duchess, you will be confined in your home. No one may leave or enter until I send for you tomorrow. You will spend the time contemplating what name it was you did hear. Sheriff, escort her home and stand guard with your men."

Her curtsey gave no indication of her ire at her house arrest; only Eron knew how furious she really was. He wondered what new game she was playing, and he meant to learn.

Chapter Three

Just a few lamps were lit. Moonlight streamed in the many-paned industrial windows in his warehouse-turned-loft. He thought he heard a noise as he stepped from the shower, towel wrapped about his waist. At first glance the place appeared empty; then he saw her, half-in–half-out the window.

He hissed in annoyance. "Must you do that?"

"Darling," she drawled in her smoky voice, "however am I to convince you otherwise?"

"Not by cat-burgling my pad. Is nothing sacred to you? Do I need to bell you just so I can shower in peace? Have you not heard of things called phones?"

He watched as she slithered the rest of the way into his loft and came across the floor to him, the moonlight making her seem to glow. He breathed in sharply, glad she couldn't read his mind. She was a delicious temptress. Her yellowish-green, brown eyes, seemed greener; dark brown hair flowed down her back and shoulders in a tumble of waves and curls. Her lips were so wetly carmine. She had a crimson, draped top and tight white pants with high, strappy scarlet heels; but still she was silent as smoke. She came right up, never breaking eye contact.

"Let me show you." He felt the coolness of her hand on the heat of his wet skin at the base of his throat. If he leaned just a hair forward, they would touch, but he forced himself to keep still. She drew her hand down the center of his chest, always careful to keep a slight distance between them as she prowled to his right. He sucked in a long, slow deep breath and tilted his head down to track her hand. Her hand reached the top of the towel, and she stopped behind him. She leaned close, still keeping the bare minimum of space between them. He felt her breath tickle his ear.

"Just a little bite, a mere taste. A whisper on the lips. Hmmmm?" she purred.

Goosebumps spangled in constellations as his libido jerked to life. He turned his head just enough to see her and forced a thread of steel into his voice "Keep your fangs to yourself."

She threw her head back and laughed delightedly, clapped her hands. "One day, mon ami, one day. I shall see myself out, non?" She smiled at him affectionately, her pert nose crinkling, swayed to the door, undid all the locks by hand. She paused to look back at him over her shoulder and whispered, "Bonne nuit, mon immortel." With a last mischievous smile she closed the door behind her.

* * *

Eron waited until he saw Illyria's slaves leave the room before he slipped inside, letting the door shut with a soft thump and turning the bolt. She had started to cry out in irritation as she splashed in the tub, stopping at the sight of him.

"What the hell..."

"I could say the same, *Duchess*" he snarled, cutting her off as he swiftly crossed the room. "Or are you forgetting we still have a conversation to finish?"

"It's waited how many centuries?"

"If I let you put this on hold, you'll wipe my mind and reprogram it to think we already had it."

"If you think I'm going to have you in here while I bathe, so my slaves can spread that gossip over the kingdom..."

He smirked as he raked his eyes up and down her body, "Not so nice when it's someone else doing it to you?" he inquired pleasantly and perched on the side of the tub, down by her toes. "I remember how much you loved to pop in after I had stepped from the shower."

"I don't recall you minded much." Her smile showed teeth and fangs, and she chuckled throatily as his libido made itself known.

"Fuck you."

“Ah, darling, I do believe we’ve already had the pleasure. Not in a bath, however.” Her eyes turned honey fire in unholy glee as she rested her arms on the tub edges. “Are you sure you won’t join me? You are sooooo dirty. Unless you mind slaves’ chatter.”

“Stop with your bullshit, your slaves say nothing without your knowledge and permission,” he replied flatly and tried to ignore the water beading on her breasts. Ambushing her had been a mistake—he recalled a shower they had once shared after a battle. “Besides, this is the only way I can be assured you’ll stay put long enough to finish a conversation.”

Their eyes clashed. She inclined her head acknowledging that for now he had the upper hand. She picked up a bar of soap, a small cloth, and continued her bath.

“Excoriate me for the past.” Her tone bitter as she washed, not attempting to seduce him with the motions.

“Donny, you bitch. Do you care what you ordered done to him? Do you even remember?”

“I was cursed!” she shouted back at him, “How was I supposed to remember events forced from my consciousness!”

“We’re not amnesiac now! So don’t use that excuse! Would you even have gone to the blast site?”

“Why should I? The boy didn’t survive,” she answered. “He was an immortal, but the amount of damage? Bits of him were vaporized! You saw what was left reduced to almost nothing! You think he could have reassembled, returned from that?”

Eron flung his arms wide, steamrolled on. “You think he’s happily dead? Hell. That’s what he’s in, that’s where you put him. Do you even understand to what kind of life you’ve condemned him? Missing bits, living on the fringe of society, trying to survive with what reknit!”

He leaned closer, continued, “We were cursed!” His voice lowered, became quieter, all the more menacing. “Mica should have retrieved the boy’s soul gem and brought it to the blast site. Placed it amid the splattered remains of his protégé and released his soul. He couldn't do it because of you. Imagine someone cutting you to pieces, blowing you to bits, and yet refusing you the one thing which would grant peace. Imagine surviving for centuries, missing bits of yourself, being unable to die!”

He stopped, saw the horror in her eyes, and it was she who lowered her head in shame.

"It never occurred to me one of you could survive. I never knew how your kind could be killed. I thought that the damage alone would be sufficient to ensure the final death. So much damage," her voice a thin whisper, "to exist in such a state all this time."

He could see blood tears shimmer in her eyes, wend down her face and drip in the water, staining it a pale pink.

"How dare you cry now for him!? He would never have been there if you hadn't played your games, seduced him into believing he could have your undying, eternal love." He was standing beside the tub now, looking down at her in disdain.

Her head jerked up, the cloth floating free in the water, tears drying as a cold rage fast replaced sorrow. "I played no games in which he was not willing to participate. I had no need to seduce him. He knew I did not love him romantically, that we would not be together for all eternity."

Her eyes had gone back to being honey fire, "He was a street kid. I helped him make his fantasies come true, if only for a little bit."

Eron cut her excuses off with a disdainful, cruel laugh. "Do you even listen to the crap you spout? So now you pitied him. The poor kid. Let the rich, bored, gorgeous woman take care of you like some pet until she tires of you and moves on to the next one."

"No!" She was upset enough to shout, emotion replacing the smooth mask of her normal countenance. "He was not my pet! They never are!"

"What would you call him? Huh? Your blood stud? Your happy meal? You dropped a job he dreamed of having into his lap. You showered him with gifts and money when you took him out. When you remembered he existed at all."

She was shaking her head as he continued relentlessly, "If that isn't a pet, then I don't know what is. Toxic."

"What do you want from me? What do you want me to say? I never thought of him as a pet, Eron! And that job? I gave him a chance at it, just like all the other people who applied. He got it on his own merit. As for those times we went out clubbing? Of course, I paid for it, I knew what kind of money he made. It wasn't all expensive places, lavish food and drink, Eron. Most times we did things he was interested in."

Her voice dropped, still with its note of sorrow and pain. "I want to leave those I call friends and lovers a little better for having known me. For letting me remember what it's like to be mortal, and alive, if only for a little while." Her head bowed, and she waved for him to go away.

Eron wouldn't let her brush him off. Her motives might have been as unselfish as the undead were ever capable of being. But the boy still existed, in a horrid, twisted, pain-filled state; Eron had no idea how much might have reformed and how much still lived, buried under debris, scattered God knows where. The boy lived as a monstrosity. It mocked too closely what might happen to Mica if they didn't find out where he was hidden, if Nicky had been involved.

"No more, I will not play your games anymore." His tone meant to wound her, and he yanked her chin up, forced her to look at him, "You're not a coward, so don't act it now. When this is over, you will go with me and help end Donny's torment."

Her eyes flew to his, honey fire bright, a sign she was perilously close to vamping out. "If you didn't remember before now that Mica and I knew you, you shouldn't have realized what we are. When did you learn? And if you lie to me, I'll show you the true meaning of fear. You may not know how to kill us, but in all those legends lurks the truth of how to kill your kind."

For a moment, he thought she wasn't going to answer him, but use her great strength and speed to break free and try drowning him; he tightened his grip on her chin and braced himself on the tub lip with his free hand.

"I smelled your scent, the immortal scent, in the Bloody Knuckles one night. I didn't know what it was, or to whom it belonged. I smelled it when I was in the palace, and I knew something was not right. The person to whom it belonged was different from the surrounding mortals, only I didn't know how. I snuck into this person's bedchamber and drank while he slept. The images I got from his mind confused me. I didn't realize he was an immortal. I didn't know what your kind were, or how to find out."

He was struggling to contain his rage, breath coming in ragged gulps as he listened to her tale. He couldn't help the mocking laugh. "So you met me, and what? Thought I was some exotic you could add to your menagerie? And what about Mica and Colin?"

"No. I would have freed you..." She flinched at his laugh. "I kept you in the hopes I could learn what you were, and whether you were friend or foe. Then Mica and his brother told me their tale about the little boy named Nicky, and I thought you were wizards who had extended your lifespans. I agreed to help them because I could see what an evil shit Nicky is and I want him gone. I figured he would never know I was behind his downfall if he were too concerned with..."

He interrupted her, "Damn you! When did you meet Nicky? Where the hell is he? Do you even know how badly you've fucked us all over with your bullshit?"

She stared at him. He felt the invisible pulsing of her immense power for one shimmering heart-stopping moment. He felt he would be consumed in the blaze of it but suddenly it was gone, pulled back inside of her.

"You owe us. You owe Mica and Colin," he said quietly. "When have you met Nicky?"

Still she remained silent, staring at him with those predator's eyes. "You meet him also, many times, at the inn, here at my mansion, in the hallway tonight at the palace."

"Damn you!" He breathed again, reminding himself anger was useless if he wanted to get straight answers. "I never met any child. Nicky is between eleven and twelve."

"That can't be. He's nineteen or twenty."

Eron shook his head as they stared at each other and she said, "He has the boy's memories. I've seen Mica and Colin in his nightmares, from the past, when they first met."

The immortal fisted his hands through his hair. "No, I only met a young man pretending to be an older version of Nicky."

She was sitting in the cooling water of the tub, a frown on her face as she made a gesture of denial. "No, no. That can't be right," The water sheeted from her as she stepped from the tub, reaching for a linen sheet and wrapping herself in it. "I'm telling you..."

"Damn it, Illyria! You know Mica and I are Immortal! How

many years did you know us before we were cursed? Think!" He grabbed her by her shoulders and shook her lightly.

He saw her blink, the only outward sign he had surprised her. Eron continued to gaze at her as she furrowed her brow in thought. "I... It wasn't enough years for me to think you should have aged the way normal humans do. I suppose I thought you did age, only at a very slow pace."

"No. We don't. Like you, when we are made immortal, we remain the age we were at that point, that height and that weight."

They searched each other's eyes a long moment, "I'm telling you. Eron, the advisor, the one you met in the hall and all those other times bears the scent of the immortals. It's in his blood as it's in yours. I... I don't understand how he can be the age he is now if you swear you don't age once turned. Perhaps, perhaps he wasn't an immortal when you first met?"

He released her, paced the room, wishing she had some wine; he could do with a drink right about now. He ran his hands tiredly over his face and slumped unmindfully on the bed. His words seemed to be addressed more towards the floor.

"No. Mica told me the kid was already an immortal when he and Colin found him. I don't know how long he had been one before they met. None of us was able to discover that." He looked over to her, never able to stay mad at her for long.

She had dried herself and pulled on a filmy gown as she began to comb the knots and tangles from her hair. He wished she had just left herself naked, it was less tantalizing than the shifting material. He realized in the sudden silence she had been talking to him while he had been fantasizing tearing the gown off.

He forced himself to look in her eyes. "Sorry, I was trying to figure out what the boy got into. What he uncovered that lets him change his age and still remain alive and an immortal if what you say is true." He wondered if he were fooling her, then recalled she couldn't read the minds of immortals without drinking from them.

Her brow arched up, a sure sign she thought he was lying. "I do not lie, Eron, and I see nothing to admire in it. I'm telling you, he tastes and smells..."

He wearily waved a hand to cut her off. "I don't like him either, but he's been able to do things none of the other Immortals could do. That's damn genius no matter how you feel about him." He fell backwards onto the feather bed and let his eyes drift closed as it gently swayed on its supporting ropes.

He heard the knock on the door, her voice as she spoke with her slaves but couldn't make out what she said. The door closed, and he forced his eyes open long enough to see her sit before the fireplace as she finished with her hair. So she was going to continue their conversation after all. "Fine, explain it to me then. Our scent."

It took a moment and her voice began, "I have noticed all immortals share the same scent and taste in their blood, one exception being Nicky. You are cinnamon and ambrosia. He is both of those things, and another one I can only describe as being close to sulfur."

"Was that the only reason why you pursued us back then? Because we smelled different and you had to know why?"

After a bit, she said, "Yes," and he could hear how unapologetic she was over it.

He laughed to himself at the absurdity of it all and forced his eyes open even though he was exhausted. "He's gone, the advisor. We lost our only link to Mica and Colin. Do you know what could happen if it's found out he's not mortal by those who hold him?"

Eron watched as she walked toward the bed, the firelight outlining her body, her hair a rippling mass over her shoulders and back. "Are you sure the boy would entrust another immortal who is his sworn enemy to a mere mortal?"

"The boy may have found a way to change his appearance, but I doubt his core nature is any different. He's an angry, jealous, covetous, distrustful and manipulative kid. He loved conning grown men and women while he enjoyed the fruits of their labor."

She perched on the edge of the bed and looked at him with her unblinking gaze as he talked.

"He will want his enemies where he can strike at them, but not so close they could bring him harm, and still maintain a reasonable eye on those he's conned into doing the dirty work."

Eron watched as her eyes dimmed a bit as she mulled over all he had said. "He knew those two men. He called one his slave."

"So they tried to ambush and betray him—they cannot know

what he is."

"He might not be gone. They might have hurt him enough he's hiding, waiting to heal. If we can discover whom the other person was...they might know where the brothers are."

"No, they might think we are dead or seriously wounded. We don't know what the thing was supposed to do. Do you want to tip them off we're immortal? Let the kid be ignorant."

Her smile was wicked. "Who said I would let them live?"

His rage brightly flared, and he leapt up. "I've heard this line before. Look what it got us. There will be no more Donnys."

"Not even to save your friends?"

"Don't you dare...you bitch. If Mica gets killed because of you and your schemes...When Nicky comes back, you will let me know at once so I can take care of him. Double-cross me and you can kiss your ass goodbye." He stormed from the room, more upset than he remembered being in a long time.

Chapter Four

"Are you sure you are well, Your Grace?" Susafan asked while she unfurled my parasol as I stood silently inside the door—Mary Elana's weeping over her dead, abusive father a tiresome background noise.

It was with great effort I roused myself from my stupor. "Yes. I am fine."

"Your Grace, we should leave now. His Majesty will not wait much longer." Saizar was looking at me with something close to pity. I realized.

He had been commanded, along with his men, and the earl, to bring Eron and me to him as he still had questions about the night of the Harvest Ball. My carriage was waiting, the sun shone in a rare, cloudless day. I dreaded walking out in it, my powers already lessened; thus my choice of dress which would have made even the countess proud.

"Very well, let us get this over with," I replied crossly as I brought the hood of my cloak up over my head. Susafan stepped out first, holding the shade up. My personal guards were waiting, Jax sitting next to the coachman on the box, Jareth with the footman on the rumble behind and Criton inside.

Aranthus was waiting outside the palace for us when my escort and I pulled up. I caught the worry he hid behind his smiles as he escorted us to the king's private apartments. I noticed there was a man posted at each doorway, even one at the bottom of the stairs. The men had deep-sunken eyes, gray faces, heavy stubble. Their uniforms were dirty, and the odor of dried sweat and sour fear rose off them. They must have been up all night, guarding the king. It didn't look as if they would be able to stay awake much longer.

Aranthus announced us, telling Susafan to wait outside as he took us inside. His Majesty was pacing nervously, demanding of his men what could be taking me so long. Every window had a guard, as did the doors into the room.

"Majesty."

He rounded on me. "I trust you have thought long and hard on what you believe my advisor said?" he demanded.

I could feel the tension in the room ratchet up a notch, and despite the bone-deep exhaustion of his men, they were keyed up, on edge. I wondered what had happened, but could get nothing coherent from their minds. I hoped he would remember. What he said and did next would let me know.

"Yes, Sire. My answer is the same. He called out DiJinn's name, saying that DiJinn and the other man would pay for their betrayal. Ask my freed-man, he heard the name as well as I."

"Well?" The king turned toward Eron.

He bowed elegantly, replying, "Her Grace speaks truth. Lord Nicky did call out *DiJinn*, and seemed to think they had betrayed him. The whole attack had the characteristics of an ambush."

"It wasn't an attack aimed at me, but slaves rebelling against their rightful master." He slammed his fist on his chair arm in vindication. "And this is why slaves who rebel should be put to death at once!"

I saw the faint wince Eron gave, hoping no one remembered he had once been enslaved, however mistakenly.

The king moved onto other matters. "As for those now-dead men Sydney claims attacked you, I am told one of them was the owner of the Bloody Knuckles."

"I believe that is correct. I recently purchased his daughter for a house slave," I offered.

"His widow is claiming you stole the girl, and lied about it to the former sheriff when he tried to question you. That is why you hounded the man, to hide your own crimes."

"I have a purchase agreement signed by both the late tavern owner and myself, witnessed by none other than Jake himself. A notarized copy was duly filed with the royal tax office, and all fees and taxes paid. Shall I send for my receipts?" I inquired coolly.

He waved a hand negligently. "Aranthus will see to it. We must find Lord Nicky! Those traitors might even now be hurting my advisor, hoping to gain a writ of freedom."

Or already dead and re-animated, I know the immortal and I were thinking, *and just waiting to make his way back to the palace*. We had to get out of here, and search every place belonging to the advisor for Mica and Colin while the boy was in hiding.

"What would you have us do, Majesty?" Saizar asked.

The king brooded. "You know what goes on in my kingdom?"

He hesitated before carefully replying, "I know as much as any man can, I suppose, Majesty. What do you want to know?"

"Those traitors! How can I sleep when they are still on the loose? I must know where they went, and that they are not fomenting more rebellion among the slaves. I need my advisor!"

"Shall I send out my men to make inquiries?"

"No, you must get them trained! We must have men to guard the town. We wouldn't be having this problem if it weren't for that damn corrupt sheriff! I will order the slavers to give you and the earl more men. I want them trained as quickly as possible."

"You are most generous Sire. I hesitate to point out…"

"Then don't! Just do what I say!"

He bowed again, but it was the earl who spoke.

"Majesty, the current budget of the town guards will be insufficient to support such a rise in numbers. We will not be able to equip the men, much less feed or clothe them."

"Have the bills sent to the royal treasurer. I will authorize the expenses only so long as I see results. Now go, all of you!"

The moment we stepped out into the hall, Saizar turned to me. "Forgive me, Your Grace. I am sorry you underwent questioning, or that your loyalty to the crown was ever in doubt."

Eron gave a strangled cough behind me as I replied, "I thank you for instructing your men to not take advantage of my slaves, or property or person while I was under suspicion."

He bowed, a faint smile on his lips. "I would not want my men or myself to be regarded as another Sheriff Jake and company."

"After last night, I have no qualms on the subject." I hesitated a moment. "Perhaps Lord Nicky has gone to another of his properties to get what supplies he'd need if preparing to flee."

The Earl stirred beside me. "I know some of his properties, Duchess. We can take our men out to check. You should go home, and finish recovering from your ordeal."

I fumed as we strolled toward the front hall. "Very well. I doubt the kingdom could stand to lose any more of her brave men."

Saizar and the Earl both colored in embarrassment.

Sydney's smile was rigid, more of pain than happiness. *It's your fault our daughter is ruined! You just had to visit those whores! Well, the foreign slut can forget about what the king says! When I tell him how his advisor ruined Sally, he will have to see they are married, and forget about the duchess!*

"It would not be right leaving you without guards," Sydney replied aloud. "The kidnappers might try for you, as the king values you so."

"I have sufficient men for protection and will no doubt be staying close to home tonight." I waved his concern away.

"Yes, well. If you will excuse us, Duchess, there is work we must do." The earl bowed to me, his eyes intent on mine.

Saizar bowed as well, a speculative look in his eyes masked before both men took their leave.

Eron sniffed, leaned in close to me and sniffed again. He lifted his feet up to inspect the soles one by one.

"Dare I ask what you are doing?"

"Just making sure I didn't step into a big pile of shit."

Susafan seemed mildly horrified by the familiar tone he took with me and I shook my head at him as we continued to my carriage.

Chapter Five

Eron rode, trotting behind Illyria's mount, knowing she was made to see in the dark. Long experience had taught him that requests for midnight meetings from people who had tried killing you never worked out nicely. The immortal was also leery of what the one man had done; Eron was unfamiliar with the weapon the stranger had used, and it smacked of the irrational. He had never given credence to tales of supernatural entities, thinking there was a simple mundane explanation, and for the most part he had been correct. Though his mother had claimed to have "powers"; his mind drifted back to the day his father had confronted her.

* * *

"Woman!" The roar filled the spacious tent as Eron and his father charged up to the altar and the lady behind it. "How many times have I told you not to practice your obscene religion?"

The woman faced the warrior calmly. "It is my 'obscene religion' which has allowed you to rule so well for so long. Without my power, you would have been dead ten times over."

The man snarled, slamming his hands on either side of the small altar, "I am the only reason I survive. Me. My cunning, my brains, my skill, my might. I warned you I would not tolerate any more!"

A movement behind her had the man striding around her as she shrieked, "No!"

With a casual backhand, the enraged warrior sent the woman flying into her altar and catapulted the craven knave cowering behind her skirts to the dirt. Eron backed up a few steps so the noxious brews atop the antimins didn't splatter his fine sandals. The young man was pleading with his father, struggling to get free of the man's grip.

"What did I promise you if you disobeyed me and continued this foolishness?"

"Da, no! I can prove she speaks the truth!"

The big, muscled man slammed his fist into his younger son's jaw. The howl of pain caused the woman on the floor to look up at her oldest in disbelief, "Eron! He is your brother! Help him!"

Eron hesitated, giving his father time to drag his youngest around by his hair, and to nail his oldest with a fierce look. "Are you my warrior son who'll rule after me? Or are you as useless as a tit on a male camel like your brother?" He shook the boy's hair.

"No, my son, no!" his mother wailed, clutching at Eron's legs. She ululated in her native tongue and began a sing-song chant.

A growl of rage culminating in a scream cut through the tent. In a maddened rage, the big warrior let his youngest drop to the floor and charged the woman groveling on the ground. He gave her a solid kick in the ribs which did nothing to dislodge her, but had her clutching tighter as she fought for breath.

He ordered his sons, "Go tell the other warriors to gather for a judgment."

"So it finally comes," the young warrior thought and with some difficulty extracted himself from his mother's grasp to do his father's bidding.

* * *

On the night of his mother's death, she had cursed him with her foresight, thinking it would help teach him compassion; at odd times, he heard her in his head and felt compelled to obey. It annoyed and angered him until he began to see the wisdom in following through with the nudges. They had ofttimes saved him, and helped him get closer to his goals, though he was not sure his mother would have appreciated the precise methods required. As time went on, her presence faded, but not the instinctual nudges.

On the two rode, the miles flowing behind them.

“Illyria!” Eron hissed. “Do you even know where you’re going?”

Her eyes flashed and gleamed in the moonlight, and he was reminded once again how other-worldly she was. “You know of what I am, and you ask?” She nudged her horse into a canter, and he was forced to follow or be left behind.

* * *

Lightning flashed across the sky, the small park before him luminescent in the glow as thunder growled through the dark, angry clouds. Eron peeked between the boughs of the tree he hid behind. He couldn’t understand what he was seeing. Four very tall men and one equally tall woman, all cloaked, arguing with another woman in tight black leather. Her curling mane glowed softly, but much brighter when the lightning flared and flashed. He looked across to the other grove of trees where his friend was hidden, and turned his gaze back to the group.

The leather-clad woman made a gesture of frustration, though Eron heard nothing of their speech. After a few more minutes, it seemed they came to an agreement. The cloaked group walked off, out of the park, and the man knew his friend would follow them. He stayed, waiting for the woman to leave. She gazed after the departing group until they had moved out of sight, strode down the path which would take her past his hiding place. She disappeared into the shadows, almost as if she flitted between them. Eron hurried to keep her in sight. She passed statues of unidentifiable eighteenth-century men mounted on implausibly deep-chested high-prancing steeds, brandishing swords at or gesticulating toward now-invisible foes. On the street beside the curb rested a gleaming red crotch rocket. She mounted, turned the ignition and the bike roared to life, though the engine noise was drowned out by a growl of thunder. She eschewed any helmet, gunned the bike out into traffic, hair streaming behind her. The Immortal sprinted to his SUV, but she rapidly shifted gears and was out of sight, only the fading roar of the bike remaining. He knew his friend was not going to like that development. Eron drove to the pre-arranged meeting spot.

* * *

Eron blinked in shock, the scene fading before his eyes. How many more memories of her had he? How long had they known each other before the curse? He was so lost in his thoughts, he almost rode upon her. Hurriedly he stopped his mount as she dismounted and let her stallion browse. Eron watched her hide behind a rock outcropping. He thought he heard voices, so he dismounted, tied his horse to a low-hanging branch and gave the animal an absentminded pat. When he looked back, she had disappeared.

What the hell? Where'd she go? Eron cautiously approached the rock outcropping; there was a small opening at eye level, and he peered through.

Holy shit! That's a fucking army! Eron counted the campfires scattered about. *Not a professional army, judging by the spacing of the fires.*

He concentrated on the men and camp followers moving in the firelight. *Ragtag clothing, where's...Ah there. Weapons, furs, and blankets in piles, a few small tents. Hired men.*

Eron watched a fight break out, growing to engulf another group of men before officers broke it up with difficulty. He was unfamiliar with the dialects, but guessed that more than one was being spoken.

Mercenaries, anyone who can hold a sword and swing it, and loot and rape and...Great. Does that damn kid think he's going to lay siege to the town and throne with this bunch? There won't be a town left when they get done. Amateur...crap! I'm going to get caught up and probably killed. Again. Hell no! It's time for me to make plans and leave, as of yesterday!

Eron gave a quick look behind, to make sure no one was sneaking up on him. *I have to find where she went. The day for the attack may have been set, so I will know how much time I have left to pack and leave. I don't want to be around when she tells the king. It has the potential to be the mother of all fuck-ups.* Staying low to the ground, he slithered back to the tree line, using it as cover to move further down the camp, disappointed he didn't have a chance to test his skill against any sentries. *Sloppy and over-confident. I could lead this rabble more effectively. I'd have the town under control in a day, and Lira would be my queen. What the hell am I thinking? I'm not that person anymore. Focus!*

The man came to the edge of the tree line, and saw a tent which could only belong to the leader of the rag-tag army. He had still not seen Illyria anywhere. *What did she do? Walk right into the camp? Just like an arrogant vamp. Mind-whammy their way past the support. Why the hell am I even here? It's not as if she needs me. Now how to get near the tent? It's too well-lit, I may have to give it up. Wait, what's this?*

Eron saw a cloaked figure escorted into the camp as Illyria exited the tent, followed by a large muscular man and his personal guards. *Damn! I really want to know what the hell they're saying.* He looked around for a better route to approach.

* * *

I faced Lord Nicky's slave; even close up, I still could not see inside the cowl. A wet guttural laugh issued from under that all-encompassing hood. I and the men behind me took an involuntary step back. "You would do well to fear me, more than Lord Nicky."

Fleeing was looking like a better option than staying, but I would not be scared until I knew why I felt the need. "Why?" I calmly asked.

"You have not learned from the last time you crossed beings of power. They cursed you. Your memories are only now returning."

I didn't know how much power he and Nicky had; they were not like the other immortals I had known. Whatever was before me laughed in sibilant amusement.

"My servant accomplished his task with what I taught him. The pain of breaking it fed me well, and for that you should be thankful."

I still couldn't pick out his mental signature. "Stop playing games like the boy. You claim to have information I need. If you have anything of value to report, do so."I could smell the fear-sweat of the men around me—intoxicating until I caught another whiff of the person before me, then it became nauseating.

"I think not. I like this way better," Nicky's slave said.

I felt a twisting in my gut, which almost brought me to my knees It felt like another being trying to invade me.

I tried to force the strange sensation away, but my body was out of my control. Had Lord Nicky's slave done this? Was he a witch? How could he take over my body and power?

"Wrong, little vamp." My mental shields crumpled from the brute force of his mind against mine.

He knows what I am?! How the hell?

He said, "Hell indeed, little vamp."

To my utter horror, and may I say there's not much anymore which can cause that sensation in me, a rotted hand shot out from the cloak, grabbed my upper arm and spun me about to face the growing circle of men ringing us. Every muscle in my body seized as if in one nasty cramp. I saw the men before me freeze, then jerk and scream as if in unimaginable pain. The other rotted hand rose from the sleeve of his robe and touched the chest of the man in front of him, right over his heart. I saw a blackened circle of flesh blossom, deepen, encompass the heart within the man's chest. Each man I could see developed their own matching hole.

I couldn't reach up and draw my swords. Damn it! Stupid vamp! Soon to be dead stupid vamp if I didn't get free. I fought for control of my body, felt his dominance over me lessen and with all my speed I let myself fall onto my ass, twisted, and brought my legs around, slamming at the arm holding me with every ounce of strength I could muster despite the pain. I heard his elbow snap, then a wet, ripping sound, and I was free, though I still had half an arm attached to me. Grimacing, I gave a vicious tug at the wet ends of the bone, felt the fingers spasm. I slid the forearm down my own arm, and as I felt it clear my fingers, I flung it out from me. Without being able to touch me, the slave couldn't kill me. The men screamed in terror as they fled. Others tried to attack us, but strangely were repelled. I looked to Lord Nicky's slave and recoiled as the thing before me laughed and laughed.

"It would be a mistake to attack me. Look closer," the voice hissing like steam from a kettle.

At first I saw only the rotted, dead person, but a hazy outline coalesced around it, bigger than the body before me, more massive, with muscle, horns. Okay, I got the point. Hell indeed. "Demon, I see?" I was pleased with how calm I sounded.

Another laugh was all I got. I felt fear give way to majorly pissed off. "Just who the hell... fuck holds whose reins here?"

The demon gave an angry hiss, much better than my own; I almost felt jealous. "This meeting was your idea, not mine. I have no interest in being tricked into any bargain. So whatever you want, forget it."

I got another hiss and a guttural growl. "Without the answers you seek?"

"I wasn't aware I had questions," I tartly replied, beginning to back away toward the trees.

"Phillip."

I caught myself before reacting and continued my slow backing away. "What of him?" I would not give him an opening.

"Your mate. Wandered off, dazed, amnesiac." The tone sly. "I can bring him back, and you will get rid of the little boy."

"No bargains, especially if he's truly dead." I was proud of my calm, how I permitted no iota of emotion to leak through the shields I had re-erected around my mind. Get away from the demon first, then weep and scream for the loss.

"Those men will never be able to kill the boy."

I couldn't help but interrupt, "And I'm the only one who can do it, blah, blah, blah." Why did these conversations so resemble one another?

The corpse's bulging eyes popped, and yet the thing could see me just fine. I crouched, readying for battle. I had no idea how quick the demon before me was.

"Stupid vampire." It sounded bitter and dare I say it? Disappointed? "You cannot kill the boy either."

"If no one can, what the fuck is the point of all this?" I moved to an all-new level of pissed-off.

It seemed he was going to respond when to my utter surprise I saw him stiffen in shock. I decided to take the opportunity presented me.

* * *

Nicky stopped short, gripped in fear at the carnage before him. The bodies of his men lay strewn about the ground like broken dolls. Those who still lived fought each other or fled. In the middle of the carnage were the last two people he expected to see: his demon and the duchess. *How could he get free of my bindings?! How dare my slave refuse to answer my summons! How dare the conniving bitch steal my slave!?* Nicky drew his sword and, slamming his spurs into his horse's side, charged. He had just enough power left to show them he was to be reckoned with.

Nicky watched surprise overcome his slave at sight of his master, realizing he had been outsmarted. Nicky's smirk of satisfaction became a yell of outrage as that damn woman moved in a blur, plowing into his slave.

* * *

Eron felt all the hair on his body raise in a spine-tingling rush unconnected with the impossible scenes unfolding before him. He saw the blur Lira became, watched as she and that whatever-the-hell-it-was disappeared into a patch of shadow. Eron could only stare as Nicky rode his horse past the man's hiding place.

The kid was yelling in an unknown yet familiar language. *Holy shit! Holy crap! Holy fuck! Yo! Stupid! Opportunity is knocking!* Nicky halted mere feet from another handy-dandy rock outcropping, and Eron bolted for it, using the trees for shelter and praying to all the forgotten gods the boy wouldn't see him. He gained the top, loose rocks clattering down, just as something shot like a firework rocket out of the end of the sword and exploded in a ball of light. *Not another one of those damn things! What the hell did he do? Attach it to his blade to launch it?* He set the impossibility out of his mind, squinted his eyes against the growing light, and launched himself off the rock in a flying tackle. Nicky was twisting in the saddle when the man slammed into him and dragged him off. The horse reared at the nasty yank on its reins and toppled onto his back, nearly crushing the two men.

* * *

I felt bones snap, flesh slid off as we hit the ground. The sun burst out in the middle of the night. Not again! I was only marginally better prepared for the pyrotechnics. My hand flung up, palm out, and I turned my head while closing my eyes to shield them as I tumbled off the man beneath me. He screamed, a noise high-pitched enough to burst a bat's eardrums. I felt my body hit the ground and through squinted eyes, I saw smoke rise off him, or maybe me? It sure felt as if the sun was burning me. Vision blurred, I spotted a white blur well away from the spreading glow. I hoped it was a tent. I scrambled up on all fours and had started to lunge up into a sprint for the blur when the man or sorry, demon, yelled something unidentifiable in a guttural tongue. It was like flicking a light switch. With a pop and a rush of cool air, the light vanished. Inky darkness without light of star or moon.

* * *

Eron grappled with Nicky for control of the boy's sword when they were plunged back into darkness. He let out a yell, partly because he couldn't see, and partly because of the elbow in his gut. He was left blinking, trying to keep a hold on the child. He felt a foot slam into the side of his head. He tried to grab it, but felt the kid's leg slip through his grasp.

"You'll pay for your interference!" Nicky snarled.

Everything still a blur and Eron had no peripheral vision. A wave of pain tore through him as he felt Nicky's sword slide out of his gut. He backed away as he staunched the wound with his left hand, forcing his guts to stay inside and the pain to the back of his mind while drawing his sword out. The man heard chanting. Silently he launched himself toward the source. Nicky saw the man come toward him, twisted, but was a tad too slow. He felt a searing pain in his left arm as blood trickled down.

Impossible! He'd dealt a death blow. The little boy froze for a moment but backpedaled. Straight into the rock behind him.

Nicky heard a whoosh, rolling away again just in time as Eron's sword rang against stone. He couldn't be too mad as the damn rock saved his other arm from getting sliced.

He gritted against the pain in his left arm as he placed pressure on it, trying to lift himself up. He almost lost his grip at the strength and force as the other man's sword rang against his own. The boy kicked out, making a lucky connection with his foe's knee. He felt it give and the man slammed down onto the ground. Nicky took the opportunity to spring up and slice the other man's back. For his trouble, he took a cut to his upper thigh. He made a limping run for an abandoned wagon. Slid under it and risked a glance back at the man gimping toward his hiding place.

Nicky sneered, lay panting to get his breath back. Swordplay was difficult against longer-armed heavier opponents. He preferred to ambush or let the people he tricked into caring for him defend him from others.

He had let his sword training grow lax when he learned how to make himself bigger, and his magic expanded, relying on his guards to take care of pesky details. He would have demanded DiJinn help him if the damn demon hadn't betrayed him again.

I ought to have kept punishing him the way my old masters told me I should. But no, he seemed to have learned his lesson early and well. Why waste my fading magick on something I didn't think I needed to do anymore?

If only the men around him would quit behaving like pussies. He had to get back to safety. Grab one of the horses running around, avoid the other men who would no doubt see him as prey.

Finally! The men saw Nicky's wounded attacker and were trying to overpower him, providing the perfect distraction. The boy scrambled out from underneath the wagon and ran as best he could toward one of the wandering horses. Eron saw the boy go as he hurried to dispatch the men attacking him.

Nicky veered just as a blade whistled past his head. He jumped the log seats surrounding a fire pit but caught his foot and went sprawling close to the fire. Ignoring the heat and flame, Nicky snatched a burning brand up and twisting, thrust it at his foe. The man grunted as the branch slammed into his stomach, and his sword blow at Nicky's chest went wide. It did slam off the kid's sword, scoring his shoulder; he was rewarded with a scream of pain. The man frantically beat at himself with his free hand as the brand caught his shirt on fire. Nicky fought to remain upright, but he would not pass out! He slammed his sword into the man's gut again before drawing it out, and painfully stumbled toward the milling horses.

Nicky sobbed in frustration at the slow pace of his retreat, what with fighting the pain from his cuts and defending himself. The boy clumsily blocked a blow intended to split his head open, losing his grip on his sword in the process. Eron's backswing with the pommel clipped the little boy upside the head and sent him flying into the dirt. Nicky's ears rang from the blow but swam back into consciousness as Eron knelt to finish incapacitating him. The little boy shot both legs up in a last, desperate effort and managed to kick the man full in the groin. Eron couldn't even scream, so great was the agony.

Nicky scrambled to his feet, a triumphant grin splitting his face. He snatched his sword up and plunged it into the back of the man before him. He looked toward his demon but it was still locked in combat with the woman.

* * *

The Thing/Demon? snarled as I drew my blades out.

"Get back to your hell-pit!" I snarled.

The demon grinned at me, muscles and tendons snapping with pops from the effort. "Surely you don't think that's going to work?"

The shriek I let out had nothing to do with the demon's sending me flying backward and everything to do with its stubbornness. I landed in a crouch as it materialized by my side. The demon lifted me by my throat, rotted bits sloughing off as it raised its arm. I shuddered, revolted.

"I will send you back," I gritted out. The stench this close was overpowering, but I rammed one sword into his gut and severed the arm holding me with the other. I dropped, yanking the second sword up and out. Rotting organs and trapped gases rushed out. The stench was enough to make anyone who must breathe to live bend over and puke.

I could hear Nicky yell something to the demon before me. I think it was annoyed; reading its expression was difficult with the few features remaining. It cursed, whether at me or the little boy, now fleeing toward a horse, I couldn't be sure. "You better hope he doesn't order me to kill you."

"If you don't know where I am, you can't," I gritted out.

"What makes you think I need to be near, vampire?" it hissed back. "Your maneuvering hasn't impressed me."

Oh, fabulous. Here I was, with no clue how to get rid of demons, and it was under the control of a vengeful, immature little boy. "Have you seen whom I have to work with?" I snapped, moving away from the body.

The thing's laugh was guttural, promising pain and other unpleasantries. I don't know how it did it, having no arms, but I felt claws rake down my face, leaving blood and searing furrows. I brought a sword up to take his head off and felt a brief burning sensation on my wrist, causing me to misstep.

"Run, little vamp! Before I am commanded otherwise." I brought the sword up and sliced his throat. Dark clots of blood and other bodily fluids came out. I looked for Eron. I still had uses for him, and capture by my enemy was not high on my list.

I thought I heard a howl of rage, or perhaps agony, in a voice which didn't seem like Nicky's as I kept moving, fighting off men as I looked for the immortal and risked a glance down at my throbbing wrist. What the? A pattern of red lines had appeared upon it in a newly formed excoriation. The damn demon had marked me! I could not keep a demon mark on me.

Pounding hooves brought my gaze around., Nicky sent his horse charging, men running like chickens from his contorted visage. My eyes followed his intended path and saw Eron feebly moving on the ground, trying to defend himself from men intent on killing him. Crap. The boy had a bigger head start, and I had half an army between me and the Immortal.

* * *

Eron heard the horse, even as a sword cut slashed across his chest when Nicky slammed into the group. Both combatants fell under his horse's trampling hooves. I saw the brat rein his mount around and put spurs to the animal's side for another pass.

“You stupid POS demon! I wanted her unharmed!” Nicky shrieked in rage. I didn’t know who he was yelling at, as the body the demon had occupied had collapsed from the loss of its puppet master.

The boy made one more pass over the prostrate forms of the two men and galloped off, avoiding the men running to intercept him. I had a quick scent of blood, and knew Eron or someone had harmed the advisor. Those men who had managed to capture mounts made a half-hearted chase attempt, while others turned their attentions to me.

I had to get the immortal out of here. I knelt by his side, putting the swords away. As I turned him over onto his back, the world wavered, melted, reformed. I was still kneeling beside the man, but his clothes had changed. He wore a long-sleeved worn purple t-shirt, dark blue jeans, and boots. He lay crumpled before me, having fallen from four floors above. A man stood glaring down at me, leaning over the metal railing.

“You won’t escape me easily!” He had brown eyes, an old scar running from his hairline diagonally across his nose to the left side of his chin. His eyes widened for a moment, and he laughed, a chilling, delighted laugh. “Oh, I’ll enjoy cutting your head off.”

I could hear the lap of water from somewhere, and a creak of metal. “Don’t,” another voice spoke softly, a woman’s voice. “If you fight him, you will lose all. Remember your promise.”

A man stepped from the gloom surrounding us; he was tall, lean and muscular with long shining blond hair and green eyes. He seemed young but his eyes held ancient wisdom. His brow creased briefly as he looked from the crumpled man to me, and his voice was velvet. “Let his kind see to him. You need to help us get back.”

I could not trust myself to speak. I had seen the man almost die. I had shoved him out of the way of the explosion. I barely noted the gleaming short swords in both hands as I felt another presence come up behind me.

A world-weary voice spoke, “Now is not the time for revenge, young one. Already your kind discusses your involvement. Leave him for another day.”

I knew I should trust one who had seen more centuries than I, but he neither liked nor trusted me. The crumpled man before me gasped. I heard bones realigning themselves.

The man above me shouted down, "This isn't over yet! I'll find you one day!"

The men around me didn't react, merely kept gazing at me. I could sense more people around us in the gloom, and the smooth female voice spoke, "We must go. I sense one last trick from the man above. A deadly one."

The concrete beneath us shook, the man above laughed, turned and ran, boots ringing on the metal walkway. I caught the scent of smoke, burning things, plastic.

"Bomb!" I screamed as the shaking intensified.

The men understood now. Horror flashed across their faces.

The world melted once again, and I was back to kneeling in the valley, with Eron before me. I sucked in a harsh breath I didn't need and stopped the attack a hair's breadth from my head. My new scar itched and throbbed in an unfamiliar pain. I didn't need any more flashbacks.

There was no time to be delicate; I hauled Eron up in a fireman's lift over my shoulders, snatched up his sword and sprinted for the tree line and our horses. Why did the fuck-up fairy have to choose this night of all nights to visit? Double damn.

Chapter Six

Mica felt himself floating on a sea of blackness, images swimming behind his eyes. He was remembering every time he and his brother spent together. His brother. *Where was his brother now? They were supposed to be doing something very important. What was it? Think, think!*

"I can't let the boy live, Colin, not after what he's done to us."

"I don't know, bro. Eron seems to think if we forget about him, Nicky will come to us. We could waste seven years of our life searching for him. What if we can't find him? How long do we search before we say we won't find him and take the gem back? Are you willing to risk your life?"

"Yes! He must be destroyed! We must see that the Immortal Wolf didn't die in vain!" Mica was insistent.

Colin, where was Colin? He heard chanting, saw him through a glass cell.

"Mica! Mica!" Colin screamed from his prison.

Mica banged on the glass, but it wouldn't budge. The pain in his brother's eyes! The accusation!

"What have you done to me? We're family! How could you condemn me!? Mica!"

"Colin! I swear, I never intended for it to happen!" Mica pleaded through the glass. "This was not supposed to happen!"

Screams. Someone was screaming in terror and horror. Colin was reaching out to him, his mouth moved, but Mica couldn't hear him. Something held him from his brother, some invisible wall.

"Colin! Help me break through!" Colin raised his arms and placed his hands flat, palms making prints on what he realized was glass. Mica mirrored him. His arms and hands were sinking through to meet those of his brother, and he grabbed hold of his brother to pull him through.

Colin looked at him, pleading with Mica. What was he saying? Mica braced himself and yanked hard. Colin toppled through and landed in a heap beside Mica on the grass.

His younger brother looked up at the sky, so blue with happy puffs of cotton clouds. A sweet wind blew across the grass, making it ripple gently and bringing the faint scent of wildflowers. He turned his head to look at his brother lying next to him with a long blade of grass between his lips.

"It's good to be home again. Will you not stay awhile?"

"To be sure but only for a small time. I still have things to do."

"It can't be that important. Nothing ever is." Colin smiled, "You haven't been home in so long. I saw Sarah making eyes at you last night.'"

"I wish I could, Colin, but the matter is necessary to me." Mica knew their conversation was not right.

His brother studied him, "Don't let it obsess you, bad things can happen when you let something consume you."

The clouds started racing across the sky as it darkened to pitch. Lightning ripped across as thunder gave a hollow boom. Needle-like drops of rain slashed down. They were no longer in a meadow but a vast sea. The wind rose with a howl, sounding like a thousand voices chanting a death knell. A wave rolled over Mica and when he surfaced, Colin was being swept from him.

"Colin! Colin hold on! I'm coming!" Mica struggled against the heavy swells but the pull of the current sucked him down.

Mica struggled endlessly in the roiling sea, the bitterness of the waves far less than that of his own failure to save his brother. He swam toward a glow from far ahead only to realize it was the bottom of the sea. Instead of sand, it was made up of thousands of clear plastic cubes. Each one contained an image of Colin, laid out in death. Mica opened his mouth in denial, but only bubbles emerged.

Mica found himself back in the home of his childhood, staring at Colin laid out on a bier. Around him were the mourners. He looked to see who had come to pay their respects. Eron stood, gazing sadly at Colin. His eyes moved to meet Mica's.

"I'm sick of your quest! It'll only end in death and destruction! Look what you've done to your brother!" Eron reached out and took the hand of Illyria.

Mica felt a black rage, wanting to scream and smash her as she spoke, "You stubborn, foolish man. I told you to trust me. His death could have been prevented if only you had followed my orders."

Colin regarded Mica with dead eyes. "It's too late now. You can't bring me back, move on."

Their voices mingled, each repeating the words they had spoken.

"No! It's your fault, you hell-bitch! You'll pay for my brother's death with your life!" Mica roared out his denial.

He charged, ramming his blade through Illyria's gut. She looked down at it and then up at him; only it was Colin he saw instead.

"What have you done to me, brother?" Colin whispered painfully before sliding off the blade. His body collapsed and red bloomed.

"Nnnnnnoooooooooo!" Mica howled, backing up. He bumped into an invisible wall and looked down as the blood kept rising. His shrieks rang out, and he swept his arms out only to encounter two more walls. He was in a cube.

Mica looked up, screaming denials as his brother's blood rose higher, faster, and he began to choke on it.

* * *

Mica sat bolt upright, heart pounding, sweat drying on his body, chilling him. For long moments, he could only sit and breathe harshly in the darkness. When his panic subsided, he looked around in confusion. Mica dimly remembered his nightmare, and his thoughts flew to Colin. He tried to stand and swayed at the movement. Spots danced in front of his eyes.

As Mica's head cleared, he felt he had healed completely from the repeated torture. He tried to count how many days it had been since his captors had done their best to get the immortal to reveal the location of Nicky's soul gem. He just didn't know. Mica had drifted in and out of consciousness; they had left off drugging him and tried starving him. He knew how long it would take a man to starve to death, and he was close to the danger zone. The Guardian of the Cave should be coming for him any moment. He could swear he heard chanting, and a rushing sound, as his final death approached.

A deep terror awoke in him. He had told Eron repeatedly he was willing to die to see the boy's life ended, yet he'd believed Nicky would precede him in death. He had failed, not only himself, but Colin, as well. Mica didn't know if his brother were alive, or if the men who had captured him had also caught his brother.

Mica couldn't let the little boy win, but he didn't trust the men with what they asked. Why was his brother not looking for him? The kingdom wasn't large, unless he had been moved outside of it? Perhaps his captors kept moving him to prevent his friends from discovering where they held him.

He rubbed his head, which started in on a low, throbbing ache. Mica didn't understand why it plagued him, or why it wouldn't go away. There seemed to be something just on the edges of his consciousness, trying to break free. Voices, echoing and thundering in his head behind locks. He had to concoct a reason why he had to be taken to the spot instead of just telling them where to look. If he did, mayhap he had a better chance of trying to get free.

Mica yelled in a voice hoarse from long disuse and lack of water, "Hey! Hey! Lemme out! You piss-faced vultures!"

He yelled until he was exhausted, but no one came. He sat back down on the floor and drifted to sleep. The immortal didn't know how long he slept, only that when he woke, he was strapped into a wooden chair. He wasn't sure if it were an improvement.

A rough voice spoke in a strained whisper, "Ah, you are awake. I hope you are in a cooperative mood."

Mica tested the straps, trying to see where the man was. Several paces in front of him, standing like silent sentinels, the two torturers. Since he hadn't been asked a question yet, he decided to remain silent. The Head Questioner walked out from behind the chair to stand in front of him.

The flickering of the brazier illuminated his milk-white eye and half-burned face and he took great care not to let his right hand or arm be seen.

"I am...disturbed." The man gazed upon him before resuming, "It seems I have been lied to, by not one but two people. This vexes me."

Mica remained silent, trying to remain calm, even though his heart pounded fiercely inside.

"I distinctly remember torturing you, and quite a masterpiece of work it was if I do say so myself." The man laughed at the shudder the sitting man couldn't quite conceal.

The noise soon died into a hissing, hacking sort of cough. When he had it under control, the man strode forward and thrust his face into Mica's. The stench of burned flesh curled between them. His voice thrummed in anger, and spittle hit the immortal. "You should be in pain. Writhing from it! Begging for release from it! And yet what do I find?"

His good eye wild with rage. "I find you acting as if nothing happened to you!"

Mica didn't like where this was going and kept silent, waiting for the question he knew had to be coming.

"So why do you act the way you do? I want to know, and you will tell me!" He drew back, and slashed down the side of Mica's face.

The man ignored the burning pain, his situation much worse than he had anticipated. If he told what he was, he had no illusions: his jailor would demand to be taught the ritual. He was prepared to give up the soul gem, but this was more than he was willing to concede.

Mica retreated into his head. It wasn't until the man left off slashing and moved onto breaking bones that Mica roused out of his stupor. Eventually, screams of agony tore from him.

The immortal sat, pain lancing along every nerve end, head lolling forward, clinging to consciousness when a thunderclap of sound echoed throughout the chamber.

A guttural voice, which seemed to come from everywhere demanded, "You dare to disobey me, slave?"

The man dropped down on one knee, bowing his head. "Master. No, Master. I thought only to impress you with breaking the man and getting the information you needed from him."

Mica was dimly aware of a long scream of pain from his torturer and couldn't keep the smile off his face.

"The only thing which will impress me is my slave following my orders!"

Screams followed the words, then the man sobbed out, "Y...Yes Master."

Fingers cold as ice grabbed Mica's chin and yanked it up. He found himself staring into blazing eyes. He tried to blink the sweat and blood out of his vision; something seemed to be wrong with the person's face. His head was left to drop back down, and the man before him turned his robed back to the immortal.

"He is of no use to me today. Because you choose to ignore my commands and overstep your bounds, I must punish you," the guttural voice continued in pleasant enough tones, but currents of fear ran up both men's backs.

He made a gesture which had the Head Questioner writhing on the stone floor in agony. The master stopped only when his slave screamed himself hoarse.

"I have need of one piece of knowledge this man holds, slave. He is not to be touched unless I command you. All other matters pale before mine. If you cannot obey me, I shall find one who can. Think carefully, and remember our bargain." The master didn't sound as if he cared what the man's decision was—either way he would win.

Mica's smaller cuts had healed already, and the deeper ones starting to re-knit along with his bones. He forced himself to hold off on letting his body sleep so it could repair itself.

"Yes, Master. I hear and obey."

"Excellent. Convey him to his cell. Tomorrow we begin anew." The master left, door shutting softly behind him in punctuation.

The burned man hauled himself painfully off the floor, walking over to stand swaying in front of his prisoner.

He spit on Mica. "You bastard. One day you will be mine to do with as I please, and there will be no one to interfere."

Mica didn't reply; he was hoping to be free by then. Dimly he was aware of the two hulking brutes unstrapping him and carrying him back to his cell. He let himself fall into a healing sleep.

* * *

The meadow was blooming with wildflowers, the sun shone in an azure sky. Mica squinted down at his village spread below.

"It's time to leave, brother. Time to start a new life." Colin spoke calmly.

"I don't know if I can," Mica confessed.

"You must. You agreed when you asked to be made what you are now. Please don't force me to undo the ritual. It'll kill you and I couldn't bear the thought." Colin was soothing and patient. "You have to journey still and place your soul gem in safe keeping."

"Do you ever regret having it done?" Mica asked, still gazing to the village.

Colin looked out over the sunlight meadow to their village below. "Sometimes. But then I think of what I can do, see and learn and sorrow vanishes, regret evaporates. I can always die. I need only find someone to do the correct ritual."

Mica turned to his brother and saw where his heart should be an empty hole. His ruined soul gem hung on a chain. Mica felt a mild horror and a profound sadness at the sight.

"I've failed you. I'm so sorry. Can you ever forgive me?" He gestured to the wound.

Colin's mouth quirked in a smile, "It's not I who needs the forgiveness, but you. It was bound to happen. Too many bad choices made. Don't make another, please. I'd hate for you to end like me."

''But it was my pride. I betrayed you," Mica began.

Colin shook his head. "We all made the bargain. This happened because of treachery. If we had never made it, it would be you who died. Do what you must, brother."

"I don't know how I can anymore. Look what the murdering bitch's done to me." He gestured to his ruined body as it struggled to heal.

Sorrow filled Colin's eyes. "You cannot blame Illyria for things other people have done to you."

A heat filled Mica and moved all through his body. "It's

because of her you're the way you are and I'm..."

"Then I cannot help you, brother. Do what you must. For I cannot, not anymore. I'm sorry." So saying, he started to walk off.

"Colin! No! Wait!" Mica cried out, chasing after his brother.

But his brother seemed not to hear, and the distance between them widened until Mica found himself running alone through an endless meadow. He stared up into the blinding sun and screamed his fury and pain to it.

* * *

Mica woke to the darkness once more; he was fully healed, yet still had no clue what day it was, or how much closer to expiration his opportunity to use the soul gem had moved. He wasn't sure he could handle any more torture—his extremities twitched and jumped from all the healing they had been forced to do. He wasn't now in pain, but he remembered it whenever he moved.

The immortal gritted his teeth and rolled over on the cold, damp stone floor, creaked up on hands and knees. He felt his way around the cell, but the stool was empty of food, and only a little water in a crock. His prison of unyielding stone. He would have to wait. Maybe when those men came to carry him to the torture area, he could slip past them and run? It was a plan, the only one he could come up with, but having even one made him feel better.

A low grinding noise woke Mica. He lay against a wall. Slowly and carefully, he stood as the door swung inward. Though he'd adjusted to no light, but still, he was for all intents and purposes blind without it. He listened to the steps of the two men as they entered his cell.

He used the sound to aim his kicks, and what he could remember of their height. He clocked one of the men before the second man clubbed him over the head, knocking him out.

When Mica could focus again, pain swam in brightly colored streamers before his eyes, and he was strapped down in the chair. The sibilant voice of the burned man spoke.

"You have damaged my slave. This displeases me greatly."

The man paced in front of Mica as if in thought, then whirled and demanded, "Why do you heal as you do?"

The immortal let the silence stretch and lengthen.

"You will answer my questions, or I will punish you."

Mica refused to answer, secure in the fact the man in front of him couldn't harm him without angering his master and receiving punishment in return.

"Perhaps you think I won't dare? Do not let the words of my master make you foolish. I would dare anything for the secret of what you are."

Still the immortal said nothing, merely looked at the man before him.

"Very well. You have been warned. Don, Jon, the right hand, open it flat upon the chair arm."

The men shuffled over, and even though Mica held his fist clenched tight, his strength was no match for the two before him. They pried his hand open and the burned man came over with a hammer and a nail.

"No!" Mica yelled, trying to jerk free, but the leather strap prevented him from moving his arm.

The pain was sharp and immediate. The immortal did his best to ride it out. When his vision cleared enough for him to see again, he looked for his tormentor.

The man was holding a dagger to the base of his pinky, and even with the light amount of pressure, Mica could tell the blade was very sharp.

"What, what are you doing?" The Immortal hated the whiney tone of his voice.

"The truth, please. Why are you as you are? Why are you still not hurt?"

"I don't..." He had to stop and lick dry lips. "I don't understand the question."

The blade pressed enough to bring blood welling up. "I think you do. Quit stalling."

Mica's brain raced frantically; if he told, he might never get out, but if he bargained...

"Need you think about your reply?" the man asked, pressed harder.

"Wait! Wait! I'm just, I, it's been so long, I don't... I can't... I'm not sure anymore how it happened." Mica stalled.

The man waited, dagger held in a steady hand, ready to finish cutting. "How long?" he said flatly. It wasn't a question.

"Years, centuries."

The man hesitated, then sheathed the knife and sat behind a table, parchment and pen and inkwell before him. "How many centuries exactly?" He dipped the quill into some ink.

Mica didn't need a written record of what he was, but the more interested the man in his story, the better. He would play Scheherazade if it delayed pain.

"At least, as best I can recall, pre-cataclysm. Over...over 5,000 years ago."

The man's head snapped up sharply, his gaze narrowed. "How did it happen?"

"That's the part I have trouble recalling, it's been so long."

"You'll have to do better," he was sternly told.

"I'm trying!" Mica snapped. "I have a lot of memories to sift through."

"I would think something so momentous would not be an event easily forgotten," his tormenter replied.

"It was not a happy, or pleasant occasion. Just give me a bit to think. I haven't had to remember back that far for, well, forever."

The scarred man scowled. "Very well. But my patience is not infinite. I needn't remind you what will happen if you lie?" He picked up a goblet and took a sip, watching Mica.

Mica briefly closed his eyes; perhaps a half-truth would be acceptable. It wasn't like the man before him could verify any of the information. "I don't remember when I became an immortal, or how. After I had been half-crushed by a falling tree, I noticed wounds I received healed faster."

"What type of wounds? Where were they and how severe?" the man asked.

"My, my lower half had been crushed—both my legs, and my pelvic area," Mica replied.

"How did you get back to your...dwelling?"

"I was with a team of loggers; they loaded me onto a cart, took me to the local medical man. He was the one who said I would be dead after a few days. He could do no more than give me something to dull the pain until the end came."

"So they were fatal wounds?" The man dipped his quill in more ink and finished his writing.

"It is what I can remember him saying. But after a few days I woke and saw the wounds were reduced, less severe than they should have been."

"Interesting," the interrogator said, making a notation. "What did the medical man say when he saw you?"

"He was not around. The hut was empty when I woke. I didn't see anyone for days after. I lay there until I noticed my legs had healed enough for me to get up and walk."

"And what happened to the medical man and the others who were logging?"

"I don't know. The place looked like it had been raided and abandoned. I surmise rival loggers."

"Hrm." The man recorded Mica's answers.He scrutinized the man strapped down before him, finishing his drink. He walked around the table, standing before Mica, toyed with the dagger he had taken from its sheath on his belt.

"You know, I think you're a liar," his captor remarked conversationally. "I wonder: if I were to ask you the same questions days from now, would you give me the same answers?"

"Why would I lie?" Mica just barely kept from shouting.

"I once asked Lord Nicky, after he had consented to make me his apprentice, how he came to be what he was. He only would tell me bits and pieces, as a reward for learning some particularly difficult task he had set me," the man mused.

Mica had a feeling he wasn't going to like where the confidence was going.

"His story, you see, would change. Oh, not the significant parts, but the details, as if he couldn't remember what he had said from one telling to the next."

The dagger's edge came to rest back at the base of Mica's pinky, and pressed. The cut, which had been healing, slowly oozed blood again.

"You can understand how I would view your tale as just an interesting fiction you are making up for my benefit. I have no doubt it may contain some small kernel of truth, but I am not looking for pretty lies."

"Why the hell did you ask me?" Mica gritted out.

"So you should know what happens when I am lied to," the man replied and brought his full weight down on the knife.

Mica felt the blade slide through his flesh and muscle and grate on the bone of his finger. He screamed long and loud. Where his pinky finger had been, was now a stump. He could not tell if the skin had healed over the wound already or not.

"Why, oh why did you do that?" Mica could not help sobbing.

He screamed as the nail was pounded out of his hand, came to, lolling in the iron grip of the two men. His torturer held up the severed finger so the immortal could see it as he directed his slaves,

"Take him to his cell. When you are ready to tell me the truth, we shall talk again."

"When your Master finds out what you have done, I hope he kills you," Mica managed to grind out around the pain.

The man bent and whispered in Mica's ear, "He may be too late to help you by the time he does show up. For every meeting where you do not tell me what I want to know, I shall cut another piece off. It would excite me to see a limbless torso with a head."

Mica knew he was screaming in horror before lapsing into semi-consciousness. Mica knew the finger could never be re-attached. He had seen an immortal lose a limb once. The man had forever been without a leg. The assistants half-dragged him moaning to a cell and, dumping him on the floor, went back to the torture chamber. Mica lay where he had fallen and shivered.

How was he to tell the truth? If he recanted now, the man might cut more pieces off because of the immortal's lies; but if he didn't tell the truth, it was certain he would lose more body parts. Mica was doomed either way. It was only a matter of how many parts he was going to lose before he was rescued, if he ever was.

Just the thought made him nauseous. "No! I will not despair!" Mica told himself. To despair was to invite madness. He would have to plan his escape, he would have to break their hold once in the torture chamber.

The man had a feeling there would only be one chance to attempt escape. Mica lay on the floor, and tried to meditate on what he had seen of the chamber. Eventually, he drifted off to sleep.

* * *

The streets were wet, and the pavement glistened as Mica walked in the gloaming, melancholy. He had just broken up with his girlfriend, and even though he knew it was coming, the parting was still bittersweet. The streetlights had halos of light around them. People hurried, some trying to get to vehicles or subway to go home, others to dinner and drinks.

He envied them, their brief lives, and wondered if he had truly made the right choice all those long years ago. He stopped at a corner with a crowd of people, waiting for the light to change, and let himself be carried along in the tide, idly glancing at the store fronts as he walked. Several times, he was sent dazzling smiles from women passing in the crowd, and once, a man.

Mica wanted to be alone, yet he didn't, and he toyed with the idea of calling a friend, or maybe his brother. He kept walking uptown as dusk turned into night. Still he aimlessly wandered the streets as the night wore on. Up ahead, he thought he saw someone he knew coming out of an expensive and popular restaurant.

He stopped abruptly in surprise, and was bumped and cursed by a few people. It was Illyria, not in any of her regular flashy-couture clothes, but rather business chic with a smart bag. Her companion looked like a slick businessman or lawyer.

Mica moved closer, and saw a glossy black Rolls Royce Phantom, the extended wheelbase, with a chauffeur holding the door. He watched as she parted with the man, already engrossed in the phone in the few steps she took to the car.

He couldn't help himself, even though he despised how she had tormented Devon—she was still someone you could confide in without the information being used against you. Mainly, he mentally corrected himself, as long as you weren't an enemy and she wasn't gunning for you. He started over to her, calling out her name. An eyebrow raised when she saw who hailed her, though she gave a dazzling smile. Her hair wasn't in its usual curling mass down her back but tamed in a sleek French twist.

"Bonjour, Mica, to what do I owe this pleasant surprise?"

"New look?"

"Even party girls must work from time to time," she said with an amused glance. "And what have you been up too?"

He hesitated, not sure how to frame his request. Sometimes she made him feel to ask anything of her was akin to asking for a favor, and she would and did often collect on them.

He shrugged and gave a smile, not realizing how sad and bitter it was. "Just enjoying the nice spring evening, you?"

She gave him a piercing stare as the phone in her hand dinged with an annoying rapidity which spoke of incoming messages.

"I am heading to another interest of mine, one I think you might like. If you wish, ride with me and stay as my guest. I can have my driver take you home when you want."

She named a spot he was unfamiliar with. Mica told himself it was reconnaissance, know thy enemy and all. They got in the limo, and before it had even pulled away from the curb, she was busy with her phone. He stared out the smoked windows as the city slid by, the dings and beeps of her cell a background noise to the otherwise silent space.

The limo wound further uptown, before slowing and double-parking in front of one of the city's newest hot spots. By the time the man came around to open the door, she had dipped into her bag and had brought out a VIP pass and employee ID. The pass she gave to him to wear around his neck, and he silently cursed her as they slid out of the car.

She put on a pair of expensive sunglasses, and he pasted a bland expression on his face as they bypassed the line of hopefuls waiting to get in.

It was much, much later when Mica, slightly drunk now on expensive scotch, followed her into her multi-level penthouse in one of the city's most desirable buildings. The pad was quiet, with the smell of rarified air all such places had. He followed her into the living room, and saw the city spread out before him like a sparkling jewel.

He was busy admiring the view and didn't notice when she went to a hidden bar and brought out another bottle and a glass, and a crystal bucket of ice.

"What is wrong, Mica?" She sat on one of the couches,

delicate feet tucked underneath her, her fashionable, very expensive high heels lying on the rug.

He left off examining the city and plopped down at the other end of the sofa, noticing the bottle contained a very nice scotch.

"No matter what, you always treat your guests like royalty." He savored the single-malt, one he had been able to afford only once.

She remained quiet, waiting for him, her phone on her lap, her head propped on one hand, elbow on the back of the couch. How could you talk about the eternal loneliness which came with being an immortal with someone who hadn't even lived a century yet?

"You would not understand," was what he said.

"Because you think me so young?" she asked, just a tinge of annoyance in her voice. "I promise I shall listen only."

He gave her a jaded look, savored another sip before speaking. "Yes, you are young. It's not just the way you look and dress. Have you lived a century yet?" He knew he was insulting her, he remembered when he was a new-made immortal; questions like that from older immortals had always irked him.

She seemed to take it in stride as if expecting it, her eyes never leaving his face. "If your problem deals with this age, I can be of some assistance."

He snorted and muttered into his glass, "It's a problem no matter what the age or time-period."

Her eyebrow quirked up. "Disappointed in love, Mica? I would not have believed it of you. I am sure I shall be as jaded as you, wondering why I cannot find loooove, twuuuu loooove." She snickered.

Was she making fun of him? It was a reference with which he was unfamiliar. He set his glass down with a snap, and made to get up.

"No, no, no!" she protested. "I am sorry. You must admit though, that the romantic love the human race talks about today does not exist and has never existed. It is something created by troubadours, Hollywood, the diamond people and the wedding industry to brainwash the masses into thinking they can find it."

He thumped back down. "It doesn't seem to have taken you long to become cynical."

"You know I'm right. The most we can hope for is someone who makes us want to be better versions of ourselves, someone who will be there no matter what curveballs life throws us."

"It took me centuries to discover the love they sang about was bullshit. Do you know how many times I've found someone who could be called my true love? Just once, and she died in my arms."

"Why should it bother you if you've been abandoned by some woman who couldn't appreciate the real you? Why not just enjoy what was, for however long it was?"

"You'll see, should you live more than a century or two, how tiring, how exhausting, how disheartening it is to be forever searching, always saying good-bye."

The laughter faded from her eyes, and she suddenly looked much older, much wearier, than her apparent age of thirty years. "Perhaps if we ever learn to trust each other, I shall tell you just how long I have lived, how many lives and loves lost to time." Anguish crossed her face before smoothing out to its young mask.

"Perhaps," he replied noncommittally and sat back with his drink, content for the moment to be with a person who understood after all.

* * *

Mica woke with a start, the dream, no, even that didn't seem right, fading from his mind. It had the feel of an event he had lived a long time ago. Why was Illyria, Her Grace, the Duchess, in it? It wasn't something he needed to dwell upon—it wouldn't free him.

Chapter Seven

Colin woke to silence, darkness, the smell of old blood, mold, and cold. Tentatively he flexed fingers and toes, before testing the rest of his limbs. He was unbound. A fading ache all through his body brought back memories of being beaten with cudgels. Colin sat up, patting himself down. His captors had taken his belt and pouches but left him his boots and clothes.

The man felt around the stone floor and only encountered flags. Carefully he turned over onto hands and knees, slowly crawled, feeling the floor, the air around him.

"Mica!" he hissed, waiting for an answer.

"Mica! If you're awake, answer me!" None came.

Did it mean his brother was bound and gagged? Was he in the same space? Was he even alive? Colin kept crawling until he bumped into something wooden. He felt the object, hands tracing the outline of a crude human shape, a brief touch of metal bars. Upright, he kept one hand on the unknown object and probed the floor in front of him.

More cold stone, rough underfoot. His hands busy sweeping about his body as he slowly moved forward. He came across more wood, what felt like rough rope, and icy metal chains. He didn't like what he was feeling. Colin didn't know how long it took him to make his way around the room. Eventually, he felt the outlines of what had to be hinges and a door.

He tested the handle, it turned easily, and opened inward. Faint tendrils of light appeared, and when the door was fully open, he saw a lantern hanging from a hook on the wall. He took it up, unsure how much oil was left in the well. The Immortal knew he needed to get out of whatever prison he was in, find his brother.

Curiosity, however, overcame him.

Just a quick look. I've gotta be sure my brother isn't inside.

Colin ventured back into the room, turned the lamp up a notch more and held it up by its handle. The flickering glow showed a torture chamber. Each device appeared well-used, if not well taken care of. Blood and other fluids crusted on the wood surfaces. The iron maiden held a skeleton in rotting clothes.

Metal chains dangled from the walls, along with tackles, pulleys, and stone weights. There was no sign of Mica.

"Come on! Why put me in here and not lock the door? Or chain me up? What's the point of it all?"

The man left the room and shone his light up and down the crude stone floors and walls. Two more doors interrupted, both shut. He picked one and tried the latch. It opened under his touch. The room did not have an occupant, only a hole in the floor smelling strongly of feces and urine, a set of chains upon the wall. The room behind the second door an exact duplicate to the first.

"O.K. private torture chamber and cells. But where am I? More importantly, where is my brother?"

Colin continued down the hall to a door which closed it off. It, too, opened easily to show another room, which contained many doors and a set of stairs. Freedom stared him in the face, only...

"I wonder what's behind the other doors? I may never get a chance like this again."

He ignored every instinct screaming at him to get out, and explored. Behind the doors lay pantries, a kitchen, workrooms for the care and upkeep of the building. One room held a jumble of detritus that accumulates in large dwellings. Colin wiggled his way through the piles and stacks of rotting wood, cloth, and wicker. Mica was not chained inside, and the cursory inspection the immortal gave to the junk didn't reveal anything useful. He left the room, ignored the stairs, and opened a door underneath them.

Another hallway led into a second, longer wing with many doors. Each one opened easily to his touch. Each room, no, cell, held a bed, washstand, chamber pot, and pegs on the wall for clothes.

"Slave quarters." He dismissed the barren rooms and turned back to the stairs. His curiosity still over-riding his common sense.

"Why toss me down here and not restrict my movements? Where are the guards? None of it makes any sense."

He started up the wood steps, which creaked under every footfall. At the top he encountered another closed door, it too unlocked. The cool basement air was replaced by warm, stale air.

"Bizarre."

The door led out into an open curved space with stairs to a second floor and the main entrance hall. The floor was a mixture of stone, marble, and mosaic tiles in no discernible pattern. A massive brass chandelier overhead held remnants of candles, and pools of hardened wax dotted the floor beneath. Stone bases with nothing on or in them except a few holes stood against the orange painted walls. The front door a massively, intricately carved piece of wood. It, unlike the others, was locked tight.

Colin patted his clothes. He had no tools on him to force the lock. Its lock needed a key both inside and outside.

"There has to be a back door, or windows even." He scratched at his skin, pushed up his sleeves to look at his arms. It felt as if millions of tiny bugs crawled and bit. The skin was red from his nails, no bugs, still the feeling persisted. He set himself to ignore it and explore.

Colin felt jittery and uneasy, sweat broke out on his skin as he moved from room to room. Spaces heavily and richly furnished, despite the poverty of the times. More of the stone bases stood against the walls, and in the center of each room was a knee-height wood platform. Thick velvet or brocade drapes covered windows. Colin tried each one, but shutters covered them, locked like the front door. A few had what looked like scratch marks on them, perhaps from fingernails of people trying to claw or pry them open without success. Each room spoke of wealth, though the taste of the owner questionable at best. If it wasn't for the empty bases, the house would just be a rich noble's fancy hunting lodge.

He found himself back in the main hallway after exploring two short wings, one with servants' rooms.

"The second floor it is. It would be nice if a hinge were loose, or even a key left lying about."

Slowly he made his way up the stairs but hesitated at the top. The landing had doors opposite each other, no doubt leading into separate hallways. They seemed heavier than the ones downstairs, and he had a fleeting thought that, with them closed, any screams or sounds would be muffled, if not blocked completely. He didn't relish investigating each hall. He swiped his arm across his forehead to blot at the sweat which soaked him.

The immortal turned to the left and entered the closed-off hall. Each door heavily carved, with scenes of couples or groups engaged in various positions of copulation. Behind, the rooms still richly if perhaps sparingly furnished. The accoutrements suggested whoever used them was into bondage games. Colin continued checking behind all the drapes, testing the locks on the shutters, hoping one had been overlooked, but no such luck.

He exited the hall, crossed the landing, and entered the right-hand side. There was only a few doors in the wing, the rooms much larger. He could only surmise it was Nicky's private area, as the decor was lush and rich. The feeling of wrongness intensified, and Colin realized that for several minutes now his breathing had become labored and fast, as if in fear, heart pounding. Back on the landing, he almost didn't see the concealed door, painted to look like part of the wall. He spent many minutes searching for the catch. When it swung inward, a steep set of stairs led up.

Colin mounted them, and found himself under the eaves of the roof. He could only stand upright if he stayed in the middle, due to the sharp slope. Metal grilles had been placed in the floor at regular intervals. He peered through, noting he could see into the rooms below. The wooden floor had dust thickly over it, except in places where someone had knelt to spy. The air up here was fetid and humid. His clothes soaked in sweat. He swallowed, throat feeling tight and raspy. Now his curiosity had been satisfied, he needed to get out.

The man stumbled down the stairs to the first floor, dots appeared before his eyes, a high pitched whine buzzing in his ears. The hall spun before him. Colin didn't realize when the lantern fell from his numb fingers and hand. It smashed against the floor, what little oil remained catching fire and burning briefly as he slowly tilted forward. The treads met him with a bone-jarring rattle. He stared, dazed, at the painted ceiling of flames, smoke, writhing bodies, before passing out.

* * *

Voices greeted his ears. Languages which to him sounded as if they had once been Russian, Ukrainian, Polish, German. The man inhaled: the scents of wood smoke, wet livestock, horse and human manure, unwashed bodies, and food tickled his nostrils. He lay on wood, curled into an uncomfortable ball. Colin let his lids open a bit at a time. He didn't know what poison made him die back at the hunting lodge. He saw metal bars before him, and when he rolled over, saw he was in a small cage roped to the back of a wagon. Nighttime greeted his senses. He shivered in the cold air, noting a thin film of ice on the bars.

The immortal couldn't even stand in his cage, only kneel or sit cross-legged, no space for his stretched-out legs. He idly listened to the different dialects, trying to make sense of the words. The languages had changed so much, that he only understood one in twenty words. Dogs yipped, howled, men shouted, argued, laughed. Occasionally female screams arose, sometimes as if in pain, others in ecstasy. He heard the shuffle of hooves, the sleepy snort of a horse. The man strained with all his senses, but learned no more. He explored the confines of his cage, hoping there would be a flaw permitting escape. It seemed there was none.

How many days have I been a captive? Where is my brother? Who has him? Colin struggled to keep calm.

He could only wait, for food, water, a chance to relieve himself. None came. Only the relentless cold, the night unending. The man curled into a ball, shivered uncontrollably, drifting in and out of sleep. He was not aware when dawn broke, only the slow lightening of sky, illuminating the camp.

It was a rag-tag, makeshift place. Fires burned low, or not at all. Very few possessed tents or beds; most slept outside on the ground, buried under mounds of fur, heavy cloaks, or with females next to them. There was a few more cages like his, but they contained women, on the edge of childhood into young adulthood. All dressed in rags, sporting bruises, cuts, welts and other signs of ill-treatment. A young male barely into adolescence made his rounds. He had a scraggly mustache and beard, all gangly limbs and pimples, his clothes too big for him. He banged on the bars, shoved bowls and mugs inside. If the occupants still slept, he tried to thrust a hand in to stroke unkempt, greasy, dirty hair or skin. A few of the females cringed away from him, some never stirred.

The boy made his way to Colin's cage, shoved in the bowls, and continued on, deaf to all requests, all questions. Colin looked at the food, a watery, thin gruel and sour wine. He forced himself to eat, knowing he had to keep his strength up. He was not even given a pot to piss in. That function had to be performed by aiming through the bars, for both needs. It made for a messy, smelly cage.

Slowly the camp woke, women booted out from underneath warm furs or cloaks to stir the fires, cook the food, or satisfy carnal needs. The horses received better care than the prisoners.

When the meal was ready, the majority of men took care of personal business before sitting down and grabbing at food and drink, breaking their fast. Once the males' appetites had been satisfied, the women were allowed to eat while cleaning up. No one would talk to him, or even acted as if they understood a word he said, though he tried different languages. He continued to observe the camp, hoping he could discern a pattern which would help him escape and get back to town to find his brother and warn of the threat which remained nearby.

Another day and night passed, then a second, a third, a fourth...The immortal found it harder and harder to remain calm. Why wasn't his brother looking for him? Why wasn't Eron? Surely they couldn't all be prisoners? He tried to make conversation with the women, the kid who fed him, the men who cared for the horses. They spit at him, cursed him, or poked him with various implements until he gave up.

He had long ago lost track of how much time his brother had left to grab the kid and complete the ritual. Time had no meaning when you were treated as a non-entity. On the uncounted last of an uncountable string of days, he ate another sorry bowl of gruel, drank another mug of sour wine, curled into a ball trying to keep warm. Colin thought he had drifted off to sleep when he was awoken by shouting and screams of terror.

The clang of steel upon steel greeted his ears, fires blazed bright. He could see shapes rushing about, men calling and shouting. The horses whinnied in fear, rearing and trying to break free. A bright light illuminated the entire camp. Colin thought he saw Duchess Illyria and a robed person fighting before all became enveloped in a stygian darkness.

He felt his cage/wagon rock violently, then it lifted up and tumbled backward. He could do nothing but attempt to brace himself as it crashed back to earth. The bars slammed painfully into him, wood splintered, screams echoing and distorting. The Immortal blacked out.

* * *

When Colin woke, it was to find himself buried under a pile of splintered wood and scattered iron. Slowly he made his way out, blood caked his clothes. He surveyed the camp. Bodies lay, as if they had been tossed like so much garbage. A few horses grazed near the entrance to the valley, most having run off.

He picked his way through the mounds of wood, dead men and women. Animals had already come to feast—he had to avoid carnivores who tore chunks out of the bodies and growled at him, showing bloody teeth and muzzles. A heap of dirty canvas spoke of a deflated tent. Colin picked up a sword, and set about to catch a horse. Briefly he wondered if his pack was still wedged in the tree he and his brother had hidden in.

Chapter Eight

"You dirty little whore!" Caroline slammed into her sister's bedroom.

Sally looked up in shock, her eyes red from crying, nose running with snot. Before the youngest could do anything, her sister's hand flashed out and cracked across her face.

"He is mine! Mine! How dare you seduce him away from me!" she shrieked. "It's me he plans to marry! Not you!"

Sally let out a howl of rage and raked her nails down her sister's face as she screamed, "He loves me, you nasty old bitch!"

Caroline shrieked and yanked her sister's hair out of its updo. "You stupid, stupid child! Why would he want an idiot like you! You keep away from him or I'll kill you!"

The youngest cried at the pain and grabbed a handful of her eldest sister's hair with one hand as the other clawed for her face. They struggled, pulling hair, kicking, slapping each other as they screamed insults.

"We laughed at you! He said you kept pushing yourself on him like one of the dockyard women of easy virtue! So he took his pleasure of you like the whore you are!"

"You bitch! You have no idea how to please a man! He thought you a stupid, silly little girl. He told me he fucked you to teach you a lesson."

"He said your cunt is stretched out like an old sausage casing! He said mine is tight and perfect and he loved the feel of me!"

Caroline shrieked loudly and ricocheted her sister off the wall. "Sausage casing? He said you felt like a brood mare!"

"He said you just lay on your back like a turtle, a beached fish!" They crashed to the ground, Caroline on top, and they continued to slap and scratch at each other.

Caroline's words were cut off as she was pulled off her sister by her hair.

"What is the meaning of this?" their minder demanded. "You are sisters! Not slaves to be rolling around the floor fighting! What would your mother say if she could see you two? This is not how gentle-bred, noble-born ladies behave!"

"Yes, let's tell Mother that Sally is proud of her disgrace! You'll never be allowed out again!"

"You tell her and I'll tell her what you did! She'll banish you!"

Caroline shrieked and tried to charge her sister but the grip her minder had on her hair brought her up short. "Let go of me, old woman, or I'll tell Mother you're abusing us and she'll see you sold to the meanest slaver she can find."

"I'll take my chances," the woman spat back. "It's a disgrace the way you two behave, like a pair of cats in heat! Lady Caroline, you are a grown woman with children. A true lady does not brawl on the ground and shout filthy things like a common trull. As for you, Lady Sally, a girl who wishes to retain the appearance of virginity does not lie with a man to whom she is not married. You have jeopardized your chances of finding a decent husband."

"Have not! I'm marrying Lord Nicky! He told me so himself!"

"March. Now. We shall end this nonsense once and for all. Your parents will sort this out."

* * *

"Elizabeth, please, now is not the time; not with the advisor missing," Sydney wearily pleaded.

"Our daughter has been ruined! No one of import will marry her! Not when it is found she is no longer a virgin! How could you allow this to happen? It's your fault for even needing to visit those whores! It's revolting, a man of your age!"

The earl stared at his desk and his hands lying flat on top. *I would not have to visit them if you weren't such a frigid bitch. I am a man, I need more than just procreation, especially now you are too old to bear children.* But he remained silent as she raged.

"I will speak with His Majesty on the subject. I don't know why Lord Nicky thought he could use her and discard her. She isn't some whore, or a slutty duchess, to pleasure himself with."

"Elizabeth," he tried again but she ignored him.

"I have had enough of being humiliated, Chadrick! Do you understand me? I wish your father was still alive; he would have nipped in the bud your tendencies to stray."

"Elizabeth."

"As if that wasn't bad enough, the whole of this town is a morass of sin! And you know why? That damn foreign duchess and her free, sluttish ways! I shudder to contemplate how her family was made nobility! I will not have her around my family! Do you hear me! I will not!"

Sydney felt detached from himself, the rage in him seemed to belong to someone else, as was his hands clenching into fists.

"Then the whore goes and acts as if she cares what happens to Lady Anne! How dare she pretend! I was and still am the only woman Anne trusts! I told her how to be a proper wife! But did she listen?! No! And now she cries and whines there is no one to help or protect her! All she had to do was be a good, chaste wife! Is it the marquis' fault he has to keep correcting her behavior? And the damn whore acts as if it's not natural at all!"

She took a breath in, trembling in rage as she paced, her monologue continuing. "No doubt the whore seduced the marquis, the two-faced bitch! Disgusting how they act like they hate each other, when she is no doubt as depraved as he is! I tried my best to educate her, to instruct her in a proper lady's ways, and look how she repays us! By ignoring my advice, ruining our family!"

"Elizabeth," he tried again in desperation but she would not heed him.

"You, you coward of a man! Our family had pride, and power, and, and respect once! Once! When your father was alive! You've done nothing but drag the name of Sydney down! Do you know what they say of our family? That you're a fence-sitter! You have no balls. They all think you're a joke!! How is Martin supposed to marry a girl of consequence now, I ask you!

"And Caroline! How is she supposed to find a man to be a father to her children? Are you even listening to me? Where do you think you're going? We're not done! Don't you dare think you're going to some whore?"

"You want to know where I am going?" he asked coldly, his tone and voice like his father's when displeased.

His tone stopped Elizabeth in her rant long enough for him to continue."I am going to visit the duchess, and fuck her. Yes, that's right. The foreign whore you blame for all your problems. I plan on fucking her for a very long time, and unlike you, you frigid bitch, she enjoys it." He rejoiced in the horror and shock on her face.

"We've been fucking each other since the mask, and I don't care who knows anymore. I'm leaving you for a woman who isn't a castrating bitch! For a woman who knows the difference between being cautious and being uncaring. And know the name she screams is mine."

Sydney stormed from the room, ignoring the look of shock on his wife's face. Elizabeth felt the blood drain from her body. He had promised her! He had signed the contract his father had drawn up! He could not do this to her! Not again!

The countess could barely breathe; she flailed about for a chair and weakly sank into it. Her humiliation would be complete once it became known around town. It couldn't be! It mustn't be! If only Lord Nicky was not chasing after disobedient slaves! She could make sure the king would command his advisor to marry her daughter, and punish the foreign whore for bringing disgrace upon her entire family. At least Martin had sense enough still. She could only hope he would not show signs of her husband's disease.

Dimly, Elizabeth was aware of voices, and she looked up to see both her daughters and their minder standing in the doorway, staring at her in alarm and curiosity. They must not know what their father had done.

She cleared her throat and waved off the minder who was fussing around her. "Stop it, Dennela! I am fine. It is only my usual complaint. Why are both my daughters here?"

Dennela curtsied and said, "I do not like to interrupt m'lady during her travails, but you should know your daughters have been fighting and screaming things no lady should know."

"It is your job to see they behave! I will not have any more disgrace brought upon our house."

"Yes m'lady, only, it is more serious. Both your daughters think Lord Nicky means to marry them." She kept her eyes downcast and thus didn't see the slap coming. It left her ears ringing and her nose bleeding.

"How dare you tell lies? I will see you whipped."

"No disrespect meant, m'lady, but I speak no lies. Ask them."

Lady Elizabeth looked at her daughters coldly, and for the first time noted the defiance in their eyes, the scratches from nails down both their cheeks and the rumpled hair and clothes.

"What is the meaning of this? I warn you both, if you do not want to be whipped, you will tell me the cause of this fight."

The two burst out at once, voices slowly rising in accusation. The things they said, the things she heard, brought a chill to the countess's spine. She stopped them with a few cold words. The enormity of what they said lay before her.

It could only be because of the foreign whore and her sluttish clothes and her disrespectful ways. Her daughters had always been mindful and pure, and now that woman had all the men panting after her, her children had been driven to desperate, unnatural acts. She knew now her family was cursed. There was only one way to keep complete and utter humiliation at bay.

"I cannot speak of how deeply your behavior has hurt me. You will return to your rooms at once, and not leave them. Your meals will be brought to you. You will not speak with anyone but your body slave. You will not have contact with your brother, nor your children. If I hear one word of protest, I will disinherit you and eject you from the house. Do I make myself clear?"

Sullenly, her daughters nodded. Elizabeth stopped Dennela. "Minder, I have tasks for you. Should you fail in even one of them, or speak a word to anyone else in this household, I will see the flesh flayed from your back and sell you to the slavers."

Dennela knew her ladyship always followed through on her threats. "Yes, m'lady."

Elizabeth did not know if the people she wanted would do as she requested without speaking of it to others but she had no choice. Just the thought of having to treat with the likes of those people made her ill. "You will take a note to the marquis's body slave telling him to present himself to me after dark."

The countess stood, proud she did not faint or stumble as she crossed to the earl's desk and scratched out a note. Dennela left with it, and Elizabeth managed to make it upstairs to her room before she stumbled, retching violently into her chamber pot.

* * *

Matters had not got any better when Lady Elizabeth met with Jenabram's body slave. He was an odious sly man, with a roving eye.

"Seeing as you need me more than I do you, it should be you what treats me like an equal." He smirked. "Earl not joining us?"

She could feel her rage start to pound in her temples but she merely compressed her lips and ordered food and drink brought for him. "His lordship is sick at heart from these matters, and can't bear to lay his eyes on them. It falls to me to deal with the mess."

"That's mighty nice of you, your ladyship. Such a shame. I always heard he had no balls. Now what can I do for you?" he said after he had seated himself and tasted of the wine and a morsel of food.

"I need your knowledge. My daughters..."

He chuckled. "Oh, everyone has heard about your youngest. But you mention both of them."

She couldn't keep the contempt out of her voice. "It has come to my attention they have been doing things which bring disgrace and humiliation to the house of Sydney."

The snicker he gave almost had her ordering him flogged. "Lady Caroline. Your eldest is quite an accomplished bed warmer. No doubt she taught her younger sister how to please a man. My master mentioned many times how he was amazed you managed to produce such exquisite ladies."

The slave laughed uproariously at the look upon her face at his words and he couldn't help goading her, "Oh ho! You didn't know? Lady Caroline has fucked every officer in His Majesty's army. Why, it was bantered about those children may not even be her late husband's. She fucked my master many times; he even let me take my pleasure of her." He grabbed his crotch and licked his lips.

"She knows how to suck a man's cock dry, even..."

"Enough! I will not listen to such... such filth any longer! Say one more word, and I will have you flogged."

His eyes grew mean and small and he pointed his finger at her, "You need me, don't forget, you high and mighty bitch. So you'll shut up and listen if you want my help."

Lady Elizabeth trembled in outrage, "If you expect to leave this room alive you will not speak such filth to me."

Their eyes clashed and held and then resentfully he muttered an apology and sipped and nibbled after saying in a sarcastic tone, "What is it you wish me to do for you, My Lady?"

"Since my eldest daughter, it appears, does not care to be a lady, she can earn her living on her back. Not, however, in this town. I want you to find me a traveling slaver who will meet outside in the forest and give me the best price for her. I imagine you know of quite a few, and, with what you know of her, can find one adequate to the task."

He licked his lips again, in anticipation. "I suppose you want one who will not blab of who she is?" She merely inclined her head. "And your youngest? I have nothing to tell you which would make Nicky marry her."

"He will marry her if the king tells him to."

"Your pardon, my lady," he corrected her, "but the young man is hot for a dukedom. He won't give it up easily."

"It is because of that whore that disgrace has been brought upon my family." The trembling was visible now.

"It would be a tricky thing to kidnap and sell her to slavers. My reward would be greater than arranging matters with your daughters," the slave said.

"I will not chance her escape and return to denounce us all."

He paused in eating and looked at her in some small shock, "You wish her to be made silent? To cut her tongue out and sell her? It will diminish her value somewhat."

"No, you fool! I want her dead! With the whore out of the way, Lord Nicky will have no choice but to marry my daughter."

The man sat back and regarded her. "You are desperate indeed. The Advisor is not likely to forget her easily, not when his chance at being Duke Nicky is ruined. He would bring great pain and suffering to any who took part in denying him his prize. No, you have not the money nor power to pay the price it will entail."

"I will have her dead!" the Countess hissed in fury.

"You had best take the risk yourself," he replied tartly.

"I can't," she replied bitterly. "She knows I hate her."

"Then you have a problem indeed." He drained his goblet and gestured for more. "The youngest has only lain with one man. I can find someone here to take her who will not complain of used goods, if she can obey his orders. If she is a fast learner and clever, she will have an honored place in his household."

"You talk of making her some concubine? Surely not the king's?"

He laughed, and almost choked on his wine. "Are you daft? The king will not have a disgraced daughter of one of his nobles in his harem. No, I speak of another man who keeps one. He is very discreet about it—few even know he has one. He will consent to remain quiet, but it will require paying him what he asks."

She sat a moment in thought. "Very well. Make the inquiries."

"As you wish, my lady. You understand it will take more than a few days? You'll see they do not run off?"

She nodded curtly, telling herself not to think about the next part. "There is one other matter."

"My Lady, you have no other children in disgrace, unless your son..."

"No. He is innocent. It is...my...Lady Caroline's children." She paused and pushed the sick feelings down.

His eyebrows raised and he tsked, "I know you are hard and frigid, but it is extreme even for you." He mocked her.

"I cannot condemn children to a life of slavery. However, they are bastards, if what you say is correct. I will have no bastards in my house. You will find me a poison gentle yet effective."

The slave contemplated her over his cup, smiled evilly, "Done. Now, as to my price..."

* * *

The Earl was by turns sick and exhilarated. *Yes! Finally I have done it! No more will I be held a slave to my father's bargain. I care not what people will think of me.*

He entered the courtyard of the duchess's house, shocked at how many people swarmed over the buildings. He saw men and not a few women he knew. They called out greetings, but he could tell they laughed behind his back over his daughters' foolishness.

I don't care. They will have more to mock when it is heard how I left my wife. Nothing matters but my love for Her Grace. Once we are married, there is nothing Lord Nicky can do.

Sydney dismounted and handed his horse's reins over to a waiting slave and asked to see the duchess. He paced in her receiving room, slapping his riding gloves against one hand. The wait seemed to be a long one, more so than usual, but then, when he had come to her not as a lover it had always been thus.

There is no need to worry. It is nerves from finally having the wherewithal to pursue something I really want.

He had almost convinced himself she didn't love him by the time a slave came back and escorted him into the room she had chosen to make her office. Sydney bowed to her, until the slave left; he hurried to close the door, rushed to catch her in his arms.

He kissed her, one part of his brain noting she held back from him. He stepped to arm's length, still holding onto her, "I thought you would be happy?"

Her voice was distant. "You mentioned we need to be discreet."

Sydney smiled at her concern for them and drew her close and kissed her mouth, even though it was still unyielding. "I have left the cold, unfeeling, uncaring, castrating bitch. Now we can be together and out in the open and free."

Lira placed one hand on his chest. "But I am not. You know that. You know what will happen if..."

"I don't care!" he burst out and clasped her closer, or tried to. "Don't you love me? Did you not hear me? I have left her, for you! For us! We can marry, be together."

She regarded him, no emotion or expression on her face. He was beginning to feel a sinking feeling in his stomach as she carefully and gently replied, "Chadrick. Tell me you are joking. You didn't really tell her about us, did you?"

He stared at her in shock, not believing how cold she sounded, "Of course I did!" He was indignant and started to pace the room in jerky steps. "She just kept hounding me, denigrating my manhood, our marriage, my honor, all I have done for our family. I...I couldn't take it anymore. I just blurted it out, told her I was never coming back. I came here to you, my love."

Lira briefly closed her eyes and opened them. "Oh Chadrick." He paled a moment at the thought it had all been a lie.

"Explain yourself." He had meant to be cold but it came out hurt and wounded.

She closed the distance and taking his hand, urged him to the loveseat against one wall and sat beside him, keeping his hands in hers.

"Chadrick, I am afraid." She looked down briefly, then back up. "It is not an emotion I feel often, but I feel it now. I am afraid of what will happen to us, is all."

Her wonderful yellow-brown, green eyes searched his as he swallowed painfully, and before he could say anything, she was speaking quietly and deliberately.

"You told me the countess is proud, and vengeful. What if she won't give you up and instead demands I be punished? What if His Majesty refuses to grant you a divorce? Lord Nicky, he...I am afraid of what he will do to you in retaliation."

"He and my daughter! Ruined her! He will have to marry her for the insult done to my family. You said you loved me, was it just a lie? Surely you can't tell me you want to be his wife after all his accusations of you? You would be jealous to deny her marriage to the man who took her maidenhead."

Lira raised one brow. "Don't be silly. I bear no ill will toward the girl, but..."

"But what?" he burst out. "I thought you would be happy, and I am hearing nothing but excuses and denials!"

Sydney watched her take a breath in, breasts rising as if he was a complication to her day she didn't need.

"I am trying to point out reality, which will come crashing down on us all too soon, and for which we need to be prepared. I don't want to lose you."

He stared at her, something about her words not quite

convincing him even though her tone was sincere. “Then you must go to the king and plead for us both. He cares for you, he will grant whatever you ask of him.”

She stared at him, searching his eyes. “Very well. I will ask.”

“When?”

The frown was back. “Soon. There are things here I must take care of first.” She hesitated, then added, “Chadrick, you will not like what I have to ask of you next, but I must do it all the same.”

The sick feeling of dread was back as he nodded stiffly.

“You should stay at the sheriff's barracks until His Majesty grants our requests. He will see you mean to leave Lady Elizabeth with whatever dignity is possible still intact.”

Chadrick felt like refusing. There was no reason he could not discreetly stay here until they could marry. He was about to say as much when she squeezed his hands gently and pleaded, “Please, Chadrick, please, my love. It may help us, however little.”

“I...” he cleared his throat. “If I do this, you must spend a part of each night with me. I want...I want to make love to you.”

“Of course, as long as we continue to be discreet until we are free.”

He leaned forward again and kissed her. This time her lips yielded under his.

Chapter Nine

The soft groan broke the silence of the chamber as the figure on the floor stirred. Another groan came along with an exclamation, “Oh my god! I shouldn’t be hurting! Where the hell am I?”

Eron squinted in the half gloom. He remembered the boy. There was a battle. The damn kid had ran his horse over him! Twice! He had felt things break inside, and he had died...Eron sat bolt upright. A pure shot of terror and adrenaline coursed through him. The best thing was to approach his dilemma logically. That meant finding out where he was, and getting the hell out of there. He was on top of a musty pile of straw, still in his dirty clothes with his sword strapped to his side. Whoever had dumped him down didn’t care if he remained armed, and usually that meant there was no way out. Eron made his way across the detritus-covered stone floor toward the light. He saw a window embrasure, such as castles had, with a warped and rusty metal door with many glass plates. He undid the latch, saw the metal had warped and gave a tug. The latch came off in his hand in a shower of rust, and the glass shattered and tinkled to the floor. He wrapped his hand around the metal and it crumbled to pieces. He pried bits of the doors off until he had created an opening. The shutters behind looked to be metal as well, and rusted full of holes. He tested them, and they flaked apart. Eron gave a hard push, and they plummeted to the ground. He barely kept from following them. Eron felt wind tugging at him. He was up three, maybe four stories. Despite his precarious position, the view was breathtaking. From what he could see, the keep was U-shaped, and sat up high in the mountains, which sloped steeply away. He could hear the muted thunder of water. That alone let him know this was the hidden castle the three men had seen through the spyglass on their hike in to town. It also meant he knew where he was, and who had brought him. His biggest worry right now was finding the ground floor.

He needed some sort of light, but there was no candle or torch. Their conspicuous absence only ratcheted up the curiosity and alarm he was feeling. He searched the debris and found a few lengths of wood which appeared to have petrified. He could wrap his cloak around them for a makeshift torch. Eron set to work tearing strips off and using some of the straw to bulk it up. Crude and wouldn't last long but better than nothing. At least he still had his belt and the leather purses on it, one of which held his flint and strike stone. All the furniture in the room was slowly crumbling, as it had been thick wood and protected to a degree from the elements. He found a heavy wooden door, hanging off one hinge, which looked to have been heavily carved at one time. Slowly he eased the door open only to have it crash onto the floor and shatter. He stepped over the wreckage to find himself in a stone corridor. Lights made to resemble torches were either hanging off the walls by what looked like moldering wires, or smashed to bits on the floor.

"How does it still exist?" He shook his head, glanced around again. "Trust a damn vamp to build something remote which doesn't need modern conveniences. Some fucking torches would have at least been nice! A candle even," he shouted into the silence, wondering if she was awake and could hear him.

The light from the nearby window didn't penetrate much past his feet. Eron started down the hall, one hand trailing on the stone wall to guide him. Eron passed many crumbling doors, many of them shut; but when he tried to open one, it fell inward with a crash. He saw it had completely rusted off its hinges. The room was gloomy inside, but again light streamed in brokenly, letting him know shuttered windows were rusting. He didn't want to go inside, and risk tripping over debris, as his nose twitched at mold, mildew, and rot. Soon Eron came to stairs; while there was small windows to provide light; it wasn't enough so he worked on getting the first torch lit. Once that was done, he gathered up the extras and descended the stairs gingerly, ignoring landings and hallways branching off until he came to the bottom and found another hallway. He didn't know how long he wandered, as he had only been here twice and his memory of the layout was a little faulty. Everything in the castle was Pre-Cataclysm, and slowly breaking down into dust, dirt, and other detritus. His stomach growled, reminding him he hadn't eaten since sometime late yesterday. He kept inspecting, his mouth very dry, and he swallowed constantly.

"Screw this, why bring me here if there's nothing to eat or drink?" Eron muttered to himself. He couldn't even find a damn wine cellar, and he knew she had one.

"This is bullshit! Dump me at the top, leave me without food or wine! You bitch! Fine, I'll just, just," he didn't know what he was going to do. He picked another door at random off the hallway he was in. He found a banquet hall.

"What the hell? This furniture looks new. The place looks like it was cleaned up."

A layer of dust and cobwebs covered everything. There was a wealth of candle stands and candles which he went about lighting. The chairs had faded cushions. The windows had frames, glass in them now spotted, with heavy drapes and filmy curtains open. There was a balcony, what looked like... "Yes! Finally!" Eron strode over, saw bottles in a small rack. It was hard to tell what was inside.

"Let's see what you are." He had to use one of his daggers to pry the melted wax off, then dig a wood cork out. The first sip he swirled. "Would be better with food. Maybe with some liquid I can find the larders." He took another swallow and then picked up a branch of candles and some of the bottles and moved with more confidence. "Although why the hell wouldn't you just dump the food here? Damn vamp."

He never found the way to the larders, but Eron did stumble upon what he knew at one time had been a spectacular library. It too bore testimony to having been recently cleaned and refurbished. He was drunk: whatever was in the bottles was potent, doubly so on an empty stomach. The remaining bottle thumped down on a table being used as a desk, also new. Yet everything had a layer of dust and cobwebs over it. He got the candles lit and used them to start a fire in the fireplace. He poked around in the desk, piled with a variety of writing material, and saw what looked like a list but whoever had wrote it used their own code. The immortal realized it was all in a man's hand.

"Phillip." The name came back to him with startling clarity. He had yet to see the male vamp who had been with them the night they had been cursed.

Where was he? "I hope if you're about, you're in your right mind, 'cause I'm not in the mood to flee from an enraged vamp." Eron sank with a sigh into a surprisingly well-upholstered leather chair before the fire, now roaring, and proceeded to finish off the last bottle.

"OK. Some hospitality, some good wine. Damn you, Lira, I hope you don't plan on sleeping the day away," Eron continued to mutter to himself, dropping off into sleep.

* * *

The fire flared and crackled in the gold-veined marble fireplace. The lights had been turned down low, so the stacks looked to be in darkness. Painted literary scenes encircled the perimeter of the room, above the tops of the bookcases. Tasteful spotlights shone down from the ceiling onto the artwork. The room's two massive, many-paned windows stood open to the gentle night breeze. There were many comfortable reading nooks scattered about the room, lost to the general gloom. The high ceiling and the upper stacks blended into the darkness.

There was a plush deep-pile rug in front of the fireplace, along with two cushiony leather sofas, and a pair of chairs.

Eron lay on his back in front of the fire, a bucket of ice with two wine bottles chilling in it, one opened. An exquisite cut leaded wine glass, half-full, sat on the low table to his right.

He gave a sigh, his eyes closed. An observer would be able to see the lines of fatigue and misery drawn on his face. The woman paused in the shadows before padding over and gracefully crouching down at his side.

"You're blocking the light, and the warmth," Eron said without opening his eyes. "Even in death you try to suck the life out."

"There's no need to be ugly," she replied, but switched to his other side and lay down beside him. "Now you can have the light and life all to yourself."

"Is there something you wanted?" he asked in dull tones.

It hurt her to see him in such obvious pain. "No, I only came to see if there was anything you wanted or needed."

He didn't reply, then: "A woman who will love me for me. Who won't recoil in horror and disgust when she learns what I am. One who won't care I stay the same as she ages, withers, dies."

The woman smoothed a lock of hair from his forehead. "If I knew where such people existed, I would request one for myself."

He paused, in a slightly lighter tone, said, "I didn't know you wanted a wife. I thought you looked for a husband."

"Men are like candy, women are dandy," she joked.

He gave a weak smile. "Of course. It must be easier if you're bisexual before the turn isn't it? More opportunities to feed."

"There are very few of us who started out bi or same-sex oriented. Those who never learn the necessity of feeding off their same sex have a tough time without leaving tracks."

"Dear Illyria, practical as ever. Equally adept at evading the subject."

"I am merely stating the truth," she replied. "I do wish you would tell me how I can help you. Would it be better if I left and let you alone?"

Illyria knew he had come here to heal. He had found a woman to love him, and she learned from Mica, her friend, he thought she was the one.They had started to plan a life together. He had told her his secret, she accepted him, they married. Life was great, rainbows and unicorns until one day he found her in bed with another man. A man older than she. Mica had gone on to say Eron was devastated. His wife had begun to resent him after all, as she aged and he remained the same.

It was possible they might have been able to divorce with a minimum of acrimony, but one of Eron's enemies had told Eron's wife that she too could have been immortal, forever young, but Eron selfishly wouldn't turn her.

Mica had said Eron still wouldn't talk about it to this day, nearly ten years later. He had been there when the woman accused Eron of keeping immortality from her. She was bitter, vengeful, and tried to drag Mica into the spat. Her final revenge had been to empty their savings account and have extensive plastic surgery in an effort to make herself younger.

It was during one of the surgeries that she died on the table from complications. It was later found out no legitimate doctor would operate on her anymore, so she had gone to one with a shady reputation, and paid the price for her vanity with her life.

Personally, Illyria thought Eron worth better than a woman so petty, selfish, and narcissistic but wisely kept such opinions to herself.

They lay in companionable silence, until he said, “You never did answer my question.”

She turned on one side to face him, propping herself up on one arm. “I did not realize you asked one,” she replied, disgruntled. “I don’t need a baby-sitter. Why don’t you go and play with one of your men?”

“Because they all found someone they want to live with...” She almost added *and grow old with* but stopped. He said it for her.

“So we’re both freaks and outcasts, forever single.” He was very bitter. “Oh wait, people nowadays are obsessed with vampires. You at least could announce to the world what you are and they would line up to offer you their necks and be your slaves for life just for the chance they would be the one you’d pick to make immortal.”

Oh yes, he was very, very bitter. “They wouldn’t believe me, I’d be just another human sharing in a mass delusion.” She sat up and curled feet under in preparation to leaving. “Besides, you know as well as I do sheep are not candidates for immortality.” Now they were both bitter.

She knew better than to think any of the men and women she loved would be special enough or able to handle the long, dark nights to stay with her forever.

His arm moved, hand clamping on her wrist, “Don’t. Please. For once, let’s just be two people lying here in misery.”

“Such a tempting offer,” Illyria replied drily but lay back

down. They stayed, each drifting in thoughts of all the people they had known and loved.

* * *

The sound of drapes opening rattled in the room, and pale moonlight filtered in. There was the sense of movement about the room, though no other sound was heard. I was in a foul mood, and Eron lay passed out if the empty bottles surrounding him were any indication.

"Damn you, Phillip! How dare you leave me!" I had a sinking suspicion that the advisor had ordered him killed, after learning Lord Nicky's slave was a demon, and the memories from the old woman who once haunted the Fishton Mansion. So did the boy know what we were?

It looked like Phillip had been trying to figure out what the advisor was. I thought back to what Mia and the demon let slip. I had a suspicion my mate had entered a whole new dimension of hell. I didn't know if the demon tried to break the curse and failed, and Phillip wandered with wits addled as it slowly lost its potency. How would I even begin to look for him if he was in such a state, assuming damn peasants hadn't killed him? I wanted to cry at the loss, rage and smash things; but I had already done so to no avail. I had to do something else to get over my grief. I had more problems piling up, more questions. How to find out for sure? I didn't know how to achieve my goal without resorting to bargains I didn't want to make; so I paced and I thought, turning over possibilities.

* * *

The listener floated up out of his drunken stupor, he could hear a soft, scratching noise. *What the hell? It doesn't sound like rats.* Cautiously he peeked around the arm of the chair he lay in; the library was in darkness except for the streams of moonlight coming through a large window. He became aware of Illyria flitting in and out of shadows. There was something about the sight which tugged at his memory, but he couldn't bring it to the front of his mind. Eron was horrified as he watched her blur in and out of darkness. *I've never seen when she wasn't trying to at least act human. She's pure vamp.*He sat bolt upright in blind panic yelling, "Fuck!"

He found himself staring into a pair of silent yellow-green luminous eyes. He felt a mix of amusement and menace coming from her. His eyes darted frantically between the woman and where he thought the door was, noting the utter stillness. He wouldn't know she was in the room if he wasn't looking directly at her. Cautiously he felt for his sword and slowly slid off the chair.

"Uh, uh, bad dream?" Eron offered lamely. He took a shaky breath in. She could have been a statue, there was no sense of life about her. "Simon says, talk to me?" Eron tried for humor, but trailed off as she stalked forward with a panther's grace.

Every hair on his body rose as if electrified, and the primal lizard hindbrain shrieked *Flee! Predator!* Eron automatically backed up and drew his sword before he stilled himself in a fighting stance. S*he knows me, assuming she remembers or cares.*

* * *

I didn't feel like myself anymore, or perhaps this was how I had always been and didn't realize until lately? Mayhap the mere fact of the demon being in our realm caused things to happen which otherwise wouldn't. Whatever the demon had done to get his mark on my wrist permanently was causing bad side effects.

I saw Eron blink as I appeared in front of him. He was tensing up, ready to defend himself when a crackle broke out behind. Eron jumped a foot in terror and half turned before remembering the threat in front of him. He looked back to see me a hands-breadth from his sword point.

"Um...please don't go all Spike on me, or was that Angelus?" His eyes roamed to my face, which should have been cut and bruised and swollen from the demon's attack. Then down to my hands, curled into claws, and back up my body.

All he saw was tight black leather: lots of it. *Mmmmm, leather,* his mind channeled an old Simpson cartoon. *No! Bad man! Bad Eron! Potential Evil waiting to kill you. But leather, make me feel cheap. Damn it! Focus!* Eron dragged his eyes up from my perfectly revealed cleavage to see anger sparking in my eyes.

Eron sucked in air, his mind a welter. *How the hell to get out?*

His fear was a delicious scent perfuming the air; before I could stop it, an animal growl trickled out between my lips. I watched emotions chase themselves across the man's face: lust, longing, and fear before the brain he was born with kicked in and he blurted out, "Would it kill you to have some damn food in this place if you're going to kidnap someone?"

I cocked a brow, knowing it made me look even more dangerous and sexy as I flowed forward, stopping with the point of the sword touching the skin over my heart and tilted my head, like a bird of prey looking at its victim. He was sending out mixed signals, fear and lust, and it was driving me crazy. I could feel the thirst start its slow rise.

"I knew this was going to be the mother of all fuck-ups. I don't know what the fuck is wrong with you, but I bet it's hard to pronounce. Now, get me some damn food. I'm hungry and I'll sit and answer questions all damn night long if I have food." His being switched to fight mode helped clear my head.

"You'll answer them, no matter what," I let my voice go from mellow whiskey to smooth silk.

"Don't bet on it, fang face."

I slinked in a circle around him. Eron tried to maneuver to keep me in sight. "Come on, Lira, I know you're in there somewhere, so cut the scary vampire crap. We've been there, done that, blah, blah. We have big problems, and you doing this is not going to help solve them."

I stood staring, as his words sunk into my brain, and attempted to shake off whatever was gripping me. I barely succeeded. "Fine, come." I started for the banquet hall. After a moment I heard his footsteps following me.

Chapter Ten

I let him eat, and gazed out over the mist-shrouded mountains with my arms clasped behind my back. The night was sprinkled with stars, silvered by moonlight. Behind me, Eron gulped down more drink. At the rate he was going, he would be drunk again.

I turned my head to look at him, and he said, "I'm getting sick of your bullshit, have I mentioned that? You play games. You're playing them now. You still won't tell me what you want, and you have clandestine late-night meetings with the head of an army."

My smile was cold as his. I stalked closer, leaned over so our faces were close. "I told you, the note I was given said I would learn of interesting things if I showed up. I suppose my interlude with the boy's slave was a figment of all our imaginations?"

"I..." He trailed off, considered, conceded the point. "Very well. Perhaps you wish to tell me what he really is? And why you have an army hidden?"

"Secondly, that is not my army and firstly: A demon."

"A...Demon? Okay." He drew the word out, thought about it. "I suppose that would explain a lot." He drummed his fingers on the table top in thought, leaned forward. "Whose army is it?"

"The boy's," I replied.

He sat back, eyes narrowed. "And this doesn't concern you in the least little bit? Mica's still missing, probably still cursed. The only good to come out of it is that the boy showed up. Bastard, I can't believe he trampled me twice! As if once wasn't enough!"

"Of course his having an army concerns me! Tell me, which way did you enter the town?"

"Huh? Why the hell would that matter?"

"Just answer the question, please; it was something one of the nobles mentioned at a dinner."

He barely kept from rolling his eyes. "Over the mountains and through the woods, from..." he took a moment to orient himself and pointed, "that way."

"And did you see any army men? Forts? Scouts? Anyone who looked to be patrolling the borders?"

Eron's mouth formed an O. "I'm, I'm having a bit of trouble."

My tone was impatient, did he ride the short bus? "Did you see any signs which indicated the town had an army?"

Eron remained stunned, mouth hanging open. I was irritated: if I had wanted an imitation of a fish, I would have asked for one. He seemed awed, or perhaps it was disbelief? "Well?" I demanded.

He spoke, after his eyes had started watering from the effort not to blink. "Thinking back on it, no. Our journey was fairly uneventful, if you don't count the bandits we ran into right outside of town. They killed Colin, then we managed to kill them."

The man decided to eschew the cup and started drinking straight from the bottle. "So what you're trying to tell me is the whole town is fucked. Nice." He sighed and rubbed his eyes with his hands and ran his fingers through his hair.

Eron continued, "Let me get this straight. Nicky has an army waiting to raze the town, and Mica with it, the ability to change his age, and a demon whom he believes plotted with you. Oh, and he knows he killed me, so if he sees me, he knows I'm part of the club." He thought a moment and continued, "Yup, we're fucked, royally and with sandy Vaseline; bend over and kiss your ass good-bye, buttercup." He began to laugh.

I'm afraid he saw how un-amusing I found his glee; his laugher died suddenly and he unknowingly shrank back. Oops, needed to tone down the fear factor.

"Lira, we've seen what he has with him. What he commands. He didn't have those powers before. So I say that makes it your problem now as well. Especially if you plan on staying here since it doesn't seem he's going anywhere anytime soon. Did I mention he's a vengeful bastard? He'll remember you opposed him and won't stop going after you until you're dead. It won't matter if you pull stakes to live elsewhere, he'll send people after you and when it doesn't work, he'll come for you himself." Eron smirked. "Just ask Mica and Colin, oops that's right we can't, BECAUSE NICKY HAS THEM!" He threw the bottle at me in rage.

Oh this was too much! Suddenly I was in front of him before he'd seen me move. I felt my blood coursing through my body. My canines itched with the need to plunge themselves into veins and pull the warm liquid out. What the hell was wrong with me? It had to be the taint of the demon causing this to happen; even where we were. I must control myself! This is not the way to convince him!

It was a great effort for me to stalk away from him over to the window. I stared out; trying to ignore the blood lust singing inside of me. One Mississippi, two Mississippi, it took several dozen repetitions before I could get my emotions back under control.

I tried to speak as casually as possible, though it was a great effort. "If we kill Nicky, how do we get rid of a demon? I do not think they just roam our world at will. The boy... I think the boy is controlling it."

I felt Eron trying to bore holes in my back, as if willing me to turn around. Not going to happen.

"Why? Did his pet demon tell you that? Why would you believe anything a being like that says? Legend speaks of them as nasty, lying things best kept away from and not to make bargains with."

I continued to stare sightlessly out a window. Damn the thing the little boy had trapped! It made it hard to keep my emotions in check as the beast welled up. The urge to rip into him, smash him, destroy him nearly overwhelmed me.

"I don't trust a word it says, but what it has said contains grains of truth." I swung away from the window and stalked back to a chair. I wrapped my hands around the back, staring at him over the top. "I wish we could discern truth from lies."

Eron sat transfixed, staring at me. "I don't think that's a wise course. We need to concentrate on finding the brothers, unless you're planning on becoming an evil overlord?"

Oh for! "I have to have something to do with my time. I can't always be a noble with a lot of business interests to pass the years until I am forced to move to another place where I am unknown. As I'm sure you must know, traveling takes money, as does setting oneself up somewhere new. I'm afraid I've become accustomed to a certain standard of living."

Eron stared at me in disbelief, "What, is it too hard for your kind to live like peasants every now and then? I hear it's good for one's soul."

"Yes, I can see the effects poverty's had on your soul," I replied drily. "What does Mica have which you and Colin need? We know where Nicky lives. He's desperate for my title and standing. Why don't I just lure him somewhere you can ambush him without interference?"

"Because it worked so well the last time?" He needled me and gestured for a bottle of wine.

"At least we are no longer cursed!" I shot back as I picked up a still-corked Traminer half-way down the table and set it in front of him.

He worked the cork out and tasted it. Then ticked points off on his fingers. "One, we will work together to get rid of our common enemy; known as Nicky. Two, we will not let Colin know what you are. Three, we find the brothers. Four: the demon."

I mulled this over, it all seemed rather reasonable to me, "Five, I wish to hear your story."

I startled him. "My what?"

"How you came to be. I wish to hear it, if you please." I regarded him steadily.

I could see he didn't know what to say, "What does it have to do with anything?"

"What if there is something in your origins that will let us know how Nicky is able to change his age and do the things which smack of magic?"

"I doubt it." He was adamant.

I smiled sweetly, "Humor me."

"I really don't think that would be a good idea." I could see he was considering something. He looked toward the window. "How old are you?"

"What does that have to do with anything?" I asked. If he could play, so could I.

"Fine. My story for yours."

"My story?"

"Humor me." He gave me a smirk.

“Fine, but after this is over. My story is not as important as yours could be.” He stared for a moment at my face. Then, he began:

“My tale starts when Africa was the cradle of life and Egypt was only a baby. I’m not Egyptian though, I don’t remember what I was, Sumerian, Babylonian, Mesopotamian; I’ve forgotten, it’s been so long. I wasn’t always the man you see now. I was...” He paused, “Well, I suppose you could say I was poised between evil and goodness. I was a young warrior, who thought he knew more than anyone.”

“What happened?”

“I won’t bore you with my whole life’s story. Know I had an overwhelming amount of ambition and pride. I was a young soldier under a very ruthless general. I had been born into a family of warriors. My father was a trusted general in our King’s army, and by dint of hard work, a lot of backstabbing, I quickly rose through the ranks to be the king’s second in command. Now, our sire wanted more than he had, wanted to rule over vast numbers of people, vast tracts of land. Because he was so bloodthirsty, we went on many a raid, conquering neighboring tribes and bringing them under the man’s rule. I believed I could rule better than my king, and one day, I was finally given the chance to usurp him.”

* * *

Eron galloped into the desert camp a three months’ ride from the palace. Women and children screamed and hid in tents. The men ran to meet the invaders with whatever weapons they had at hand. Eron saw the first man, covered head to toe in a white garment. He fell under the slash of Eron’s sword.

“Don’t touch the women! All who surrender will be shown mercy!” Eron bellowed as he rode over men and sliced them down.

As he turned his horse’s head to go back through the camp, an old man stepped from a tent with a staff and his daughter. Everything seemed in slow motion to Eron. One of his men rode up behind the man, slice his sword down, but was flung away before it even touched the man. The horse he was on shied suddenly, dumping the rider on the ground.

The old man held his staff up and cried aloud in an unknown language. The air seemed to shimmer and pulse around him and his daughter. Eron's men seemed unable to target anything. Their horses started to plunge and snort in fear.

"Hold! Hold, I say!" Eron screamed to his men. For a few tense seconds he thought they would not listen and then the cry went out.

"Round everyone up, bring them to me," he commanded and his men hastened to obey.

Eron walked his horse up to the old man. He was so bent and wizened he had to look up at Eron on his mount. There was complete calmness in his eyes as he meet his attacker's.

"So you have come at last," the old man croaked out.

"Silence, I will do the talking," Eron demanded.

The old man merely smiled, and Eron felt something invisible twine around him and the horse. It tried to rear in fright but Eron kept a firm hand on the reins. He could hear his men mutter in terror as the same unknown thing swirled around them too.

* * *

Eron paused at the memory, seemed ashamed of past behavior.

"Now, there had been many times when I had considered taking my king's place; I was only held back by the thought many had tried and died horrible deaths. I thought once again about betrayal. Here was someone with real power. If only I could learn what it was, learn how to use and control it, I could be king. I of course did not let any of this show on my face. I remember, as the sun burned down upon us and my men shifted restlessly, the old man threatened us with his power."

Eron seemed lost to me and the room. "I don't remember exactly what he said, but a strange thrill ran through me when he spoke and something whispered in my mind, telling me how to capture the old man and his strange power."

* * *

The hot sun beat down on Eron and his men, and even though

it was a cloudless, breezeless day something still stirred the air. He moved his eyes from the old man to his daughter, a lush beauty, and she did not lower her eyes but stared boldly, almost defiantly, back.

The strange breeze pulsed around him again and he thought he heard his dead mother's voice on the air.

"Show them the medallion, speak the words," that instinctual voice whispered. Eron drew from underneath his breastplate and tunic a worn, carved medallion. He held it up to the old man and spoke the words his mother had taught him went along with the metal.

He saw a faint flicker of fearful dread in the old man's eyes before he could control himself. The next thing Eron knew, the breeze had gotten stronger, swirling sand about. His men cried out, but Eron only raised the medallion again and in a more insistent voice cried out the words. Suddenly, the medallion grew hot in his hand, so hot he felt he would be burned. But the heat subsided, the metal was nothing more than a harmless medallion.

"Where is your power now, old man?" Eron taunted.

The daughter plucked at her father's sleeve and whispered to him. He gave her a harsh command and she fell silent once more.

The old man lifted his staff, and cried aloud his strange words, but nothing happened. He lowered the staff and in a voice creaking with age, addressed Eron.

"You have won this round, general, but do not think the medallion will hold my power forever."

"It only has to last until you are dead, old man. Take him and his daughter. They will be a gift for the king. No one is to touch or harm them. The rest of the village shall be slaves. You may have the women."

Eron's men rushed to obey him. That night, they dined well and the next morning started back to the palace.

* * *

"During our trek back, I worked at getting the old man to teach me his power. It wasn't until we were at court, and he had been tortured by the king that he agreed. Or, it would be more accurate to say he agreed after I saw him die from the torture and was assigned to get rid of him."

* * *

Eron grumbled to himself as he dumped the old man's broken body in a cart. He should not have to do such menial labor!

"I will be sure next time I question the King's judgment, it will be with him spitted upon my sword point."

Eron pushed the cart out the archway. He knew of a spot right outside the palace which would do nicely. Let the vultures feed on this offal. As he trudged along, Eron thought the heat must be getting to him; he could swear the old man's body was healing itself, and was it breathing he heard? Eron tumbled the body from the cart, saw it land in the pit smooth and whole again. The old man looked like he had never gone through the King's torture. Eron's eyes narrowed as he inspected the body. Giving a quick look around, Eron took off his outer robe and wrapped the old man up in it. He slung the body over his shoulder and made his way back to his chambers. There, he chained the body to the wall and sat to wait with a cup of wine.

It was not long before the old man's chest heaved and his eyes flew open. He looked around him and hurled curses in his native tongue at the soldier before him.

Startled, Eron flew up from his chair, his hand clenched involuntarily around the medallion hidden beneath his tunic.

"You can't die! How wonderful! Tell me, old man, did you plan to sneak back into the palace and free your daughter? Perhaps sneak away with her and live somewhere else? This is marvelous, you will tell me how to become immortal."

"It is not for greedy fools such as you!" He spit on Eron.

"Why you... you'll regret that!"

* * *

After a brief pause to moisten his throat with wine, Eron continued, "But it was not to be. After what I put the old man through as well, he was ready to do anything I asked; and to have his daughter released from my men's tender care. Now, the shaman taught me all he knew. But there was one great secret he still would not tell me, how to be immortal. I eventually tricked him. I got what I wanted and I was so...overwhelmed. I was glorying in the rush of invincibility! Not even the king himself could harm me! So greedy was I, my thoughts showed themselves plainly on my face. The old man must have seen what would become. He tried to undo the ritual but it was too late. I threatened to maim his daughter as a way of forcing him to do the ritual on himself. I almost didn't believe it would work, but it did. I killed the old man in front of his daughter."

He closed his eyes and fought down a strong wave of emotion. Illyria felt her heart beat faster at his revelations.

When Eron continued, his voice was rough with suppressed emotion.

"I slaughtered the current king and all those loyal to him and kept the daughter as my personal slave, little knowing she too knew the secret. The old man had been wily in that respect. I wanted people to hear my name and tremble in fear and dread. I got what I wanted, but at a terrible price."

* * *

Moonlight streamed in through an ornamental screen across the windows. The young woman in the room heard voices outside the door to the chamber. She stopped to listen, but as the voices continued on, she relaxed. She stepped to a cedar table upon which rested a tray bearing a decanter and a goblet. The young woman fingered one of her rings thoughtfully, and opened a secret compartment underneath the jewel. She poured the powder into the drink as the door flew open. She tried to appear normal, though her pulse was throbbing and her heart beat madly in her chest.

"Cassiopeia, bring me some wine." Eron swaggered in as the guards shut the doors behind him.

Taking a deep breath, Cassiopeia poured the wine into the goblet and kneeling before the man, she offered it up. He moved past her and still she stayed where she was, as he had taught her. After several heartbeats she heard the golden goblet thud to the floor and a choking, gasping in front of her.

"You hair of a cunt! What have you done to me?"

Swiftly the woman drew a dagger from a hidden pocket in her sheath as he crouched on hands and knees on the marble floor. She plunged the dagger into his back until the poison and blood loss caused him to die.

Once he was dead, she backed up and looked around. She would not have much time to find the medallion in which he had imprisoned his soul before he woke to life again. She must do things in order; if he woke, he would kill her. She was mortal still, this was her only chance. Cassiopeia drew off one of her arm bands. A golden snake with ruby red eyes. She dumped the ritual herbs into a bowl and ignited them, placing the band on top.

Cassiopeia held her arms up, palms out, and began the chant her father had taught her. So engrossed, she failed to see Eron revive, see and hear what she was doing. He reached for the dagger at his waist and threw it, but his aim was off. Cassiopeia felt a sharp pain in her shoulder and cried out, her concentration broken. She fell to the floor in pain.

Eron struggled to his knees and crawled to the traitorous bitch. He jerked the dagger out, drawing another cry of pain. He leaned over and hissed,

"So you think to outsmart me like your father did? But the ritual is not finished? Tell me what I want to know and I'll make your death a quick one."

Cassiopeia thought quickly. She only had a line or two more to chant; perhaps if he got what he wanted, she could finish the ritual without him noticing. If she could, it wouldn't matter if he killed her. She would be able to come alive later.

"Well?" Drawing her arm before her, Cassiopeia watched as he slit it. The pain a bright thing. He knew how to make someone suffer for a very long time without killing them.

"Y...yes, yes whatever you wish, Majesty. For a clean death."

"Good," He went to a chest and took out a tablet and held it up so she could see. "On this is how to make one immortal. You remember how I had your father teach me it, and the correct lettering, as evidenced by the many living immortal birds caged about the room?"

He waited for her nod and continued, "You shall teach me the Ritual of Undoing and how it is written." He walked over to his writing table and prepared a new tablet. On the desk sat different fruit seeds in a bronze bowl; these held the souls of the birds.

Eron held up the bowl. "In here, you know what I have. I will give you your clean death when I can release the bird's soul from its seed, and kill it. If you don't give me the correct ritual, your death will be long and painful."

He smiled cruelly. "Now begin."

It did not take long for her to tell him, or for him to write it. He chanted over a seed and picking the bird to which it belonged, killed it. He waited and the bird did not come back to life. She whispered the last words of the chant and felt her soul leave her and enter the snake armband.

Now to grab it. But she did not move cautiously enough. He spotted her and came over and his foot sent bowl and band skittering across the floor. She lay gasping up at him. He took out his dagger. "A clean death, like I promised." He slit her throat.

Once she was dead, Eron cleaned his dagger and picked up the armband. He looked at her once more before secreting the band on his person. He shouted for the guards, ordered them to take and burn Cassiopeia's body. He followed them to make sure it was done, and watched as they buried the remains in a sand dune far beyond the palace walls.

* * *

Eron paused and I filled his goblet with wine again. He thanked me and took several healthy swallows before continuing, "It wasn't until centuries later I found out the truth. Cassiopeia had managed to complete the ritual and had started a cult. They were good immortals, gathering in strength and number so one day they could stop me."

Here Eron laughed.

"She almost succeeded, but she herself had been betrayed yet again. I learned of her plans and life from a man who had turned evil. He had been one of her acolytes, and he wanted to kill me and take my spot as king."

Eron paused, reliving ancient days in his mind. I was astounded. To think! These people had discovered a way to become immortal which didn't require them to restrict their movement according to the time of day. How many of them still existed? I realized he knew how to do both rituals! Excitement coursed through my veins, then doubt; if it was easy, he wouldn't tell me outright. He was leaving something out, some crucial bit. He had mentioned it, what was it?

"You do not think evil of me? You do not think I should die along with Nicky?"

Why tell me his story if he was going to ask? I said as much.

"I can't get over the evil vampire, I suppose. I guess by telling you, I'm convincing myself you're good, the way I changed to become good."

Oh please. "You seem to have gotten stuck on the concept of one must be either wholly good or wholly evil. When what we all are is shades of gray?"

He paused for a moment. "I think it's because of Mica. He has such convictions of right and wrong, and even though I know better, it's so hard not to get caught up in his vision sometimes. Then I get disgusted with myself and dissatisfied. I can't believe you never noticed that about him?"

"No, not really. We didn't spend oodles of time together the way you and I did."

Eron paused to brood a moment, before picking the thread of his story back up. "There had been great wars between our kinds. My side had gotten lucky and we captured Cassiopeia. I wanted to personally execute her. But when I saw her, I couldn't. I'm not sure why, I think it was because she was the only one who had been with me from the beginning of my Becoming. I had been growing disenchanted with life, with what I was doing, only I didn't want to do the Ritual of Undoing yet. Perhaps Cassiopeia sensed it, or she just couldn't find where I had hidden my soul. She wanted to talk, a white flag of truce between us. For some reason, I dismissed everyone there except her."

* * *

"I sense a sadness in you; do not tell me the great scourge of the earth, the Destroyer of Nations, regrets the path he has taken."

Eron poured more wine for himself, offered her a goblet which she accepted. "No, not exactly. I have enjoyed my time and the things I've done. Only…" he paused to search for the words he wanted.

"Only you grow tired of always destroying, always being the tyrant. They rebel eventually don't they? Those you've conquered. You do not have their love, their honest respect, only their fear and hatred."

"Yes," he mused, "I suppose that's it." He gave a wild bark of laughter which threatened to become hysterics. "You've cursed me, haven't you? Wished upon me, this ennui, this boredom, this never ending torment. This is your revenge isn't it? Well, are you enjoying it?" and he continued laughing wildly.

She raised her brows and looked into her cup a moment. "No, I thought revenge was what I wanted, but seeing you, I'm not so sure. It makes me wonder if the things I've done have truly been for good, or if there was more harm in them."

"You are trying to get rid of me, the Great Evil; how can any action springing from that be wrong?" He groaned.

She stood contemplating again. "I don't know. It's why I wanted to be caught, I suppose. That and I always wondered: you took my snake armband all those years and years ago. If you thought I had completed the transformation, why didn't you do the Ritual of Undoing on it just to be sure?"

He was not sure why and said as much.

"I think, even then, something buried deep inside you was waiting for this day. Waiting for you to make a choice which will change both our lives." She paused and drawing away from him, knelt. "May I show you something?"

Eron nodded tiredly. He watched as she took a small pouch out from under her tunic. Opening it, she looked for a bowl and finding one, emptied it on the ground. Dried herbs, spices, flowers and other unknown powders filled the bowl. Cassiopeia took a sliver of wood from the brazier in the tent and ignited the mixture. As it burned it smoked, filling the air with a seductive scent.

He watched in fascination as she raised her arms, palms out

over the smoking bowl, looking at him. Eron felt his instinct buzz; he had a feeling he would not like what she was about to do but didn't care anymore.

"Unlike you, Majesty, I have continued my education in the occult. I have found something I think will help us both." She began to chant.

The smoke swirled and seemed to dance and pulse in time to her chanting. Then he felt it, little whispers of air, like on the day he had stolen the source of the old man's power. The smoke seemed to gather in the middle of the tent, the air swirling it into a column and out of that column a shape formed. It was wavering and indistinct but when it spoke, its voice was musical and made Eron think of Paradise.

"Why have you called me forth, human?"

"I have need of your race's help. My father taught us how to make immortals, and how to undo it, from your teachings."

The shape nodded. "This we know of. The power is not used wisely; many wield it who should not."

"For which I am sorry, O Great One, and wish to make amends."

"There is no way to undo what has been done, but it can be changed."

"Let it be so." She turned to Eron, and the shape seemed to hold him in its gaze.

"Yes, let it be so." he repeated, ignored his instinct for once.

The shape seemed to nod; they felt its approval. "It shall be done. Henceforth, every immortal made shall make a journey to here," a map appeared and showed them a spot, out of which grew an image. "This journey must be made in one year's time. The living immortal must bring their soul gem with them and place it in the cave. My brethren will guard the spot.

"If this journey is not made within a year's time, the guardian shall come for the living immortal; their immortality and their life shall be forfeit. The Ritual of Undoing will remain. One who wishes to end the existence of another living immortal must make a journey to the cave and say this phrase to identify and retrieve his enemy's gem after acknowledging the guardian." Another scroll appeared beside the first.

"Once the soul gem is taken out of the cave, the one who took it has seven years to end the life of the gem's true owner. If he fails to do so, a guardian shall come for the one who took the gem and their immortality and life shall be forfeit. As I say it, so shall it be."

Eron felt a bubble of panic. "Wait, does this mean we two shall have a year as well to make the journey?"

The shape regarded him. "Yes. You are tasked with spreading our words and agreement. Those who chose to ignore it will have their lives ended a year from now. You may not call upon my brethren or me freely without consequence. We are now the Guardians of the Cave of Soul gems." So saying, the smoke thinned and the shape disappeared.

* * *

I must admit I was amazed he had voluntarily told me the immortal's origins. He either thought there was nothing I could use out of it, or was beyond caring. Eron poured more wine and drank deeply before continuing.

"We made our journey. Not every immortal to whom we passed the words believing. True to the Guardian's word, all those who ignored our warnings lost both their immortality and life. After Cassiopeia and I had handed our soul gems over to the guardian, I vowed never to remove her gem as long as she would grant me one favor. She would never try to hunt me down again nor tell people my secret of who I really was. She agreed. I disappeared as part of our bargain. I took on a different name, a whole new life. I gave up who and what I had been. Oh, I could never become wholly good, no, but I was not the great evil I had once been."

Eron paused, his gaze drawn from the past and he looked at me.

"Are you atoning for past misdeeds? Is that why you let yourself be drawn into Mica's quest?"

Eron glanced at the palms of his hands, then reached for his goblet. He took a healthy swallow before answering. "It must be, why else am I still here? Why else would I let Mica guilt trip me into staying?" Suddenly he clenched his hands into fists and pounded the arms of the chair. “Goddamn it Mica! You and your white knight complex!”

“I... see.” I had a feeling he was leaving out chunks of information but didn’t press the issue. I was confident that in time he would tell me. He had spoken quite a lot already. “And how does Nicky fit into all this? He knows the ritual?” I surely hoped not.

“No, from what I was able to find back then, in modern times; he only knows how to destroy us. He... he was a mistake from the beginning. After the restrictions were placed on the becoming and undoing of living immortals, Cassiopeia and I passed one more, children were not to be transformed. They would not be able to properly defend themselves or make their way in the world. As you saw for yourself, one of my kind decided to ignore the rule. I’m not sure how he managed to survive so long without someone retrieving his soul gem and speaking the Ritual of Undoing.”

“Very worrisome, as few people change who they really are at heart. It seems to me the little boy should have a great many enemies. One of them should have gotten rid of him before now.” It was a point I found nagging.

Eron’s brow creased and his answer, when it came, made him seem unsure of what he said. “I can come to no satisfactory conclusion other than killing us does not confer power. So there would be no benefit in destroying him, other than to get rid of an enemy. Nicky is very good at appearing to be one’s friend, then backstabbing his benefactor.”

I believed I understood. “By the time a person knows Nicky is their enemy, it’s too late, isn’t it? He’s killed them.”

“That’s what I think too.” We fell silent for a while.

“I still don’t see how any of this helps us,” Eron prodded me.

I swatted at his booted foot. “It does, I’m just not sure how yet. I have to think.”

“Great, and while you do, people will wonder where we have got to. I bet a whole new slew of rumors will have made the rounds. We need to get back, at least you should. If Nicky shows, I know you can talk your way out of anything.”

“And say what?” I wanted the pimple on my butt gone.

“I don’t know. You’ve seen his power and might, and you

tremble in fear at what he commands." He laughed at the expression on my face. "Please tell me you brought the horses?"

When I indicated I had, still stewing over the role I was undoubtedly going to have to play, he said, "I'll saddle them." He gave a quick glance through the window. "But it would go faster if you helped, sun'll be up soon enough." Then he left.

I had a feeling he knew more about my strengths and weaknesses than was safe. I made sure the candles were out and the fires extinguished before joining him in the stable; I wasn't about to let my haven burn to ash as a result of my own carelessness.

Chapter Eleven

The Marquis lit a cigar, and calmly smoked as he enjoyed his wine and watched the earl pace. How had a man as weak and cowardly as Chadrick managed to have an affair with the duchess? But for now, the marquis was more interested in the havoc he could cause now, and the rewards he could gain for it.

If I knew who to thank for causing the uproar at the Harvest Ball I would. The opportunities they've created by getting the damn advisor out of the palace is nearly priceless!

Kendall held his glass out, and his body slave filled it with wine. He had no more need to speak; soon enough the earl would let him know of his plans without realizing it.

"I find it preposterous that my lady wife asked such a thing of your body slave. She doesn't approve of your lifestyle. Why would she confide in a slave, and your slave at that?"

"My dear Chadrick, I suspect she asked it of me because of the very way I live, which she so freely denigrates. I have told you before, if you took your fist or a whip to her from time to time, she would obey you, instead of the other way around. She is more of a man than you, but then it does explain why you prefer whores for your pleasures."

"What I do in my private life is no concern of yours," came the savage reply.

Kendall merely sipped again, sneering, "Is it true, what your slaves whisper? You are having an affair with the duchess? You believe she will marry you if you can wriggle out of the countess's claws?"

"Leave her out of this!" Chadrick stopped and shot a glare to the other man. "Why have you told me my wife's plans? What do you hope to gain from it? You do nothing without a reason."

"If the rumors are true, she is the reason why your lovely ball-busting, frigid cunt of a wife is doing what she will. Tell me, how does a man like you manage to win a prize like Her Grace?" The marquis leaned forward, glass and cigar dangling from his grasp, eyes glittering in poorly concealed rage and jealousy.

"Do not speak of Elizabeth so..."

"Don't be a hypocrite. I know the bargain your father made with you. I know you think me an unprincipled, hedonistic bastard, but at least I am not ruled by my wife. Nor do I let others take advantage of me." Kendall drank and took another puff as he sat back, lips curling in contempt for the man before him.

The earl turned his back on his fellow peer, and gulped down his wine as he stared out a window, trying to master his rage. From behind him came the drawling voice speaking words he didn't want to admit to himself.

"She won't marry you, no matter what you think. Even I know that. A woman such as her? You are an amusement. I suspect you treat her as an equal and that's why she let you fuck her, but you are weak. At heart, you know you are."

"We have different concepts of what makes a man weak. I ask again, what do you want?"

"I thought it would be obvious, even to you: what I have always wanted."

"Her Grace will never consent to sleep with you."

The earl missed the look of hate which twisted the face of the man behind him. "You are a fool. If I want her, she will be mine, no matter what you think or feel. In exchange for information on your wife's plans, you will support me in becoming advisor to His Majesty. It is time the nonsense of a foreign orphan guiding our country is stopped."

"If I don't?" The earl turned around, his eyes glittering with suppressed rage.

The smirk was evil. "Lord Nicky will receive proof that the idle rumors of your affair are true, as is the one you want to marry Her Grace. We both know that what he will do to keep from losing his chance at a dukedom will be more terrifying than anything your bitch of a wife can come up with."

"You call me weak, and if I am, you will need more than my help to achieve your goal."

"Which is why you will convince the duchess of her need to assure His Majesty gives me the appointment, rather than doing it directly yourself."

"When Lord Nicky comes back, he will crush you."

"My, my, you really are a fool. Naturally you will stand with me against the boy, otherwise your line will end when he learns you helped. If you don't care for your own skin, think of your heir, and the duchess. The orphan will have his revenge," the marquis mocked.

The earl's hand tightened around the stem of his glass, snapping the stem. A slave hurried forward to clean the mess up.

"You.are.despicable."

"I'll take that as a yes."

"Her Grace..."

"Had better do what I want, so you must be at your most convincing. I suggest you start with tonight's dalliance."

The earl stalked from the room and out of the mansion. He fumed as he waited outside for his horse to be brought around. He had no illusions Kendall would do, could do, exactly what he threatened. The ride home was short. He loathed himself and his wife for putting him in the position of crawling, of begging her not to take her displeasure out on their children and grandchildren.

* * *

"My Lord! We didn't expect to see you here, not after, after..." His steward trailed off uncomfortably.

"My grandchildren, where are they?"

"Where they always are, my lord: in the nursery wing being looked after by their slaves."

"They are well? They have not been sick?"

"No, of course not, my lord?" The man was puzzled.

The earl continued, "And my children, what of them?"

"Ah, uh, yes, the ladies." Here the steward gave a nervous little cough. "They have been confined to their rooms. Her Ladyship said their behavior since the ball was unacceptable, and until they could learn to be proper ladies, they were not to join the rest of the family."

"And the countess? Where is she?"

"She is working in her garden. Shall I tell her you are home?"

"No, I will tell her myself." The earl made his way through the house and out back.

His wife sat at the white painted iron table in the middle of the denuded garden, directing the slaves on how she wanted it prepared for winter. The slaves saw him coming and bent their heads, working even more assiduously. Dennala's eyes widened in shock. The countess didn't even look around; she sat rigid, and continued her instructions.

"Elizabeth, we need to talk."

"I said I wanted the paths raked in straight lines; those are curvy. Re-do it, properly this time."

"Elizabeth, now is not the time to punish me with one of your silences. We need to have a private discussion."

"Dennala, my juice is insufficiently cold. Have a slave re-chill it and bring me a cold bottle at once."

"Yes, mistress," Dennala scurried off with the bottle, having seen the new look in the Earl's eyes, which boded ill for all nearby.

"Damn it, Elizabeth! If you don't agree to talk with me in private, I will be forced to shout the matter aloud for all the slaves to hear. Do you really want your daughters to know the lengths you are willing to go just to punish me?"

"I am doing what needs to be done to prevent further humiliations to our family. I wouldn't need to do so if you were even half the man your father had been."

"What you are planning is not right; leave the children out of our quarrel. They have done nothing to deserve the fate you seem determined to bring them."

Finally she turned to look at Chadrick; her eyes flashed with the force of her emotions and her voice shook. "Surely that vile man told you what is being said about our family. Am I the only moral member of this family?"

"Please, talk to me, instead of condemning me for whatever it is you think I've done. You cannot betray our family this way."

She gave a short bark of laughter which swiftly segued into

weeping. The earl, helpless, tried to speak comforting words but her tears soon turned into shouts of rage.

"How dare you talk to me of betrayal! I should have known when I married you I would only get children who were capable of being traitors themselves. Both your brothers were traitors, and now you, after everything your father did to save you."

"My father," Sydney interrupted coldly, "did nothing of the sort. He was a bully. He cared only for his precious reputation and the honor of the family name."

"Which all three of his sons have now firmly ground in the mud! I will not let our daughters drag the name down any further."

"Why did you marry me if you thought I would turn out to be a traitor, and our children as well?"

"Why? Because your father swore he had finally gotten you to see the need for being an honorable man of good repute. If he had lived, he would have kept you on the right path. I see now all my attempts to guide this family were in vain. You ignore my good counsel and insist on acts which bring shame upon us all. Well, I will put it right."

"You are not selling our children into slavery. I don't know what it is you think they have done to disgrace us..."

"Of course you wouldn't!" the countess cried contemptuously. "You only see what you wish to. I will have our honor and good reputation back."

"What is it you want?" Sydney roared, startling her for a moment. She sniffed and straightened her spine.

"You will stop sleeping with that wretched woman, you will stop staying at the sheriff's office and move back home. You will stop your whoring. All those trollops! Our daughter will marry Lord Nicky. As for our eldest, she is beyond redemption."

"And why is that?" the earl asked icily.

"I cannot speak of it, it makes me ill just knowing about it.

"Elizabeth..."

"No. I don't care what you call it, it's disgusting. We are too old to have children. I will not be confronted in my elder days by possible by-blows claiming they are yours."

"Elizabeth," he began again in desperation, as he had back in his office, when his world was falling to pieces, and still was.

"You will do what I say, or when Lord Nicky returns, I will go to him and denounce you as a traitor. He knows I am loyal."

"You can't, you don't dare." Words failed him. He felt old and worn away.

He sat down heavily, and placed his head in his hands. He loved his children dearly, and would do anything to see them safe, but he was being asked to give up the one person who had brought a bit of light back into his life. How could he stay away from her?

"I do and I will. I will tell your whore myself. I don't trust you will do the job properly, or be further seduced by her." The countess stood. "Do not think of leaving this house, Chadrick. If you are not here when I get back, I will go to His Majesty." With those parting words, she left the garden to dress for her battle with the whore.

* * *

Sydney sat in his office, a half-empty bottle of wine to one side. What was the point of trying to remain sober? He was not sure the duchess would defend their love; ever since the attack at the Harvest Ball, she had become distant. Surely he had not misread her intentions? She loved him, as he did her; this affair wasn't just a diversion, but something deeper. The earl drained his glass, then with slightly unsteady hands, he poured another drink.

He was sipping and staring at the wall, only hearing the commotion in the hallway when it stopped right outside his sitting room door. His daughters' and his wife's slave's voices rose.

"You are being punished! You get back to your rooms this instant! Your mother will hear of your disobedience!"

"No! You get your hands off of us or I'll tell mother and she'll have you whipped!"

"How dare you! When I am Countess, I will make sure you regret every single unkind thing you have done to me!"

"Dennala!" the earl called out. "Bring my children in."

The two girls flounced in, satisfied smirks on their faces. "Father! You're home! Mother has been just beastly! We don't know what she is upset about, but she keeps us locked in our rooms! She won't even let me see my own children!"

Their voices intertwined in complaint as the slave defended her mistress. “Your Lordship, the ladies are being punished for their sins. Surely her ladyship explained to you why she told me to do as I have been trying to do!”

“I will have silence. At.Once.” The earl drew himself up as he gave his commands.

His daughters and slave fell into startled silence, never having heard his army voice directed at them.

“I will have no lies in this house. Your mother wishes an even harsher punishment laid upon you than the one you already endure. She is concerned your actions have brought great shame upon our name. If you wish that punishment to not happen, you will tell me what I want to know.”

He singled out his slave to begin first. She drew herself up, curtsied, then launched into her tale. His daughters tried to interrupt, but he silenced them with curt commands or hard glares.

“And that is the whole truth of it, your lordship. I have told all to her ladyship, and she has learned I bear no ill tales. All I have said is true. I wish it were not. You may order me punished if you like, but I will not change what I know and have heard.”

Sydney gripped the chair before him, more horrified than he let on. While his daughters tried to deny or make light of the slave’s tale, he realized they were indeed guilty. He felt heartsick; had his need to find even temporary solace and companionship in whores, and then Her Grace, let his daughters think it was permissible that they behave like loose women? They must be shown the error of their thinking, but not in the way his wife wanted.

“Sally, you will return to your room, and continue your lessons on being a proper lady. Caroline, I am...disgusted. You have two children to raise. This type of behavior is beneath you. I must consider what is to be done about this state of affairs. As it is, your mother is correct in keeping your children from you.”

“But, Father,” the two began.

“Out. Not another word, or I will consider methods more drastic. Dennala, see to them, please.”

The slave curtsied again and ushered the women out the door. Sydney couldn’t return to life with Elizabeth as it had been before the duchess, but neither could he let his children's mother continue her mad plans. He did love them dearly, after all. His idea on how to put things right would be the hardest thing he had ever done, but it was time for him to stop being a passive spectator in his own life.

A firm knock on his door brought him out of his reverie, and at his invitation, his son stepped into the room. The young man, around Lord Nicky's age, was being groomed to inherit the earldom.

"Father." The young man stood before the desk, hands clasped behind his back at parade rest. His hair was combed, and his clothes pressed. "I was hoping to speak with you about the family. I am...concerned over what has been happening to us."

"Tell me, Martin, do you feel our family has lost honor? That the family name has been dragged irreparably into the muck?"

His son hesitated. "I have heard disturbing things of late, sir."

"You will inherit the Earldom when I am gone, including public opinion of our family."

"Yes, sir."

"You are old enough to understand what I mean, and old enough to have an opinion on the matter. There may come a future time when events such as the one troubling our family now will trouble yours; I wish to know how you'd handle the problem."

The young man gulped, and moved his head to ease the strictures of his shirt about his neck and looked embarrassed yet apologetic. "Well, sir, by current social mores, my sisters have behaved in immoral ways. Also, as head of the household, it would be your responsibility to see their actions are corrected, unless your behavior has contributed to the problem, in which case the corrections to behavior should be shared by all."

"I see. Then you would support your mother's decisions on how punishment should be meted out?"

"I have not heard what Mother plans, other than what was said earlier in the garden," he said uncomfortably.

"Let us imagine for a moment you are the earl. Your mother and sisters must obey your decisions without question. What would they be?"

Martin opened his mouth to speak, shut it, and a smiley type of grimace crossed his face. "In that case, sir," he took a deep breath and plunged on. "If the rumors are even partially true, Caroline should not be allowed near her children unsupervised, so she does not poison their minds with her immoral ways."

The earl raised his brows, and his son bowed slightly and continued, "Furthermore, it seems to me she is unrepentant and like to remain that way. I would cast her out of the house; perhaps if she is denied the comforts to which she has been accustomed, the consequences of her actions will be better impressed upon her."

"You suggest she be forced to make her own way? Penniless and homeless? Would it not bring more shame upon the family if she chooses to make her living as an immoral woman?"

Sydney felt his heart sink as his son spoke.

"No. Send her to our country estate to contemplate the error of her ways. Ensure that the slaves see she leads a plain and simple life."

"Your youngest sister? What of her?"

Martin's cheeks stained red a moment before he said, "Some men would not marry her, considering her damaged goods, but she is not so far gone down Caroline's path that she can't be saved. If a small dowry was settled upon her, with a small piece of land as well, perhaps one of the lesser nobility would not mind taking her to wife. I think Mother is wrong about the advisor; he will not marry Sally."

"His Majesty could command it of him. Your mother is certain she can ask the favor of him."

His son bowed and replied, "If it was anyone but the advisor, I would agree. In this instance, I think we would all be wrong. He is an ambitious man, seeking power and wealth, neither of which Sally will bring him."

The earl sat back and contemplated his son. The young man was wise, but saying what he would do, and having it obeyed was not the same. "And I, Martin. What would be my punishment?"

"I'm sorry sir? Your punishment? I don't..."

"I know you are aware of my transgressions, as it seems the whole town is, I was not as...prudent as I should have been."

The young man, miserable, colored red and wished himself anywhere but where he was.

"Come, come," his father said, "I would hope you do not repeat my failings, but in the unhappy event you do, what would you do to correct it?"

Again Martin opened his mouth and then closed it and contemplated the floor for several minutes in silence. The earl waited while his son struggled with his thoughts. The young man lifted his head and took a deep breath in and spoke.

"If there was a bargain made, it would be dishonorable to ignore it; such a thing should be honored to the letter of which it was written, or renegotiated to the best benefit of both parties."

"And what if one of those parties refused to either honor it or re-negotiate? What then? What route would you choose?"

Martin tugged at the collar of his shirt. "I don't know, sir. It would be selfish to ignore the other's wishes and do what made oneself happy. But it also seems selfish to insist there is only one solution. I suppose I would try to do whatever would leave both people with as much dignity and honor as possible."

Father and son looked at each other a moment. Sydney gave a small nod. "You are wise beyond your years, despite my failings."

"Thank you, father."

"That said, it's one thing to say what one would do, and quite another to see it carried out."

"Mother has a forceful personality. The slaves listen to her more than they do you; some would say honor had been lost the moment your words and wishes became less than hers."

"Thus we come to the crux of the matter," the earl murmured.

"I'm sorry, sir? I didn't quite catch that."

"Nothing, son. You may leave me now, I have much to consider.

"Yes sir." His son walked to the door and, hand on the knob, said, "I have always thought you had honor, sir, and I still do. I'm sorry, about everything." He left, closing the door behind him.

"So am I son, so am I."

* * *

Supper that night was a silent affair. The air hummed with unspoken recriminations, bitter resentment, and uncertainty. The countess had returned from her visit with the duchess in a foul mood, and had found fault with everything the slaves did. The only words she spoke at table was harsh ones, ordering the slaves about, or remonstrating with one of the children concerning their manners, or castigating the earl. Just when the children thought they would escape, their mother crushed those hopes.

"It is time for a discussion. We will repair to the sitting room." Elizabeth rose and left the room, confident her family would obey.

The children looked toward their father, who nodded and followed his wife. The three young people glanced at one another nervously and hurried to join their parents before their mother sent slaves to drag them in. The countess was sitting poker-straight, ramrod-stiff in an equally stiff-backed chair, lips nearly invisible with displeasure. The earl stood behind a chair across the room from her, resting one arm along the back. Once the offspring had chosen their seats, their mother spoke.

"It is time for this nonsense to stop, we have lost enough honor as it is."

To everyone's amazement, Sydney interrupted her. He straightened up and walked forward a few paces, hands clasped behind his back. "That is the only thing we may agree upon, my lady, that the nonsense will stop."

"Now is not the time..."

"I am not done," the earl replied icily, "and you will remain silent until I have had my say. I am still head of this family, despite what you may know or think of past and current events."

Elizabeth stared at her husband a moment and opened her mouth for another sharp retort but he merely held a hand up and turning to his family, began to speak more forcefully than they had heard him do for some time.

"I have come to a decision regarding our family and the behaviors of various members, myself included. We cannot change the past, but it is clear we cannot continue on as we have been. Caroline, you will be sent to live on our farm. I have put new slaves in charge. You will reside in the cottage, and live a simple life. I am hoping without the temptations of the town, you will reconsider your actions. Your children shall not be joining you."

"But father! This is ridiculous! How am I to find a father for my children and a husband for myself out there? It's Sally..."

"You presume to dictate which slaves shall join our daughter..."

"You're the whore! All the army men..."

"SILENCE!" the earl roared.

His family's squabbling halted at the unexpectedness of the command and stared his way in startlement. "You will leave immediately, Caroline."

"But." Her outrage ceased as the door to the hallway opened and the family steward stepped inside, followed by slaves they had never seen before, and the family guards. The guards broke off and came over to the eldest daughter.

The countess began angrily, "How dare you make these decisions about our daughter without consulting me!"

"Caroline, the men will drag you, kicking and screaming if need be, if you do not go voluntarily."

"But, Father! My children? My clothes!"

"You will have no need of fancy outfits at the farm, and your children will be cared for by those with a stronger moral sense than you've exhibited. You are excused."

He turned from his eldest and pinned his youngest with his stare just as she stuck her tongue out at her sister; she hastily covered guilty surprise at being caught with downcast eyes. Caroline was still protesting, and at a motion, the guards stepped forward and grabbed her arms. She began to scream.

"No! You can't! I won't! I'm a grown woman! How dare you! Get your hands off me!" Her shrieks of outrage could be heard long after the men had dragged her away from the room. The sound of a slamming door shut off her voice.

Martin was sitting in wide-eyed startlement; he had never dreamed, during his talk with his father, that his parent was in earnest. The countess was trembling from the effort of remaining quiet, and her eyes flashed in rage as her lips thinned even further.

"Sally, I am deeply disappointed you thought following your sister's path a good way to catch a husband. You have damaged your worth to any noble of importance. It is best you forget about Lord Nicky and marriage to him."

"What?! No! That's not fair! If that duchess!"

"Is a duchess, with wealth and power; men of Lord Nicky's standing marry this sort of woman, no matter what they do in their personal lives. I have sent inquiries to suitable lesser noblemen. Over the next few weeks, each one will meet you, and you will be informed which one has selected you."

"My daughter..."

"Be quiet, wife. I'm not finished. The marriage will be delayed only long enough to determine whether your foolish liaison will result in a child. If there is one, it is to be adopted by another family; you will be married after you have recovered from the birth sufficiently to stand for the length of the marriage ceremony. Until such time as we have determined whether you are with child, and if you are, until you bear it, you are confined to the house and its grounds; you will not leave except as a wife to your husband's house."

"You can't, I won't! Mother!" Sally shrieked as fat tears filled her eyes and rolled down her cheeks.

"This has gone too far, Chadrick," the countess spat at her husband as a second set of guards came to stand by the youngest daughter.

"Compared to what?" the earl asked in the same icy tone. "To what you planned? I am showing them a mercy they would not have got from you."

Sally was crying and screaming as she too had to be forcibly removed from the room. Martin sat frozen; there was still a set of guards and slaves next to his father's steward. Were they for himself or for his mother? He could not think of what he had done which might have angered his father, unless it was the conversation they had earlier. Whatever happened, he would meet it with more dignity than his sisters had shown.

"As for you and I, countess, we are finished."

"The hell we are!" she snapped at him, to her son's astonishment. "You promised your father, you signed the papers..."

"And I have kept it to the best of my ability. My father is dead; what he wanted no longer matters. I care not if the king grants us a divorce or refuses it, but I will not continue to live this way."

"You will regret this, when I speak with His Majesty."

"The only thing I regret is letting my father, and then you, dictate how I should live my life. You will remove yourself and your things to the dowager's cottage. You will no longer have the running of this household."

"If you think the slaves will obey a weak man like you..."

"I expect nothing of the kind from them. I will, however, expect them to obey Martin, as he will take over the Earldom. Those who refuse to accept him as the master of the house will be sold and replaced by ones who will. My steward will see these last wishes of mine are carried out."

Martin spluttered. "I'm, I'm sorry, father, did you? But how? I mean, you can't, why?"

"How dare you have those slaves drag me off as they did our daughters? I am your countess, and they have to obey me."

"No," Sydney corrected, "you were the countess." He held up an aged scroll.

Elizabeth gasped in terror when she realized what he held. Chadrick threw it into the fire, where it flared into ash. "When Martin chooses to marry, his wife will be the new countess; I will not have her life overtaken and directed by you."

The earl turned to his son, who had been sitting in astonished silence after the outburst.

"I have arranged with His Majesty for you to legally take over the earldom. I will retain the title during my lifetime, but all the rest—lands, money, livestock, slaves—will be yours. I hope the wait, however long it may be, will not disappoint you overly much; nor will using my steward until you have inherited the title itself. At which point, you can choose to continue employing him as your steward, or fire him and find another more to your liking."

"I... I would be the most ungrateful son ever if I should allow it. But, but, what will you do if I am in charge of the family affairs? Where will you live?"

"You think you're going to live with your whore? You think the two of you will be accepted in polite society?"

"I have re-enlisted in His Majesty's army as a special liaison between the court and the sheriff's office. I will live at the barracks, with my men."

Chapter Twelve

Priester Joseph tended his small garden and chickens. He had to be more vigilant now; food was getting scarce with half the town burned away. The townspeople paid little attention to him when he preached in the street—only a scant few joined his congregation, but the vast majority continued their sinful ways. He had once been a wanderer some called crazy. He had been driven across the land by his visions, beautiful and disturbing things which whispered of people and places which held darkness inside them. The world was in ruins because of all the sin and nothing could truly flourish until it was blotted out, the Great One whispered in his mind. As he harvested the last of the offerings, his mind wandered back to how he came to the kingdom of Macina, where his visions told him the entrance to the death-lands lay.

* * *

Joseph walked along the dirt track, praying and looking for edible berries and nuts. He had a following of four or five people who believed his visions and traveled from town to town with him. When he decided upon a place to settle and minister, they joined him. They did their best to see he had food and drink and hosted him each week in turn at their small huts. Still, they were poor and he had to supplement what they gave him. Joseph saw a hollow tree up ahead, and heard humming: a honey cache. Still praying, he managed to get enough of the sweet comb to last for several days.

As he continued down the track, Joseph knew it would lead to a sheltered pond where berry bushes grew. Loud laughter, along with a child's voice raised in terror and fear, interrupted his thoughts.

Joseph stepped off the track, silently creeping through the bushes toward the commotion. Near the pond, a ring of men from the town stood. Joseph frowned sourly. All bullies who took delight in harassing him. As they shifted, he saw they were tormenting a small dirty boy of about twelve. One of the men had the boy pinioned and another was going through his meager belongings as the others laughed and drank.

Stepping from the bushes, Joseph approached, calling out their names, "Daniel, Samosa, Jethro, and Amos, a curse upon your head for your bullying, evil ways. You will be struck down for your wickedness!"

The men turned in surprise and seeing who it was, let out nasty laughs and gave off teasing the boy to advance on him. What they planned to do he wasn't sure, for The Great One struck. Joseph felt the air stir around him for a moment. Daniel and Jethro fell with rotting holes in their chests where their hearts used to be. Somosa fled gibbering from the grove while Amos dropped to the ground, holding his head and screaming in pain before passing out.

The little boy had a sly, satisfied expression on his face which did not sit well with Joseph. "Young man, you should give thanks to the Great One for your deliverance!"

The boy looked at him, coldly contemptuous for a minute before his face crumbled into tears, leaving Joseph doubting what he had seen. "I was so f...frr...frightened. I...I lost the last of my family two days ago and didn't know what to do, or where to go. Then...then those men found me. Thank...thank you for saving me."

"The Great One looks after his faithful, you must be one of them child, though you may not know it. What is your name?"

"N... Nicky."

"I'm surprised your departed family did not teach you to stay away from men of their ilk."

"Oh, oh they did. That, that was my fault, sir. I was so hungry I didn't pay attention to what was going on as I ate some berries. I heard them coming through the trees, planning on killing someone and they spotted me. I was so tired I couldn't run from them."

Joseph narrowed his eyes. The Great One was speaking to

him, telling him he needed to help the boy, so he set his basket down, "You need something to eat and drink and then you can tell me about what the men said. I am Joseph." As he talked, he filled a wooden cup from his basket with water for the boy.

"Thank you, Joseph, sir."

The two sat cross-legged on the grass and Joseph blessed them both. He shared a hard crust of bread, dipped in the honey he'd found that day, and a moldy bit of cheese washed down by the cool pond water. "Now, what is this about those men killing someone?"

Nicky looked around to be really sure they were alone and lowered his voice to a whisper. "They said they were tired of some king. He was always spoiling their fun and fining them or imprisoning them. One of them said he knew of a Lord who coveted the throne and wished the king and his family dead. This Lord would pay a lot of money to whoever killed the royal family if they did it before the spring festival."

Normally, Joseph would ignore the boastings of those men, but something about the way the boy told the story made him think it might be true for once. "You shall come with me and I will see if I can't get the King to listen to what you've heard. Perhaps he will find a family for you to stay with, or adopt you. If not, you can live with me."

"Oh thank you, Joseph, Sir!"

Joseph had gotten the boy in to talk to the king, but he just laughed and waved off the tale. No noble was willing to adopt the boy, but the king gave Joseph some money and clothes for the boy, and often had him up to the castle to play with his ten-year-old son, Maecenas. Out of gratitude for taking him in, Nicky brought Joseph small game. During the winter months, after collecting deadfall for firewood, the boy would sometimes talk of his family.

"My father taught me how to read, Sir. He prayed a lot like you do, and said there used to be great cities filled with unexplainable things all over the land. But the people who lived in them let the Dark Spirits from the Death Lands in. They ruined the world with their greed and sin. He said his father was taught the tales from his father, like all our ancestors had been."

"Did he now?"

"Uh huh, and my father said no one would make it to the Undying Lands as long as one person harbored a Dark Spirit. He was teaching me how to tell when evil had entered a person, and how to cleanse them again. My father said he was a pr...priest and the people he prayed with called him Priester." After a pause Nicky said, "Would it be all right if I called you Priester Joseph?"

Joseph was touched, and from then on the townspeople called him by his new nomenclature. As for the King and his family, Nicky had heard true and before the Spring Festival, the family was murdered except for the king's ten-year-old son. The son remembered Nicky had tried to warn him. In gratitude, he had the little boy come live with him.

The orphan seemed to have wisdom and knowledge beyond his years, and many of the nobles were leery of Nicky for this reason. The boy would have been apprenticed outside the palace but he once again uncovered a plot. This one was to get rid of the old King's son, as some found him weak and lazy. Out of gratitude, King Maecenas made Nicky an Earl and King's Advisor. Everything was fine in the years following. But now whispers had been reaching him for some time. An agent of the Dark Spirits was walking in human form and threatening the peace.

Priester Joseph thought, "This duchess who is whispered about. The Great One tells me she is a bad person. Of course, I will see to it she does not work any of her evil ways here. I will keep an eye on her for my little boy who is now a lord, Nicky."

He finished his chores, gathered what eggs he could find, and went back inside his cottage. Everyone knew Lord Nicky harbored a fondness for the man who had helped him when he was a boy. Until recently, not even the most daring riff-raff dared assault him, or steal from him, lest they face the advisor's wrath, though the most intrepid had of late been encroaching upon him. Now those ungrateful, evil, lazy townspeople dared take what was his.

Joseph heard the rumors which flew about the town; clacking tongues would be better off providing for themselves instead of looking for handouts from His Majesty. It was all the fault of the foreign woman. The whore who dared call herself a duchess. Nicky complained to him about how she bewitched the king. How she stole honest folks' slaves and children. How she seduced good and faithful men into forgetting their sacred vows to wives and family. He left the cottage, after telling his acolyte to keep a watch on the hen house.

The mud had frozen overnight, encasing the garbage strewn over the streets. A bitter cold wind knifed through the remaining buildings, and flakes of snow drifted down to create a sheet of purest untrammeled white where feet and animals had yet to trample. The man knew by next morning several inches would coat everything. He trudged onward, ignoring the groups of shivering men and women who worked to tear down buildings too unstable from the fire to be used. He passed what was left of the Bloody Knuckles, noting a new face behind the bar.

He entered, thinking that mayhap he could get something hot to eat from the sin peddler's new bartender without being chased out. Joseph weaved past tables, and greeted the man.

"Good day, brother. What fare have you?"

The man kept up his polishing of a dented pewter mug. "Rabbit stew and bread. Shall I bring you a bowl?"

Joseph stood a moment, trying to make out the man's words through his thick accent. Another foreigner come to feast off the town's carcass. "Aye, thank you, brother. And a mug of something to drink." He walked over to a table and sat.

It was early enough in the day that not too many patrons were around, nor the usual assortment of sluts. After a moment, the man came out and placed the fare before his customer, then went back to cleaning. The meat was gamey, the vegetables undercooked, the broth bland. The bread was over-baked; the ale, watery. All in all, a disappointing meal. When he was finished, he took the dishes up to the bar.

"Is the tavern mistress in, brother? I wish to speak with her."

"Problem with the food?"

"No, no. Personal business."

The man nodded and took the dirties to the kitchen. Jenfry followed him out.

"You stupid clod!" she bellowed at sight of the priest and clouted the bartender on the back of his head. "His kind ain't welcome here! And I don't waste good food on him neither! That bastard never pays, claiming he shouldn't 'cause he's a 'holy man'."

Joseph puffed himself up indignantly. “A pig eats better slop than what you serve.”

The bartender was rubbing the back of his head resentfully. “No one tole me. How’s I supposed to know?” He retreated behind the bar and picked back up with what he was doing before.

“You git outta here! And stay out!”

“My patron would be displeased to learn how you treat me.”

She glared at him, fists planted on her ample hips.

“I heard the foreign whore will not let your daughter come visit you.”

Jenfry sneered and spat, “What’s it to you?”

“I am here to do a favor for your sin-filled soul in exchange for being fed once a day.”

“The only favor you can do is get your ugly mug outta my tavern before you scare away my patrons with your crazy babble.”

“Stupid cow,” he muttered under his breath, then louder, “One meal a day will go far toward redeeming your soul and keeping it from the death-lands. I will bring you to your daughter. The foreign whore will not dare forbid me entrance to her home. Not if she hopes to keep her own eternal soul free from sin.” He could see the interest in her eyes.

“I need access to her more than one measly time.”

He tugged at his greasy beard. “Naturally, a mother should be able to see her child when she wishes. But I have other souls to whom I must attend. Once a month is the best I can do. But, if you don’t love her...” He turned to leave.

“Damn crazy. Give me a moment.”

He contemplated the foreign man before him, enjoying the way his scrutiny made the foreigner uncomfortable. Jenfry came out, wooden clogs clacking on the floor, wrapped in a thin, dirty cloak. They walked in silence to the bridge. Before the attacks, it had only had two guards, but now that had changed. Four guards warmed themselves at braziers. They searched the man and woman for weapons.

“How dare you question the motives of a holy man! I am Lord Nicky’s spiritual advisor, and the woman with me a sister in faith.”

The guards shifted uneasily at the advisor’s name. “It’s just, sir. We have our orders. From the king.”

"Bugger the king. If he wasn't a degenerate, the Great One would have protected him from attacks. His lack of faith is his problem. Now let us through, for I assure you, Lord Nicky will hear how you've treated us."

The four men shifted again, looking toward each other helplessly, before shifting enough to let the two people through. Joseph stomped across the bridge, muttering imprecations under his breath as the fat tavern keep's wife huffed, trying to keep up. The gates to the whore's house stood open; her guards watched as the newcomers walked through. They could see people working on re-thatching the roofs of the outbuildings, while a steady clack and occasional shouts came from one side of the mansion. A lone goat grazed on the cold blighted foliage of overgrown gardens.

Joseph stopped a small boy. "Where is Mary Elana?"

The kid blinked stupidly at him a moment. "Um. Inside." He pointed to a small cottage which had a plume of smoke rising from the chimney, hurried off.

The man walked the few paces to the door. Jenfry shivered, her small eyes almost lost in the fat folds of her face as she glared about in envy. The place had been abandoned so long it was tumbling down, but its former glory still showed in spots.

Bitch, whore! How dare she just steal me daughter, fuck the king, and have everyone bowing and scraping to her.

A middle-aged slave woman with reddish-brown hair and faded blue eyes answered. "Yes?"

"I am Priester Joseph, and this is my sister in faith. I have come to see the girl, Mary Elana, and minister to her soul."

The woman had the audacity to frown at him. "My mistress made no mention of such a visit. If you would care to come another day?"

"No doubt she has forgotten, with the work she does for His Majesty," Joseph announced gravely.

A crease appeared between her brows as she regarded him, then Jenfry. "A moment, please." She shut the door.

Joseph hissed in anger. How dare she close the door on him! How dare she not invite him in out of the cold as any good-hearted person should?

"Snooty bitch," Jenfry muttered.

They waited what seemed a long time. The same woman opened the door again. "Please come inside." She stood to one side as they entered a small room.

It had been newly whitewashed, and precious glass gleamed in the windows. A fire burned merrily in the grate, warming the space. The wooden floor had been recently scrubbed and sanded.

"May I take your cloaks while you wait? The girl will be out in a moment." She gestured to a couch and set of chairs arranged before the hearth.

A closed wooden door was to one side of the fireplace. Jenfry handed her garment over with what she thought a grand air. She was free-born, she should be treated with respect. The woman moved to sit on the couch as the priest took a chair.

The slave paused a moment. "Would you care for food or drink while you wait?"

"Yeah," Jenfry replied.

The woman left, carrying their cloaks with her, the door shutting behind. Jenfry wiggled back into the couch. Cushions had been placed on the seat in an effort to make it more comfortable. Light shone through the windows. A pair of candelabra stood on either end of the mantel, and an oil lantern in the shape of a teardrop sat on a low wooden table.

She was a bit surprised the slave had not told them to go around back, and had let them into the front room. *Noble bitch, my ass. She probably just some jumped-up common slut trying to pretend she be of high birth. If she really was, ain't no way we be sitting here and being served by a slave like we gentry*. Still, it was a nice change of pace from what she was used to.

After a moment, the slave woman came out bearing a tray which she set down before them and removed lids from a variety of dishes. Jenfry couldn't help her eyes popping wide. A small dish held salt, a commodity more precious than gold. A platter held a loaf of bread, fresh out of the oven from the smell rising off it. Another plate held fat sausages, still spitting fat from the grilling, a third, a small wheel of cheese. A bowl of water with herbs floating in it was set down, along with finger cloths. The last to be unloaded were two silver mugs of frothy ale and large, snowy white linen squares. The slave took up the now-empty tray and left.

Joseph glared at the offending bowl of water, and linen. He reached out a dirt-crusted hand, grabbed up a sausage, tore a hunk of fragrant bread off, cut a generous slice of cheese, mashed it all together with a large dose of salt and proceeded to eat. Jenfry wasn't raised to have any social graces, but she had heard her slaves talk of their past lives when they thought no one listened. Even though she mocked them, and took delight when they were broken in and taught their place, she enjoyed the thought the slave had shown her more deference then her status deserved.

She took the time to dip her hands in the water; it was warm, and smelt faintly of rosemary and lemon balm. The bread was yeasty, with a light texture and flavor, very different from her own hard, coarse, sometimes flat, attempts. The salt she sprinkled over it, bringing out the flavor. The cheese had a rich, buttery, creamy taste without any of the tart overtones that suggested goat's milk—could it be cow's milk? The sausage stuffed with garlic, herbs and spices she couldn't identify. The smoky flavor burst in her mouth as the thin casing gave way to tender moist meats, finely ground, inside. The ale was chilled. It slid smoothly down her throat, tasting of hops, wheat, and honey. It tasted clean, crisp.

I almost don't care if the bitch don't come. The trip alone is worth the meal. A'course, bitch better greet her ma. Maybe I can get some coin offa her.

The door opened, and she looked up to see her daughter hovering fearfully. "Well it's about time!" Jenfry snapped around a mouthful of food. "Git over here and greet yer ma proper like."

Mary Elana sidled into the room, passing in front of the fire to the only unoccupied chair where she stood, transfixed. Her fingers knotted around each other.

Jenfry sneered at her child, bile rising in her throat at sight of her. "Sit down!" she barked.

The child's face whitened in terror, but she did as bid. Her mother continued to eat as she inspected the girl, wide-eyed as any rabbit when the hawk swoops over. The woman paused to belch as her daughter sat there in silence.

Her owner had clothed the young teenager in a pale green dress, with a brown laced stomacher. She had brown deerskin slippers which peeped out from underneath her skirt and a white eyelet flounce which probably belonged to a shift. Her brown hair was clean, combed in a long braid down her back and tied with a green ribbon. Most of the bruises she had received from her father's discipline showed a sickly greenish-yellow. She still had purplish rings around her puffy eyes, and her lips had scabs on them from where they had been split. Around her neck sat a slim, ornately twisted collar etched with a raven sigil. The ends and knobs of her bones could still be seen, but not as obviously as when she lived at home.

"Looks like the bitch give you food and clothes. Your pa and I starve and scrape to make ends meet after the whore stole you. But you don't care, do you? You don't even wanna see us, think you're better than us now you serve a duchess. You whore, you don't think to ask how we are, if we need anythin'?"

Mary Elana's face grew whiter at each word, her eyes more terror-stricken. She leaned back without realizing it as her mother loomed forward, spraying food and spit with each vituperative sentence.

"You just wait, you slut, you 'ho. You'll mess up like you always do, then she won't want you anymore, will she? Maybe you'll get lucky and I'll agree to buy you back, or maybe I won't. It might just serve you right, fat cow, if she sells you to someone who knows how to treat slaves, with proper discipline."

The priest belched, finishing off the last of his ale. "Mary Elana!" he barked.

The girl flinched at his tone, shrinking further back into the chair. Her hands twisted and wrung more frantically, tears leaked silently from beneath her lids.

"You are wicked to forget about your parents and your origins. You have taken the first steps on the road to the wasteland of the Death Land. You live in a house of sin and debauchery. You must pray toward mercy and reward in the un-dying lands."

The girl shook her head, crying harder. Her sobs broke forth in great heaving bursts, sniffing snot back. Her mother shot an irritated glance at the priest.

"Listen here, girly, when that woman whores you to her male callers, you get coin offa them, you hear me? And you make sure the first man who lays with you pays a lotta gold for the privilege of bedding a virgin."

"Foul, evil minded women! How dare you corrupt innocent souls! You listen to me, girl, you lay with a man not your lawful husband, and you'll pay for it. You will be cast out to live among the whores, you will give birth to deformed monstrosities! You will be un-savable!"

"You leave my kid alone with your crazy shit! You got your food and drink, now git out and leave us alone!" Jenfry rounded on the sanctimonious man.

Her daughter curled over into herself, weeping harshly, keening and rocking as the adults screamed at each other. No one heard the inner door open, nor saw the appalled face of Susafan. She hustled the girl from the room. The door slamming shut behind her stopped the feud. They stood, staring a moment where the girl had been.

Jenfry rounded back on the priest. "Now look what ya done! I better be able to see my daughter after the trouble you caused."

"You dare threaten a holy man? Spiritual advisor to Lord Nicky?"

"Hah! We do more for him then your mumbo jumbo and hand-waving."

The door opened, a male slave stepping forth. "Your pardon, but my mistress wishes you off the property."

"I ain't done visiting with my daughter!" Jenfry hissed at the man.

"The girl's soul needs to be saved," Joseph added.

The man stepped further into the room, followed by another. Each held one of the visitors' cloaks. Both wore a thicker version of the collar Mary Elana had around her neck. Black leather boots laced up to their knees, with heavy cotton pants tucked into them, also black. Their collarless white shirts could not hide the bulge of muscles.

"I didn't make myself clear. You can leave of your own free will, or we can throw you out."

The two visitors bristled angrily.

"I'm her mother!"

"I'm a priest!"

The second man snorted, shrugged his shoulders, and moved

forward. A small mountain in motion. Jenfry stood her ground a moment before snatching her cloak back, and wrenching the door open, calling over her shoulder as she left,

"I'll complain to the sheriff about your treatment of a free-born!"

The priest continued to protest, and had to be frog-marched out the gates. He was heaved onto the icy cobbles, crusty robes flying up to reveal skinny, dirty, hairy legs. He stomped off down the hill to the jeers of the guards.

* * *

Mary Elana sat at the kitchen table, head down on her crossed arms as she wept bitterly. She was just starting to get used to being a slave when her mother had come.

"Shhhh, shhhh now." Susafan tried calming the girl, rubbing her back. "I'm sorry I ever let them in. Her Grace never said anything about them not being allowed to visit you." Her tone genuinely distressed.

The fat cook lumbered about the small kitchen, banging pots and pans as was his wont, cursing the inadequate space. "You'll have to tell Her Grace what you done," he barked out, cleaver slamming through a duck's neck.

Guts plopped onto the table with a wet slap. "Who you think gave her those bruises?" He waved viscera and cleaver, drops of blood splattering as he gesticulated.

"I thought it was just her father." Susafan's tone horrified.

The cook snorted as he seasoned the duck, clapped the clay lid on the pot, and shoved it into the glowing ashes. He swept the remains into a pail destined for the slaves' soup pot, plunged the cleaver into a bucket of water before putting it up and moving onto the next dish. Susafan bit her lip as the girl continued sobbing.

"Take the girl outta here! I got a supper to get ready and her weeping's gonna turn the food sour!" he raged, brandishing a kitchen implement.

Susafan hauled the girl up, still crying and walked her to the small room set aside for the slaves to relax at day's end. Mary Elana curled up on the couch, sobs wrenching out. The older slave left her there, and went in search of her mistress. She decided to try her office, then her bedroom. No luck. She went about her chores until it was time for the household meal. The maid's nostrils flared in distaste as they did at every sight of the outside slaves sitting to table.

Mary Elana sat woebegone in her usual place. She had stopped crying, her eyes swollen, face red, and mechanically ate and drank what was set before her. She cleared up silently, and stood waiting for Cook to give her orders.

"You git on out of here now," the man growled.

The young woman trudged down the hall, voices came to her ears, muffled behind a closed door. She heard her name mentioned and stopped.

"I'm sorry, Your Grace. I didn't understand you wanted them kept from her even here."

"I will speak with the staff on the matter. How is she?"

"Back to crying and not talking." Susafan's voice held a note of exasperation.

"Very well. Tell her I wish to speak with her."

"Yes, Your Grace."

The door opened abruptly, startling the girl out of her haze with a yip of surprise, eyes wide in terror. Susafan nudged the young woman toward the room. "Go on, don't make her wait."

Mary Elana didn't think she could, but her mistress called softly and she found her feet taking her inside the small office. She cringed, shoulders hunched inward, staring at the table top before her, quaking in fear.

A small brass goblet was held in her sight line. "Drink, child. You are not in trouble." *Drink, ease your fear, calm your worries.*

The girl hesitantly took the vessel and sipped. Sweet, spiced wine rolled over her tongue and down her throat. It felt like a little ball of fire in her stomach. She obediently drank until there was only a sip or two swilling around the bottom of the goblet.

A hand took the goblet, and she heard the chink and gurgle of liquid pouring. The goblet once more offered to her. Her pounding heart and gasping breath calmed as the wine slowly warmed her.

"I am sorry your mother and Joseph upset you today. They will not bother you here again." Her tone dark and angry.

Mary Elana shook her head, not wanting to sit before her mistress, not believing what happened wasn't her fault. She would be sold, she knew it. What owner wanted a slave who caused so many problems? She didn't realize she had finished the second goblet of wine and held the empty in a shaking hand.

A rustle sounded, the goblet taken from her. Fingers silky cold, perfumed, touched under her chin and lifted her face up. The girl kept her eyes cast down, a sliver of yellow gown all she could see.

"Look at me, please." The command gentle but insistent.

Watery brown eyes looked into green, brown gold ones. "I want you to feel safe here. I have no plans on selling, chastising, or treating you in the manner to which you were accustomed at the tavern. I have decided you shall learn to be a house slave, not a girl of odd jobs, unless there is some other work here you prefer?"

Mary Elana shook her head; she had no skills beyond being a barmaid.

"Very well. Tomorrow you will start. Go, enjoy your evening off."

The young woman sat dazed a moment, questions swarming in her brain which she had no courage to ask. She forced herself to stand, shaky from nerves and wine. It was evening, dark and cold. She didn't want to return to the cramped room she shared with Susafan, nor to the communal space set aside for the slaves. A cutting wind blew through her as she stepped outside, forcing her to fight for air at the sudden shock of it.

Her feet automatically took her to the stables, wooden clogs clacking on icy, snowy stones and dirt. A row of horses who dozed or munched contentedly. The smells of manure, hay, and warm flesh tickled her nose. A mare poked her head curiously over the stall door and nickered, hoping for treats. The nose was velvety soft, the whiskers tickled her hands. The mare nudged her shoulder, then stood quietly as the girl laid her face against the glossy brown neck, petting and crying.

Chapter Thirteen

Eron stood in worn jeans and a faded long-sleeved purple shirt. Behind him was a line of dark stone and brick buildings. Their plate glass windows gleamed in the street lights. He leaned against the side of a battered SUV, hands shoved in his pockets. Next to him was a younger man with red hair and brown eyes. He had on jeans and a t-shirt under a red leather racing jacket and heavy boots. He carried a full face helmet in his leather-gloved hands and he was looking at Illyria in awe.

"Man that is some bike." The kid's tone admiring.

Trouble, in an armor-clad leather racing suit, stood next to a shiny black Ducati which put the kid's bike to shame. Her hair stirred in the slight breeze blowing around them.

"Don't," Eron said to her.

A teasing smile curled her lips up as she looked at the kid. "So you like to ride, do you?" Her tone seductive.

"Hell, I like to race; what I couldn't do with a bike like that."

"Don't," Eron straightened up from the vehicle. "Mica won't like it. Stay away from the boy."

"Awwww, come on. A pretty lady like her?"

"Think you can keep up?" she flirted back.

"Against a bike like that? You get me a bike like that, I can outrace anyone. This one, not so much."

"Pity," she purred, slung a leg over the bike, revved it up then let it purr, though more throatily and an octave or two lower. "I was hoping for some competition."

Donny's mouth dropped open. "What'll I get if I can keep up?"

"Illyria." The warning tone low.

She slowly let her gaze roam up the kid and back down. "Perhaps a chance at a dream." She revved the engine again to drown out Eron.

The kid's eyebrows flew up. He jammed the helmet on his head, revved his bike, and flipped the face-shield down as the woman took off. The wind blew her hair back in a tangle.

* * *

Eron was in the middle of training practice when the memory surfaced, causing him to stumble enough that the woman opposite got several good hits in with her wooden sword before he could get his shield up. They finished the round, and he gave some pointers before letting them take a water break.

As the immortal turned around, a slave stood with his missing friend, who appeared exhausted. Eron walked over, "Yes, Rolf?"

The little boy was shiny-eyed with curiosity. "The man says he knows you, and since Her Grace is not to be disturbed, he asked to talk with you."

"All right, you can leave him here, I'll see he gets back out." Eron dismissed the kid, and swiftly said to his friend, "Wait a moment." He told the women to continue training, led Colin just far enough away he could keep an eye on the ladies but not be overheard.

"What the hell happened? I've been searching everywhere for you."

Colin just stared blankly for a moment at the women, before managing to lift his eyes to his friends, "Mica."

"Is missing. We can't find him either. What happened? The slaves at your dwelling came to us after the fire, let us know the two of you had gone out and never returned. I suspected Nicky, but..." He let his hands fall open.

"How long have I been gone?"

"Days, weeks."

Colin continued to stare blankly at everything and nothing. His friend sighed, "Come on. Let's get you some food and drink and a bath. I'll even find a bed for you."

* * *

Eron was exhausted from training the female recruits, barely staying awake for supper. He left word with the staff that he needed to talk with the duchess. His friend was still recovering, fast asleep. The immortal snuck into the room being used as an office and stumbled to the couch. No one would think to look for him in here. If he could just lie down for a bit...The next thing he knew, Eron was being kicked awake. He awoke to see Illyria with her brow cocked, staring down at him. She was in a scarlet dress which bared her shoulders and most of her arms.

He blurted out, "Miss Scarlet in the library with the candlestick."

She merely smiled. "The slaves will gossip if you are found napping in here, Inspector Clouseau."

He sat up and ran his hands through his hair and tried not to be angry but it came out anyway. "I pity poor Mica; he could be stark raving mad by now. Or being forced to make his captors into Immortals. Have you done anything to find him? Anything but continue to ruin the Earl's life? When the hell did you start messing with married men? Or have you always?"

She sighed and leaned back against the side of her work table, "Eron, let's leave my personal life out for once. I am trying to find Mica. I gave you the list of the boy's properties, did I not? You said you found nothing."

"He can't have just disappeared. If they notice he heals from any torture, it will be disastrous to us all."

"Is it possible he is not being tortured?"

"No, he is. It was something I learned from a former captive of Nicky's who managed to survive. The little boy loves to torment his enemies."

"Why would he want his secret revealed? If his minions inform him that Mica heals in a supernatural manner, they'll wonder why he ignores their tidbits of news."

"I'm only telling you we need to find Mica; without him, we cannot get rid of the little boy. He's the one who hid the soul gem. Non-negotiable, Illyria." His eyes bored into hers. "Speaking of which, how is it you can walk during the daytime?"

"Must we go into this now?"

"I need to know what you can do, just like you needed to know how my kind came about. I'm tired, Lira, I'm tired of all the games and all the lies. For just once, I would like someone to trust, whom I could count on to trust me in return, no matter what I have been or what I have done or what I will do."

"You are not the only one who wishes for such a person. It is very few who find a person. You, who have lived so much longer than I, should know that most of all. But I know how rare such a person can be, and when I find them, I treasure them"

"Quit resisting, quit concealing. I know you're busy trying to empire-build, but if we could put Civilization: Post-Cataclysm on hold for a night?" He could see she did not get the reference so he continued, "Give me the quick description? Quid Pro Quo."

"We do not need to sleep in coffins, but we do sleep during the day as mortals do the night. It is only with great effort, and only upon reaching a great age, that we can tolerate indirect exposure to the sun for short periods of time, and move during the daytime." She spoke in a tone meaning she would not discuss more.

"I can't believe your vaunted powers have not located the kid, much less Mica."

"To find the information in someone's mind, whoever has him has to be thinking of him as I mind-search. But there are so many people who hate, fear, even envy Nicky that it is he who consumes their thoughts, and not whomever he might have imprisoned."

"Why can't you just do your Jedi-mind trick on people?"

"I can't do an effective mass mind-wipe and still hide what I am. Even if the damn demon weren't messing with people's emotion. I'm Immortal, not Unstoppable; I need rest and sustenance as well."

Eron rubbed the back of his neck. "All right. What about the kid's slaves? Surely they of all people would know his secrets?"

"No; they're useless. Tongues ripped out, so I had to drink from each one only to find they have no useful information. Only one slave who could speak, and he was blind; what he heard was useless." She omitted to mention the gaping holes, as if their memories had been violently ripped from them.

"Shit snacks! This is a fucking disaster! He had to trust *someone* to carry out his orders!" Eron scrubbed furiously at his hair.

"I'm beginning to think his damn demon did everything for him."

"And you went and hacked apart the body which contained him, so now we've got an undetectable evil spirit in the vicinity."

"Oh yes, because I should have just let it kill me and Nicky would have captured you. Or perhaps you think I should have bargained with it? Call me what you like, even I am not arrogant enough to believe I could outwit a being of such magnitude."

She felt her blood pound, and fangs craved the plunge into a vein. She couldn't let her anger get the better of her or it would only confirm the worst legends of her kind.

"You know what I don't get? Why you didn't just rip the information about his identity from the kid's mind when you realized he wasn't like the other mortals."

"I already told you: his blood tastes foul and poisons me. Since you're so determined to cast me in the role of evil vampire overlord: if I could do that to him, then I could do it to you, or Colin, or Mica..."

He held a hand up to stop her. "Sorry I asked, ok? Thank you for deciding to trust us enough not to do that."

His apology seemed to mollify her; the angry glow faded from her eyes and she nodded curtly.

"What of the hunting lodge? Colin seemed to think it important from what Mica had said."

"No sign the boy had been there recently. There must be a better search technique." Eron paced the room, "Mica is running out of time..."

"You've already explained about the healing after torture. I am using my powers to help, but you must understand, they do not work as well in daylight."

"But there's something else: you know our souls are contained in gems, kept guarded, but there's a time limit once a ritual to Undo is put in motion with the removal of the gem from the cave. There's only three ways to stop the ritual: the person it's aimed at is Undone, the gem is replaced in the cave, or the caster exceeds the time limit, in which case their life is forfeit. The guardian takes the gem back, ending the life of the one who removed it. Mica is within days of that third option."

He watched dawning realization come over her face. "Mica was foolish enough to set it in motion before ascertaining where the kid was?"

"I wouldn't say foolish, more like overly enthusiastic. He didn't expect his quest to take so long. I never expected to discover Nicky knows the magicks he does." Eron snorted. "Or demons."

"I can't believe Colin has no idea where his brother hid the gem, or why Nicky hasn't commanded his pet to retrieve it. I would think a demon could find it, no matter what."

"Colin is so rattled over his brother's capture and his own, he's having trouble focusing. As for Nicky, I don't see him giving an order which would let his pet possess something dangerous to himself. Otherwise, he wouldn't need to kidnap Mica, unless it was in revenge for being hunted all these years. Are you sure it was a demon? And not something else?"

"I have met evil people, and those possessed by ill-intentioned ghosts, but never a real, honest-from-hell demon until that night. I...saw its true form for a brief moment...It made a point to brag of what it was and how we could do nothing to stop it."

He opened his mouth to reply, thought a moment, and snapped his mouth shut. Thinking back on what Cassiopeia had invoked in his tent centuries ago, he recalled that she'd called it a spirit, a guardian, but she could have been using a term with which he was familiar. The reality might be very different.

"I can't say I ever have met an honest-from-hell demon. Huh. If good exists, evil must as well. There used to be so much fiction about them, there has to be a grain of truth in there somewhere, kinda like the tales of our kinds. I'm also thinking, since true Nicky- and Cassiopeia-style magick is rare, so are demons. People mistook something else entirely for the demons. I remember well enough what havoc regular evil can wreak." *'Cause I was considered evil once.* Eron thought to himself and continued, "So Nicky found a real demon somehow, or stumbled upon how to call one up in his long, long life of practice." His tone a tad awed.

They both gave identical shudders and turned back to their

discussion.

"He must have found a way to trap it here, but how?" Illyria let the thought trail off.

Eron did some mental calculations. "OK, here's what I've come up with. We don't know what the little boy needs to keep that thing here and on a leash, if you will, but I know someone who is interested in debunking myths and legends."

"How terribly convenient," she replied drily.

He glared at her. "Colin. We need to bring him into this, let him know what we're up against besides a vengeful, demon-wielding, magic-using Immortal twelve-year-old wanting to bring the Final Death to his enemies."

"No! I will not have another person know what I am. I trust you because we have known each other in the past, shared adventures..." She trembled with rage, her eyes blazed bright.

The immortal held his hands up to placate her. "We need him, we need his knowledge. We need a plausible sounding reason, and Mica is most likely still cursed, one more problem to deal with. If you're so damn paranoid he'll go all Van Helsing on you because you're a vamp, I'll tell Colin you're an immortal witch."

Eron watched as Illyria tipped her head to the side, with a hip jutting out, but seated herself in the chair behind her work table as he took one of the chairs across from her. A few oil lamps had been lighted, and outside of their warm glow, the room lay in shadows.

"Did he explain where he has been the entire time?"

"We didn't get far in our conversation. I know you don't want him knowing what you are, but..."

* * *

Colin noted the chilly silence in the room, and wondered what his friend had been telling Her Grace, and why Eron wanted Colin's journal.

"Thank you for joining us, Colin." Her Grace smiled, but only with her lips and made a gesture to the small seating area where his friend already reposed. "Please. I'm sure you must have many questions." She looked past him, as a slave came in with food and drink, and indicated the small table as she turned back to him.

"I hope it is about my brother?" He seated himself and laid his journal beside him on the chair arm, accepting a cup of hot spiced wine from the slave.

"Yes. Eron told me the little boy could not be found at any of his properties. He also said you and your brother encountered an unexplained phenomena in a grove adjacent to Lord Nicky's hunting lodge?"

Colin frowned. *Why is he telling her these things? She has shown herself to be more open-minded than most, but that doesn't mean he should mention things unless he means to turn her.* He shot a questioning look to his friend before turning back to the woman. He took a sip of his beverage before speaking.

"I would not use quite the same terms, Your Grace. I have encountered such things before; if I may, what exactly do you know of them? I ask so I may fill in any gaps."

She inclined her head graciously. "I ask because I'm concerned about events for which there can be only mystical or supernatural explanations. I was told the guards were undead—altered to feel no pain, to attack mindlessly and brutally. I'm worried those things may find their way here or to a farm, causing a panic."

The chuckle could not hide the fact Colin was uneasy. "It is as good a name as any, I suppose, though I have also heard them called zombies. I suppose Eron has told you of my little hobby?"

"I would like to hear it from you."

"Yes, well. As you know, as merchants, my brother and I have traveled more than most people. In each place we traded, the locals had myths and legends, some pre-, some post-cataclysm. I started a collection of stories indigenous to each locale when I could get someone to speak with me."

He paused to sip again. "Most of them are just explanations of unknown past events or objects unearthed outside the current scope of understanding. Those creatures, zombies or undead, are one of them. Like the Haitian zombies, living men under the influence of powerful fish toxins. I have also seen plant matter used."

"Plant matter, fish toxins?" She furrowed her brow.

"I am not privy to the recipe, or what exactly goes into it, but the men were under the control of a man calling himself a life-stealer. He let me watch one of his rituals. It's fascinating and yet terrible. They are given many cups of this stuff to drink as the ritual unfolds. At the end, they feel no pain, have no idea of who they are, and are pretty much at an animalistic state. I asked him if he could bring the men back to their preceding state. He didn't know how...perhaps he never cared to find out." Colin trailed off in thought, shook his head.

"How...disturbing." She paused and continued, "The person you are searching for, Nicholas, he knows how to do what the life-stealer does?"

Eron pressed his folded hands against his mouth, elbows propped on his knees, in an effort not to give any emotion away. *Unfuckingbelievable! No wonder her kind can't be found if they all act as she does.*

"I would not care to speculate further without more information. It's possible he was apprenticed to such a person at one time, or has some arrangement with someone who does know the ritual to be provided with those poor creatures."

"The matter of the boy gets worse the more I hear."

Colin gave an apologetic shrug and smile and shot another glance at his strangely silent friend. "It's terrible to learn the kid has progressed to even worse crimes. I was hoping we could still have saved him. But, with the capture of my brother…" He spread his hands. "Have you any other idea of where he could be?"

Her Grace acted as if she hadn't heard his question. "I was given to understand the young man has been seen participating in religious rites in a grove? Unnatural rites, some would call them."

Colin glared at Eron; his friend merely tilted his head to Illyria.

"I would not worry overmuch; the religious rite is not real, in the sense nothing can come of it. No bogey men, or hexes, or strange and unexplained occurrences." He sat back with a smile, glad he could put her mind at ease.

"Odd, since a few nights ago I came across something I could not explain in other than supernatural terms."

The Immortal appeared flummoxed for a moment, eyebrows raised, as if finally understanding why he was told to bring his journal. "I will do my best to help make sense of what you saw. It is possible I have encountered something similar in my travels."

Eron's eyes ping-ponged back and forth, amazed his friend had no clue he sat across from a legend. Well, two, if he counted himself, being among the first Immortals to ever exist.

The Duchess paused as if deciding on what she would say. "The being with which I interacted called itself a demon, and even though it wore a cloak, there was the outline of horns about the head, hooved feet, red eyes."

Colin looked flabbergasted, and he sent the other man a small gesture meaning *what now?* Eron sent one back meaning *tell her the truth.*

"I'm sure there is a logical explanation," Colin began.

"I do hope so, as it killed a person by placing a hand on its victim's chest—a black circle grew over the heart. Now, for the sake of argument, if such a creature did exist, how could it be found, controlled and trapped?"

He took a gulp of drink, set the cup down and leaned forward, planting his forearms on his knees and decided to indulge her.

"Let's say Nicholas believes himself to be a practitioner of the black arts—magic, if you will—and has mystic powers. The grove about which we have been hearing rumors figures prominently in magic ritual. He would have to have a circle of men or women to help him. Now, they don't need to have mystical powers; it would be enough, I think, for them to believe they're being dangerous and different. Nicholas knows better: he uses their energy to ramp up his real black magick. He feeds off them."

"Uh, disturbing, on multiple levels. Especially if you don't know it's happening." Eron said, his first contribution to the conversation.

Colin flipped journal pages, speed reading. Finally he looked up. "Sacrifice is needed; the 'white goat', symbolizing a human, is preferred when calling demons. A circle of protection is needed to bind the demon from getting free and killing."

"Flaw in the argument: it seemed to be walking around pretty damn free to me. I was cautioned more than once Nicky's slave was just as bad as he is, and to be avoided at all costs. Is it possible people instinctively knew it was a demon without knowing that's what it was?" Eron asked.

Colin looked up, startled, mouth gaping. "W...w...what do you mean? How does his slave have anything to do with this?" He turned to Her Grace. "Is it he you saw doing the unexplainable? And not Nicky?"

"I can cause people to instinctively know they do not want to be around me, or to cross me, without realizing what I am. The hindbrain's response to predators," Lira stated matter-of-factly.

Eron made a voilà gesture while thinking, *Fuck, she's actually proud of the fact.* "Not making a convincing argument right there you're *not* an evil overlord in waiting, Queen of the Night."

His friend set his journal aside and held a hand up. "Whoa, whoa, whoa. What's going on here? Eron, you're acting like you've known her for a long time. Is she one of us or not?"

Eron watched as Lira's face smoothed out, the life leave her eyes, so she seemed a statue. He couldn't even see her breathe, and began to get creeped out. "Uh, you don't need to convince me of your superpowers there, X-man. Hello?"

He half-stood and waved a hand in front of her face, jumping when she came to life again. Both of them ignored the other Immortal in the room, who was looking suspiciously at them.

"I was thinking," she snapped as he hurriedly sat back down. "We don't know how powerful a magick user he is, as he is unique, so therefore anything is possible, even the impossible."

He thought he knew where she was going. "In other words, he could have personal protection from the demon on him at all times. I like it, a supernatural prophylactic." He thought he saw her lips twitch in amusement.

"Yes, but if it is the case, why is this entity not..." She made a waffling motion with her hand, "feeding off of those around him?"

Eron watched her face as she frowned, and wondered how he missed seeing it before. Her skin flowed like warm wax when she showed emotion. He felt a thrill go through him, exhilaration a powerful being trusted him. *I can use her, slowly seduce her into trusting me. Find out what all her secrets are.* In an even more hidden part of his mind, the part which once loved being feared as a despot, *I can try to gain her powers as my own.* He felt a warning tremble on the edges of his consciousness and kept a pleasant, inquiring expression as she re-engaged in their conversation.

"I have felt for some time now that things are not right with the town. The emotions, thoughts, and actions of the people are more extreme than they should be, as if they were under duress. I think it is because the evil of the demon is tainting the community. It is a natural part of its being, not something it can control."

Eron tried to think of a good analogy. "Like how uranium or plutonium is harmful to all living matter unless containment precautions are observed?"

He could see she was impressed. "That is precisely what I mean. Only in this case, instead of decaying and dissipating, it builds and gets stronger."

"That would mean we're all going to be fucked six ways to Sunday?" He was being facetious and got another eyebrow quirk.

He was beginning to get sick of that response and idly wondered what would happen if he tried to shave both of Illyria's eyebrows off with his dagger.

"Would one of you please answer me? What the fuck is going on?" Colin yelled. "You are acting as if our discussion is real, and not metaphysical."

They glanced at each other, and Eron began, "Sorry, Colin. Sit back down and I'll explain. Please?" He waited while his friend reluctantly sat, still fuming. "Her Grace has suspected ever since she met Nicky that something was wrong with him. When we showed up, asking questions, she figured it was a chance to find out the truth of the matter."

She continued, "I knew my suspicions were correct the night of the Harvest Ball, when Eron and I walked into an ambush. Nicky's slave and some other unknown person betrayed him, and used magic, however impossible. I was asked to meet with his slave a few nights ago."

Eron took over. "I was following her on the chance I could capture the kid and get him to tell me where he hid you and your brother. Instead, I saw some freaky-ass shit going on."

Colin tapped his fingers on his journal cover, evaluating her. "I do have one question, more important to me than our talk of magic users. Where is my brother?"

"He is still missing," Illyria said, "It would be helpful if you explained what happened to you and where you had been kept. It may give us another area to investigate."

He bowed his head a moment. "The ritual I told you about at the grove. We were ambushed. I was held for a time inside Nicky's lodge, but neither the boy nor my brother was there. Eventually I was moved. Unless you can track the remnants of an army, there would be no point. My time as a captive assured me of that."

Oh shit. Eron tried to keep the shock off his face.

"What army?" Lira's voice deadly soft.

"Why, the one you and Nicky visited and fought." Colin calmly returned her stare.

She was silent, gazing at him, as if thinking. Eron looked at her with narrowed eyes, hoping she would give him some clue as to what direction she would go. The silence lengthened and what had been warm flickers of lamp light and shadow became sinister.

"We didn't see you there," Eron felt compelled to say.

"No, you probably wouldn't have unless you inspected the camp. A man calling himself Nicky's slave, the one you two claim is a demon, made sure I was kept out of sight. I might never have escaped, except someone or something attacked. I woke to find my cage damaged enough I could escape. " He was still staring at Illyria, his tone challenging.

"Is that so?" she asked with a smooth calm which made warning prickles go up the spines of both men.

"I think it safe to say you are not human, not like those around us, nor are you wholly mortal. What are you?" Colin demanded, leaning forward.

Shit balls! Eron opened his mouth, closed it as the silence became strained, like a rubber band about to snap.

"Has it occurred to you that, by asking, you place your life in danger?"

Colin merely replied, "As opposed to Nicky and whatever he has enslaved?" He placed his palms flat on her worktable, "I won't betray you. I just want knowledge; that's all I've ever wanted, that's why I became what I am."

She remained silent, evaluating the man before her, "What if it is knowledge I choose not to share?"

"If I can prove my trustworthiness, will you reconsider?"

"Very well." She gestured to Eron. "Your friend holds some of the explanations you seek."

The sinister edge was gone from the room as Eron scrubbed his hands across his face a moment; how was he to tell his friend the impossible had happened without betraying Illyria's secret? Perhaps it was time to tell his friend a little more of his?

"This requires further suspension of belief." Eron paused, mentally editing. "Do you know an immortal named Cassiopeia?"

He could see confusion cloud his friend's eyes. "No. I feel I should; what has the name to do with today's events?"

"I'm going to tell a bit of a story. I want you to listen without interrupting. When I'm done, I'll try to answer your questions. Fair enough?" Eron asked.

Colin thought for a minute, nodded once sharply. Eron gave him a highly edited, extremely shortened version of the witch immortal he had known.

"For the longest time I thought magic was bullshit, until I was shown otherwise in ways that couldn't be explained by logic, by natural scientific laws. In all my years, I have never met another person like him and his daughter. I've never known the formula which we use to become Immortal could be changed without disastrous results. I trusted Cassiopeia enough that I never questioned her when she said she had tried. That's why this is just as big a shock to me as it is to you." When he was done, there was silence again. He could see his friend struggling to comprehend everything he had been told.

"Why didn't you tell us before? Hell, we could have looked for, what was her name? Cassiopeia, to help us with the little boy."

"To do what, Colin? I didn't even know there was another immortal like Cassiopeia, much less the little boy. I don't have what she does, did," he amended, "or like the boy does. I don't know if she's even alive; it's been centuries since I saw her, and after the second purge we had." He shook his head and fell silent.

"I always wondered why you kept insisting magic was real, even though you exposed every so-called magic user we ran across as a fake and a fraud. I thought the ritual was trappings, made to drive off all but the most sincere, that we accidentally discovered the potion. Thus the need for secrecy," Colin finally said.

Eron shook his head, trust his friend to think of the most logical explanation possible! "I've known real magic. I know how rare a user is, so in memory of her I expose them. And you are right, the trappings are to discourage those who would use it as an easy means to end their problems."

Colin mused, "I always wondered how Nicky outsmarts us all. How he's managed to remain hidden and alive all these centuries. Of course," here his tone turned distraught, "that makes it harder for us to rid ourselves of him. No wonder no one can find my brother; he could be right before us but the kid's using his powers to disguise the man."

"We have a whole new set of problems. What if he uses his magic to retrieve Mica's soul gem and kill him? What of his slave's deeds? I must consider all the implications. Clearly we no longer can ask for him openly; we must work with caution and finesse."

Eron could see the despair lurking behind the concerned face his friend wore. "If it's any consolation, Nicky can't use his magic near or inside The Cave of Soul Gems. I asked Cassiopeia before why she didn't just use what she had to retrieve and bring an enemy's gem to her magically. She told me the cave is a dead spot; the guardians somehow prevent such things from working. He can't bring the Final Death to your brother unless he goes and retrieves the gem himself."

"But he can still bring him harm, torture him, try and drive him mad. What if he has mortals guarding my brother? What do we do when they discover what Mica is? How do we know the kid hasn't made any immortals himself?"

"I don't know, Colin, but if we could find where your brother hid the kid's gem..."

"Truth to tell, I had forgotten that Mica's time is running out. I don't want him to die a prisoner, knowing everything he's done was useless." Colin slumped in the chair, as if every one of his long years of life was weighing him down.

The men jumped when Illyria spoke; she had been so silent they had forgotten she was there. "How long does your brother have, and can you find the gem if we concentrate on the boy?"

"Not long," Colin hesitated and continued, "Once a ritual to

Undo is put in motion, there's only a few ways to stop it."

Eron snorted. "I think we should just capture the punk. You can lure him away from his slave-demon thingy."

"Wait, what? Surely you're not serious?" Colin protested, "We don't even know where my brother is."

"You want to kill him and set a demon loose on us all?" Her eyebrow did the quirking thing again. It made him feel like he was being an idiot as they ignored the other man.

"I do not remember much of demons from pre-Great Cataclysm times, but what little I do recall makes them seem like a being you would not want to bargain with, or cross," Illyria added.

"Now do you understand why I do not wish to kill the little boy right away? If we knew for certain it would go back to where demons live and remain there, I would say let's capture the bastard now. But if he found a way to trap it here?"

I had the nagging feeling we were missing something still. I forced myself to ignore all the other plans I was juggling and just go over what I had been told about the kid and what I had observed. Even in his new form, he used people as he always had. We had dispersed several of his sources of information, namely the sheriff's group and the hidden army, but what if he had a few smaller ones?

"We need to discover who the second man in the hallway was, the one who set off the strange device," I spoke. "He was with Nicky's slave, so he must be part of the boy's inner circle."

"It would stand to reason the mystery person who betrayed him has to have some influence or power in the kingdom. He is in a position to be beneficial to the boy. Who do you know of, Your Grace, who fits?"

"Lord Jenabram, but my spies have found nothing indicating he is trusted by the boy."

"He passed out from drink the night of the ball; Saizar had to load him in his carriage." Eron shot my idea down. "But the priest Colin mentioned. Didn't he take care of Nicky at one point?"

"He has been known to bring harm to others in the guise of religion, and he has a cottage. I told Brother John to come to me if the priest was harming another person, and my slaves have brought me no word he has ever come back." Lira's tone grim.

"Maybe he's not harming him, just holding him prisoner for the kid. We never thought to look there," Eron pointed out. "Do you think he will let Colin in, much less tell the truth?"

"The priest? Are you daft? More like he would go running to Nicky with the tale; now, Brother John might tell me if I invite him here to see how Mary Elana is doing."

"What about the dungeon?" Colin interrupted. "I find it hard to believe the kid wouldn't have a dungeon man as part of his inner circle, especially if the sheriff was arresting and detaining people on Nicky's orders."

"I had a slave make inquiries, and he was told no prisoners of the merchant class had been brought in recently," Lira replied.

Eron hummed a bit. "Unless he was smuggled in, and only the head questioner allowed to care for him."

"He would fit the profile of at least being desirable for the inner circle," Colin interjected, "and it would explain why no one would admit to seeing Mica inside."

Eron bowed his head in acknowledgment. "Would he leave a prisoner like Mica, or any important enemy for that matter, in a place where he couldn't get to them immediately? Even if he had to use the inner sanctum sanctorum? I think the little bastard would have a hidden cell or two only he and one, possibly two, henchmen would know about."

"I take this to mean you wish me to get you inside so you may check?" Illyria asked

''It might help if you Ninja us in there and do your Jedi mind trick to the guards so the kid doesn't know we're there." Again with the blank look; he was ready to give up.

"Or bribe them," Colin suggested.

At their nods, she said, "Tomorrow night, at dusk. I will need time to gather sufficient coins."

Chapter Fourteen

"I must say, this is quite the disappointment," Eron grumbled to his companion in an undertone as they alighted from the plain carriage. "I was hoping for more Ninja, less day-in-the-park."

"He has to know we are looking for your friend, no matter what we do."

She turned as one of the guards confronted them.

"The dungeon is closed to visitors."

Her Grace brought out a small square of parchment with a wax seal at the bottom and held it out. The man took it as she spoke, "The Head Questioner himself asked me to come; said it was of some importance about a prisoner who named me during questioning." *It is his writing, and he will be angry to be denied the chance to question the woman so close to the king. She may be a traitor. You will let her and her party proceed inside.* The suggestion wormed its way into the men's minds.

One guard hawked and spat. "Best let the head jailor deal with it." He gave her a look of pity and mingled regret. "We've got to search you and your slaves first for weapons."

"Of course," she replied. *They have no weapons. They are free to pass into the dungeon.*

The second man opened the door and escorted them inside after the first nodded. It was an age-darkened door, nearly hidden in the shadows cast by the walls of the palace looming to either side of them. Colin had a puzzled look on his face, and had opened his mouth to comment before an elbow to the ribs made him shut it again as they were being admitted to an anteroom. It was lit sparsely by a few oil lamps, and benches lined two of the walls; another door stood at right angles to the entrance they had used.

Next to it sat a small desk and chair, currently empty.

The clerk fetched by the guard was very fat, and had a cloth tucked underneath his greasy chins. His eyes, almost buried in the folds of his cheeks, glittered in annoyance at being interrupted.

"Lemme see the note. Rablias made no mention of such a thing to me." He held out a fat hand with sausage fingers.

The duchess gave him the parchment, which was immediately spotted with grease. *It is the Head Questioner's writing, he suspects her of being a traitor. He will be generous to the one who brings her to him. A woman close to the king revealed to be false. You will have the guards show them the cells, then lead them to the torture chambers. They will think they are being led on a tour at invitation of Rablias, and not to their doom.*

The man let out a nasty chuckle and his piggy eyes ran over the little group. He crumpled the parchment and dismissed the guard. "I'll take it from here. Your Grace, please follow me."

The man led them in a waddle down a flight of stone stairs worn in the middle from the passage of many feet. They ended in a decent-sized room, which held more guards, who stopped their gaming to gape at the visitors.

The men called out some questions, and were told to mind their own business as the clerk called two named Dag and Jimbo.

"These three are here at the request of the Head Questioner," the clerk whispered after leading them a few paces off. "He doesn't want 'em to suspect he plans to question them. He wants you to show 'em all the cells, then take them to the torture chamber and help subdue 'em."

"Sure," the other man shrugged. "Pity though. She's the finest woman we've had in here yet."

The clerk merely grunted and walked back over to the small group. "Your Grace, I will leave you in Dag and Jimbo's hands."

"Thank you." She had a smile which would have given him pause if he had noticed the amusement lurking in her eyes.

Dag was taking several key rings from their pegs and speaking low-voiced to his fellow worker. He called out louder, "Hey, Jimbo, grab yer club." He had a short sword strapped to his waist.

Jimbo looked to be six foot and three hundred pounds of muscle. He casually laid a thick, knotted club over a shoulder.

“Ain’t we gonna search em first, Dag?”

“Guards already did,” Dag replied as he unlocked the door to the first level. The three hooded cloaked people with him followed after as the man behind them re-locked the door.

Colin misliked the whispering and the strange glances. Eron just hoped she knew what she was doing.

The air became colder, iron-banded wood doors lined the hall. “Now who did this person say yer was looking for?”

“A merchant the old sheriff falsely accused of stealing. I’m not sure how long he may have been in here, or if any one paid for his upkeep.” the Duchess answered.

“Ain’t gonna be up here, ifin no one paying fer him,” Jimbo replied.

“I prefer to be thorough, gentlemen. If there is a way I can see each prisoner just long enough to rule them out?”

“Well, now, that’s against all the rules. We got quite a bit of people in here.”

“I wouldn’t want to get you gentlemen in trouble, but I would be ever so grateful if you could find a way to make it happen,” Her Grace held out a hand, and Dag automatically took what she offered. She repeated the gesture with Jimbo.

“Aw, I don’t see no harm in it.” Jimbo replied, impressed with the gold coin worth a year’s pay.

Dag still wasn’t convinced. “Yeah, buts there’s more than one level here and that’s a lotta looking.”

“I would be quite grateful for the privilege,” Lira looked into his eyes and after a moment he nodded assent.

Each door had a grate, so she merely had to peek inside. They cleared the first level and moved down, the guard explaining, “Now, these here levels hold the less prosperous, but still generally respected prisoners.”

When the door to the next level opened, both Eron and Colin got a nose full of the stench and tried to hold back their coughs.

“Sorry sirs, My Lady, it’s pretty bad down here. Are you sure you want to do this? I wouldn’t want such an important guest as yourself to be subjected to the nasties below. And it will be nasty, lots o’ these folks have already been put to the questioner; some of ‘em more than once.”

"I thank you for your concern, Sir Guard, but we shall continue." Lira replied. "I am not sure if he has been questioned yet or not, thus I must inspect them all." She caught his eyes again.

Eron watched the man's eyes glaze over before shrugging at the whims of his betters and led them down to the next level. The process of looking in each cell was repeated for two more floors, until they came at last to a door covered in mold.

"Well, that's all there is, My Lady. I'm sorry the person you were looking for wasn't here."

"There is another door, Sir Guard."

"Well, uh, uh, um," the guard stammered. "It...It's just the, the sub-cellar. Ain't nothing down there fit for a lady's eyes. Truly, My Lady, and the smell, it's well-nigh unbearable, even for the likes of usn."

"I wouldn't have thought *that* possible," Eron drily replied and earned a glare from the guard.

"'Sides, if who yer looking fer wasn't above, ain't no chance he'll be down there."

"And why is that?" she asked.

Dag and Jimbo exchanged glances and it was Jimbo who replied, "Mainly 'cause they've gone through the worst questioning—I doubt even their own mothers would recognize them. Down there, is what we calls the disposal area. 'Sides, it's pretty wet."

"It is flooded?"

"Well, not exactly, but the water's deep enough to come over a person's shoes,"

"And there are no cells down there? No place where prisoners are kept?"

Again he hesitated but answered, "Jus'...just holes in the floor. They puts the more, uh, stubborn ones down there. But truly, My Lady, it is no place for one as delicate as you."

Eron couldn't help the snort of laughter which escaped at those words and he had to stare studiously at the floor and turn it into a coughing fit as he got himself under control.

"Nevertheless, Sir Guard, I intend to check it out."

Eron raised his head in alarm, just in time to see the guard's eyes go fuzzy. The wave of foul air that rushed out when he opened the door made everyone back up a step.

"By all that's holy!" Colin muttered in pity.

She ignored him and proceeded down the stairs after Dag. True to the guard's word, several inches of water lapped at the bottom step, releasing such an odor of decay, the men could not control their gag reflexes. Vomit splashed, adding to the flotsam and jetsam in the morass below.

Eron remarked, "I can't get past you unless you step down, or move closer to the wall." He wished he could see the look on her face.

Illyria turned half-way on the stair and said to him, "It is clear on the left side. Only stones underneath the water, but don't splash when you jump."

He stared at her a moment.

"You," he started to say, but remembered he was supposed to be an underling, and jumped. Slipped and almost went down but caught himself by the slimy stair edge and righted. Eron felt freezing droplets land on his pants and hoped he'd splashed her boots. He wiped his hands on his cloak, the hem of which he knew was soaking up the filthy water.

"Shall I stay here with the torch for you, My Lady?" the guard began.

"No, show my slave what is in each."

"I, um, uh, there's rats down here. They may come out if I leave you without a light," he apologized.

"I understand, Sir Guard. I am not afraid of vermin, animal or human. I am sure Jimbo and this other man shall keep me safe."

Eron smirked and dearly wanted to ask if she planned on having a rat snack but dissembled to look grave and put-upon as the man half-turned back toward him. The guard gave her another uncertain look but led Eron over to the first of the pits.

The man held the light close to the grill, and Eron repressed the rage which flashed through him as he looked down a deep hole in the ground. Most of them were empty, a few held rotting corpses, and two held filthy beings so nigh unto death that he hoped their suffering would be over soon. Eron and the guard kept their sleeves over their mouths and as he straightened, he saw the broad step and the door. He walked up, glad to be out of the freezing water if only for a moment. The guard joined him.

Eron jerked a thumb to the door and asked through his sleeve, "What's behind there?"

"Torture chamber, and I'm not taking Her Ladyship in there," the guard replied firmly.

"Good idea," Eron replied, "but I have to ask, any other cells in there used to hold prisoners?"

A scowl flickered over the guard's face, but he forced his face to smooth out. "No," he replied in sullen tones with only the slightest of hesitations.

The immortal sighed. "Very well, let's go back."

The guard unhesitatingly stepped off into the slime, and Eron hastened after him. Small, winking lights in the dark, and chittering, greeted their return.

"Damn it! Rats! I'm coming, Your Ladyship!" the guard called worriedly and slogged faster to the steps.

The men saw the Duchess standing exactly where they had left her, her eyes gleaming like a night animal's in the gloom. The guard made a frightened noise and Eron saw her lean slightly forward, speak softly. The man became quiet and his eyes glazed.

He woke a moment later. "My Lady, We've checked 'em all."

"We can go now, Madam, he's not in them." Eron said.

"Really?" she asked, and Eron knew there was more to come.

"I'm cold and I think my boots are leaking water."

"Very well, steward," she said and, ignoring the other immortal who had opened his mouth to protest, climbed the stairs behind Colin, Eron following sullenly.

Jimbo was locking the door behind them as Lira spoke to Dag, "How many cells are in the torture rooms, Sir Guard?"

"Huh? What? Oh, none, none at all," he said hastily; the other guard lifted his hands in a not-my-fault gesture.

"I know there must be a few." Her voice was reasonable.

The immortal merely shrugged and said, "She is persistent, and knows people who have the king's ear."

At those words both guards looked pained.

"Please, My Lady, I don't know. None of us know, only the, uh, um, Head Questioner does and, well, see, none of us question his word. Ain't too healthy if you know what I mean."

She remained silent until Jimbo was forced to say, "There are some questions you just don't ask around here." He folded his beefy arms across his chest, as if expecting a problem.

"Then fetch him to me, I shall ask them of him myself," the tone firm.

The guards looked shocked and glanced at each other. Eron rolled his eyes and murmured, "Not discreet at all."

The guard with the crossed arms narrowed his eyes. "He don't come to no one, they go to him." He shifted his weight and placed his hands on his hips.

She seemed irritated he would deny a member of the nobility. "Very well, show us to the man."

The party crossed the guard room and started back up the steps to the outside; halfway up a short hallway branched off a landing. The two men guided their guests down it. Stale, icy air washed over them as the door at the end was unlocked.

"Have you been this way before, Your Grace? There are rooms for the witnesses and other officials down here in the rare instances a trial is held. I will place you in one of the waiting rooms while I fetch Rablias."

"And there should be another entrance to the torture chamber? It seems a bit sloppy," Colin whispered skeptically to his friend as they continued cautiously down the hall.

"Who in their right mind would want to break into the place?" Eron replied. At the end of the hall, they came across another set of stairs leading down. "Wait."

"What?" Dag looked aggravated.

"I am told the torturer's live down here. I don't want them to bother Her Grace."

"They attack first, question later?" Colin asked worriedly.

Dag hurried to reassure them. "The head clerk sent word you was coming and they will be kept away from the lady."

They nodded and started down the stone stairs. Eron and Colin wondered how it was they didn't stumble upon remains from earlier times. Doors opened to small sleeping cells off each of the landings. The rooms were currently empty, but showed use. They paused outside the door at the bottom as Dag manipulated the keys to get the lock open. The tumblers groaned in protest, but finally yielded. Another massive iron-bound wooden door blocked the end of another hallway of cold, dark rooms. The guard pounded on it, tossing an oily smile back over his shoulder.

"It may take a moment for them to unlock the sitting room door, Your Grace." She inclined her head and lowered the hood of her cloak.

The man pounded once more. The door slowly swung open and Dag stepped back and gestured for her and her slaves to enter the ill-lit room. But the two immortal men yelled in alarm as they were rudely shoved inside by Dag and Jimbo, and the door was crashed shut by a hulking brute. The guards and her friends tussled as a second man joined the fight.

The second hulking brute got a lucky shot off and managed to knock Colin unconscious. The first man grinned nastily at sight of the woman.

* * *

"I need one of them alive!" I shouted to the Immortal as I met my foe's attack.

I leapt out of the way of his cudgel swing, as if I was scared of him. He fell for it; he made a noise of delight halfway between a grunt and a squeal, and launched a series of attacks. I could see at once he had only rudimentary skills, relying on brute strength and size. I let him get a few more swings in, forcing me further into the darkness of the room. I could tell from the way the brute before me held himself he was preparing to rush me. I let him, and kicked out and sideways as he went past. He howled as his knee gave way; as he collapsed with a crash, I manipulated his arm so the cudgel was pointed down and his elbow up. I brought my own elbow to bear on the joint, popping it out of place. He roared in pain and dropped his weapon.

"Duch..." the cry was cut off.

I turned to see Eron go flying backwards into a stone wall, knocked out. I was left with three opponents.

"Give up now and it'll go easier!" Dag called to me as Eron's opponent charged me.

He was a big man, like the one at my feet, but nimbler. I

moved forward as he landed, poker upraised to come down on my head. My right arm blocked his momentum. My left hand delivered an upthrust blow to his jaw. I was not husbanding my strength and the power of the blow snapped his head back so sharply I heard the crack of neck bones breaking an instant behind the sound of his jaw shattering into fragments.

Blood, bone, and teeth arced to splatter around us. He dropped as the two guards yelled in outrage, moving to surround me. I stepped into Jimbo's reach and turned sideways, reaching up to pull his arms down in front of my body. The sword deflected off the club as I kicked out and up, connecting with Dag's head. I smelled the blood as it burst from his exploding skull.

I used Jimbo's arms as a fulcrum; as my leg came down, his arms raised as he tried to shake me off. I let go and backed up as he went to swing at me. I melted into the darkness, moving to come up behind him. He was my height, but I wanted him lower, so I dropped him to his knees before snapping his neck. He fell, head twisted at an unnatural angle as the other man, despite the dislocated knee and elbow, tried to stand. No need to worry about Dag; I'd caved in one side of his head.

"How sad; good help is hard to find these days," I commented out loud and stalked over to the first brute.

I hauled him up by his hair and wrapped my arms around him to still him. No point in letting a perfectly good meal go to waste.

* * *

The man before me stood in chains as the Head Questioner sat scribbling at a table. "It says here you were caught harming your master's slaves." The voice was silky smooth.

"He lies. I was only doing my Master's bidding." He was defiant.

"Were you now? Your Master states you are...zealous. You often go above and beyond what is required of you."

"He dare complain how I get him what he wishes to know? I will crush him with my bare hands!"

"A dangerous sentiment to voice, seeing where you are. Tell me, slave, what would you do to ensure you are not sold as a rower aboard His Majesty's ships?"

"I have only one skill, but one I can do better than the mewling men you employ here."

"Indeed? You do not follow orders well, if this complaint has any truth behind it. I require complete obedience. You must not deviate from my orders. Do you suppose you can do that?"

"If you be a master what knows what he's doing."

The pale blue eyes narrowed in amusement. "If not, you will learn what a mistake it is to displease me."

The man was led away. His thoughts whirled to the first person he tortured under the Head Questioner's guidance, and further forward. Now he had been joined by his brother; under the man's tutelage, they honed and perfected their craft. Forward again. Time had no real meaning to him. He was bound on his own torture table, screaming.

"I've served you well! You'll regret it!" The man howled as his brother fought the chains holding him to the wall.

"Is this necessary? They are loyal, they will not speak of what we do here." The questioner plead with someone in the shadows.

"You dare to question me?" The voice low with menace. "You came to me asking for guidance. If you wish to be more than a two-bit conjurer, you will do as I say!"

The man on the table saw a bright white light flash about the chamber, searing his eyes so he howled in pain and shut them. His screams joined those of the Head Questioner. After a bit, he heard the man pant out in pain.

"Yes master, forgive me. Your will shall be done."

The brute saw his employer approach the table with tongs. His jaw was forcibly held open. His tongue pulled out far enough he gagged. Still the man struggled fruitlessly against his bonds.

"Forgive me, but your sacrifice serves a higher purpose." Rablias murmured.

The man felt a searing pain as his tongue was ripped out. He'd sworn he wouldn't give them the satisfaction, but scream he did with what was left of his ruined mouth, unaware of the tears of pain and rage streaming down his face. A funnel was shoved into the raw wound of his mouth, renewing the agony as he slipped into unconsciousness. His brief respite from pain did not last long. A foul brew poured down his throat. He gagged and heaved against his bonds to no use. His brother's furious threats of vengeance rang in his ears.

* * *

I let the man slip to the floor, drained dry. His thoughts at the end dwelt on his own misfortunes, only broken by the joy he felt when he was able to bring pain and suffering to another fellow human being. I saw nothing in his mind of Mica. He did harbor a grudge against the little boy for ordering his mutilation, and against Rablias for carrying it out. Colin was starting to come around. Eron was already on hands and knees.

"Holy fuck! Do you know how long it's been since someone knocked me out?" he complained.

"A week?"

"I was trampled! There's a difference."

I prowled the room and spotted a door hidden in deep darkness. It swung inward to show a darker room beyond which even my eyes had trouble seeing, but my other senses telling me the room was empty. I spotted candles, flint and steel. I got the stumps lit and inspected the office. Tablets and parchment lay scattered about. As I poked among them, I saw notes on people who had been tortured and their 'confessions'.

"What should we do with the bodies?" I heard Colin ask.

"I say we dump them in an oubliette and be done with it. It's more than they deserve," his friend replied, "Cowardly, ambushing swine."

I continued my inspection, passing into a small sitting chamber, then a sleeping cell grandly outfitted. It stank of smoke and burned flesh. I knew we had found the second man who played wizard. The question was: where was he, and where did he have Mica, if he had him at all? I could find no clue, so I started back out toward the office and realized I felt a slight breeze. By the time I found a thin crack in the wall, both immortals had joined me and with a bit of pushing and tugging we discovered a hidden door and managed to get it open.

Once more Eron took point as we followed the dark, damp,

cold hallway revealed. It seemed to go on forever, twisting and turning. I had a feeling we were headed back toward one of the wings of the palace. Eventually we came to another locked door. None of the keys on the guard's ring worked.

"The end of our journey," Eron whispered after I'd tried all the keys.

"Let me look," Colin said and knelt down to inspect the mechanism.

His friend held his torch to give him light, and turned his head to look at me over his shoulder, murmuring to me, "Can't you hulk out and bust it or something?"

I breathed in his ear, "Yes, but it would confirm for your friend I am not mortal nor natural and I don't wish to expose myself."

Colin muttered to us, "This is a basic lock. I think I can get it open." He rummaged among the pouches tied to his belt and came out with some tools. He set to work.

I was about to halt him, as my senses let me know another mortal was approaching but Colin had already swung the door open and stepped through. We came face-to-face with the head questioner for half-a-heartbeat before I sent the oil lamp in his hand tumbling into the wall. Shattering, it sprayed flaming oil across the floor, but the flickering light afforded me many shadows.

He in turn was rasping out gibberish which raised the hair on the back of my neck and caused my mark to itch through the leather sleeve and arm guard. I couldn't pass up the opportunity to battle a self-professed mage, but Eron stepped out of the shadows behind him and slammed the pommel of his sword into the back of the man's head. He dropped like a stone, whatever he had been casting cut off.

Colin joined us. "I think we know who's trying to trap us and who may know exactly where Mica is."

Eron glanced around the room revealed in the burning lamp oil, tilted his head at Colin, then to the passageway. I picked up on the clue easily enough.

"Colin, would you do us the favor of inspecting the hallway? I would ask Eron, but you have more experience with Nicky and traps he may use."

"Of course." He cautiously started off.

Eron and I knelt beside the unconscious man and turned him onto his back. One eye was milky white, in the ruined half of a face; the flesh was red and raw and seemed to have melted in rivulets. The man cradled one red-and-black arm, and a hand wrapped many times in cloth. His robe puddled around a body far too thin beneath, and the ruined flesh of his face continued down his neck to disappear inside the enveloping material.

"Is it just me, or does he look more healed than he should for an event which took place mere weeks ago?" the immortal asked.

"What are the odds of there being more people like your Cassiopeia, and the little boy trusting one enough to work with him?" I countered.

"I think you should do your vamp thing and find out what is going on before Colin returns."

"He is weak; to drink from him would be risking his life," I pointed out.

"Then let's hope your Jedi Mind Tricks work on him," Eron replied and brought out the length of rope he had attached to the back of his belt hidden under his cloak.

We waited for the Head Questioner to wake up. "What shall I do with you, Rablias?" I purred from the edge of the darkness as he woke with a start, looking about frantically with his remaining eye as he realized he was bound.

He snarled but subsided into an angry silence as I stepped into the wavering oil light. Eron and I had already agreed he would have to be killed.

"It was a mistake to align yourself with Lord Nicky, though I imagine you had your reasons at the time, didn't you? I'm sure His Majesty would love to hear them. Perhaps he will decide to use your own men to garner the truth from you?"

I paused and watched as he squinted his eyes in anger, though he still tried to peer into the darkness. I had felt the momentary flash of fear at the mention of the brothers. Why would he fear them, when he had powers they did not? Was it because of his eye? Or the stench of his burnt flesh I could smell under his clothes even though he had tried to heal himself? To show weakness before those two was to invite trouble. As long as I could keep him believing they still lived, I might get some answers.

"I intend to ask you some questions, and I need your assurances you will not do anything stupid when I remove the gag."

He gave a brief, sharp nod of assent.

"Should your answers please me and be useful, I will of course mention nothing of your perfidy to the king. You will be free to remain Head Questioner, and continue your pursuits. It should go without saying any attempts to contact Lord Nicky will bring about your demise; whether that demise is swift and painless shall be left for debate." I paused once more and he nodded understanding.

"Where is the merchant man Lord Nicholas captured?" I took out the gag, waiting.

He hacked to clear his throat and in a strained, whispery voice replied, "In the dungeon, where else would he place law-breakers?" His tone contemptuous. *Why would you want to know? Is it possible more than one person knows he is not normal? I can't let him be found until I learn how he does it.*

"Rablias, Rablias," I shook my head sadly, "it is not good we are starting out with lies."

"You should be dead, you and the damn advisor."

"Your little device was not as powerful as you had been led to believe. Now, we both know Lord Nicholas would be only too happy to see *us* both dead. What if I told you there is a way to bring about *his* end instead?"

He wheezed, and it took me a moment to realize he was trying to laugh. "You are as stupid as he thinks you are. He has unimaginable power, and you would do well to fear him."

"As you do?" I asked.

He laid his head back against the wall and his good eye blazed. I heard Eron shift impatiently in the darkness, and the head questioner glanced behind me. He thought it was Colin, never realizing there was a third person with us he had not seen. I stuffed the gag back into his mouth and glanced at the immortal.

Eron placed his lips against my ear so he would not be overheard by our prisoner. "If Mica was down here, you think this jerk'd be worried we could find him. He doesn't act it at all. That concerns me."

We felt a faint tremor in the ground, and I heard the sound of approaching footsteps. Colin came into view. From the corner of my eye, I saw how Rablias fought to keep the shock off the undamaged side of his face.

"You should come see this," he glanced briefly at the man, "and bring him with us; since he came from one of the rooms, he already knows what they contain."

Rablias groaned around the gag at the pain of movement as we walked off through one of the doorways into a short, innocuous hallway. We came out to another antechamber. Just how many concealed rooms did the little boy need? The floor, while stone, was deeply carved with designs, forming a pattern.

Colin murmured softly, "It's the same circle he's used when he pretends to be a demon-worshipping cult leader. Whenever Mica and I came across this, it meant we were close to a spot he considered important." He added, just before Eron moved, "Stay outside the circle; he always reserved the deadliest of his booby-traps for within."

We circumnavigated the etching in the floor; there was an altar within it and another door across from where we'd entered. Once more we slowly eased through and found ourselves in a private workroom. An open grimoire lay upon a table in the middle of the room. Unfortunately, the whole shebang was itself surrounded by more carvings. It was a tempting setup, but we stuck to the periphery of the room. Bookcases lined two of the walls, filled with scrolls of parchment and clay jars of all sizes To one side, an inglenook bracketed a fireplace filled with cold ashes. Eron shoved Rablias into one of the chairs; beads of sweat popped out on the Head Questioner's forehead from extreme pain.

Colin was scanning the shelves and he absently said, "Don't touch anything; it's likely to be booby-trapped as well. I never did figure out what he used, or how to undo them. There was never enough time."

Eron smirked at me as I hesitated by another door and nudged it open to see a storage area holding plant matter and non-vegetable magic supplies, none of which bore thinking about or too close an inspection.

Colin muttered, “The brat has to keep a record of all those he’s brought down here and tortured.”

I could feel Eron against my back as he looked over my shoulder into the room, “Please tell me the kid doesn’t actually use all this stuff.”

“If it’s down here, I would think so.” I was looking under the shelves, at the few chests the kid stored there. I saw one was a charred mess. The others had been moved, to judge by the marks in the dust upon the floor. The Head Questioner had already tried to loot the little boy’s stash. Interesting.

“Exactly what are we looking for in all this mess?” Eron asked.

“I thought there would be something here we could use, or would give us a clue as to what he had done with Mica. It seems I was wrong.”

The immortal poked at the two remaining chests “Should I assume since one chest is burned, that means they’re all set to burn when opened, and that therefore they must contain objects of value.” He picked one up before I could stop him. Luckily nothing happened. “It’s not too heavy. We could take them and figure out how to open them later. Of course, it’s possible that the brat’s ensorcelled them to disintegrate or some such when he dies.”

“If you will keep an eye on our prisoner, I will go back to the antechamber and see where the other doorways lead too,” I murmured to the immortal.

Eron nodded, knowing that, if alone, I would be free to use my powers if I needed. I eased out of the room under the watchful glare of Rablias and made my way back to the antechamber. There was only two doors which we had not gone through. I tested the one on the south wall. It opened easily and now I could freely smell what had only been hinted before; death wafted down the hall, but not recent.

I debated for a moment before starting down the hallway revealed within, making no footfalls to give myself away. The walls were lined with strange twisted shapes, and globes flared with a soft light. I came upon the body after only a few feet.

The corpse lay in three pieces, dried blood a wide pool around him. The edges where he'd been separated appeared clean, so something sharp. Why would the kid place deadly traps on this part, and not on the other entrance? I wasn't sure if the man preceding me, who now lay inert upon the floor, had sprung them all, so I would have to be careful. I stepped lightly down the hall, scanning for any tell-tale sign that overlooked concealed traps would spring to life.

As I came upon the next body, I felt a flagstone underneath my feet give way. I used my powers to evade the arrows and bolts, but only just. My cloak deflected some of the missiles, but others tore gaping rents in it. I undid the plain clasp and let it fall to the ground. It would only be more trouble. I continued along, until I came to a third body, I paused and tried to figure out from what I hoped was a safe distance away what the trap contained. I saw another dozen feet of tunnel before it curved out of sight.

All three bodies wore the clothes and collars of slaves I had seen before; Nicky's property.

Why would he sacrifice his slaves on traps he had designed? Perhaps someone else had, some mystery person who knew of the kid's hidden secrets. Who could the person or persons be? It wasn't the Head Questioner: he had his own access to the hidden rooms. Perhaps the traps were meant to discourage him from coming this way instead?

I eased around the turn, and saw a body-free stretch of hallway and the start of stairs. That couldn't be right; why leave a part un-trapped, unless it was to allay the fears of the unwary into thinking they wouldn't encounter any further problems? I didn't trust what I saw. I took a step forward and paused but nothing happened. Another, still nothing. I moved forward in starts and stops until I had come to the bottom of the stairs, twisting up out of sight.

It would be prudent to continue being cautious, so I slowly and carefully mounted the stairs…the trap sprung when I rounded the turn. The stairs tilted to form a slide, and only my ability to fly kept me from taking a quick trip back to the bottom. I wondered if there would be an open pit to catch the unlucky, but didn't feel like looking. I decided to fly the rest of the way up the stairs and as soon as I alighted on the landing, I heard a click. I leaped forward. Sharp points raked my back as six lances skimmed past.

Three on each side of the hall, which withdrew back into their housing. I scowled as the blood trickled down my back from my ruined corset. The last flight of stairs ended at a stone ceiling, though I could see a faint crack, which indicated a trapdoor to what lay above. The block or slab wouldn't lift, and I could see no way of making it slide.

I walked back to the spear-trapped landing, staying on the step just before the trigger, and inspected the walls. I had noticed strangely-shaped stone knobs protruding around the spear channels. They must be a way of working the mechanism to open the entrance, but I didn't have the time to work out which configuration to use, or Eron and Colin would start to wonder. I'd best leave the mystery for another day, and head back the way I came. Avoiding the traps and triggers was easy, as I knew now where they lay. A whistle came to my hearing: Eron letting me know they were coming. I didn't want them to start down the hall and made it to the ante-chamber just as they stepped through the doorway with Rablias between them.

"It leads to a locked and booby-trapped entrance which can only be opened by knowing the combination to the puzzle lock. I do not recommend wasting time on it."

"Did you try the doorway in the west wall?" Colin asked.

"No."

"Well, let's go look. This blighter refuses to speak anymore."

We re-entered the antechamber. I could tell by the tensing of muscles that Rablias was going to try something. I grabbed the back of his neck just as he tried to wrench free of the immortals. He gagged at the force and the men staggered.

"We must be onto something, if he doesn't want us heading this way," Colin gritted out.

They half-dragged, half-carried him through the west doorway. It seemed his little rebellion used up what strength he had left, as he offered no more resistance. I had taken the torches from the men so they could use both hands to control our prisoner. We saw seven iron doors, spaced evenly, down the hallway, three on each side and one at the end.

"Use these. I found them on this douche bag when I searched him," Eron said behind me.

He had a particularly intense look in his eyes I chose to ignore. I had to hand the torches back to work the keys in the locks. Five of the rooms were empty; the sixth stone cell revealed an unmoving figure.

Chapter Fifteen

The man sat before the boy, needle held at the ready, "You sure you wanna try this? That stuff sure don't look like anything I wanna be putting under my skin."

"Just do it. I'm paying you well enough for it." Nicky sneered.

The man looked at him a long minute and then shrugged philosophically. "You're the boss," and set the needle to buzzing.

The little boy grimaced as the needle traced the outline of the pattern on his skin. As the man did his work, Nicky mumbled under his breath. It sounded like nonsense words, but while the man paused to reload his gun, he inquired, "What're you saying?"

"How much longer do you have?" demanded the boy.

"It's a complicated piece, so if you don't want me messing it up, hold still." Underneath the mild warning was heat.

Nicky glared at him, but held still, and when the needle resumed its buzz, so did the boy resume his whispered words. It seemed like hours the two sat there—boy muttering, the man at his work. Several times the man wanted to stop, but the boy forced him to continue until the work was done. The man finally sat back, his hand cramped around the gun. Nicky muttered a few last words; the design glowed red and ebon.

"Holy crap! Ain't no fucking way! Now I'm seeing shit!

"It's almost perfect," the boy commented.

"Almost?" the man replied, "It is perfect."

He looked up at the boy as a knife swiped across his throat. The man tried to scream, but could not suck in air. His eyes bulged in horror as the blood sprayed out, coating the boy in crimson.

"Excellent. Your sacrifice has ensured that my body will not reject your work."

Nicky wiped his dagger off on the dead man's clothes. Then he broke into the cash register, stole what money was inside. He retrieved his backpack from under the chair and strolled into the bathroom in the back of the store, where he changed out of his stained clothes, and used a towel to clean the rest of the blood off of him. Then he piled everything in a pile by the dead man. From his backpack, he took several cans of lighter fluid and squirted them over the body.

He took a book of matches, and lighting one, let it fall on the pile of his clothes. When he couldn't stand the stench any longer, he left out the back door.

* * *

"Rablias!" the boy yelled at the man before him, "You may look older than me, but I have lived longer. When I tell you to do something, you do it exactly as I tell you, or I shall find another who wishes to learn my secrets."

"Of course, Master. I'm sorry, Master. I will do better, Master." The Head Questioner abased himself before the boy.

"You will put my special prisoner in the area reserved for our most important guests. He is not to be touched or tortured."

Nicky motioned to two burly men, carrying a wrapped bundle, roughly man sized, between them. The little boy watched the three disappear down a hallway further into the dungeons.

* * *

Nicky scowled at the slave chained down before him. He still was unable to call his demon, and that more than anything both pissed him off and scared him. He needed to be big again; he needed to take care of Rablias and that damn Mica. He continued the ritual, forcing all extraneous thoughts away.

The boy made the marks as the slave tried to thrash and scream; he gestured and spoke the final phrase. It was always an unpleasant sensation to grow big. The pain sharp as his bones, muscles and skin stretched. It took every bit of will power to stay upright through the process. In a matter of moments, the slave's life was gone and his corpse appearing to be a millennia-old shriveled mummy.

The once-little boy felt so tired, but he couldn't sleep, not now, not here. Nicky forced himself to put on the clothes made for his bigger older body. He scarfed food from the plate, and drained the cup of wine. He left plate and glass lying on the ground, and made his way back to the hunting lodge. Now he could sleep, just long enough to re-energize, and mayhap a better plan of how to deal with his disloyal slaves would come to him.

* * *

The minute Nicky entered his room, he was struck speechless at sight of the bodies and the disorder.

"Who's been in here? How dare they kill my slaves and befoul my things!" he snarled as the two palace guards standing watch outside his room followed him inside.

"Our fellow guards, my lord," answered one of the men. "Your rooms have been sealed off since the attack upon your personage, and have been under watch ever since. Have you another entrance, My Lord? We would make sure those who committed this atrocity are not still lying in wait for you."

Nicky ground his teeth; he didn't need guards mucking about in his private space and said so but they began to search anyway. "What of the others that were in the hall with me at the time of the attack?"

"They survived, and the duchess claimed you were in league with them as you seemed to know at least one of the assassins. His Majesty thought perhaps you had chased after them or they took you hostage hoping to gain their freedom."

So the damn duchess thought to discredit him? Try to make him into a traitor? He'd take care of her permanently, after seeing her plotting with his demon, killing and scattering his army.

"Your pardons, my lord, but His Majesty ordered us to inform you he wished to meet with you the moment you returned, and we are to escort you to him," the second guard said as they reached the room holding his bathing chamber which held more dead bodies.

"I will see him when I want. I have work to do still."

The guards' protests were cut short at what was revealed in the last room; even Nicky was shocked at the sight. Two hidden caches were open, one leading downward, the other between wall joists.

No! This couldn't be! The utter betrayal was too much, all the special weapons gone! His demon had shown him how to make them, and crafting them had tested his failing powers. Why was he losing his ability to do magic? Damn Rablias, and his demon!

The guards goggled in surprise at the opening with burgeoning suspicion.

"How dare they use my rooms to hide their misdeeds?" Nicky played outrage and had the guards believing him. How dare Rablias leave it gaping wide; who knew how many people had seen? He would be forced to find out who knew and kill them all.

The advisor sent the men ahead of him and paused to disable his traps before following the men. Why would Rablias and his demon do that? They would suffer for their impudence, after he got the answers he wanted.

The three men started down the passageway; Nicky noted his traps had been sprung, the bodies of his slaves a twisted trail of bread crumbs. The rage in him grew a little more with each step. Damn demon, thinking to disobey him and protect his acolyte from the effects! When the man entered the round entrance chamber, he stopped short in puzzlement. There was blood on the floor, and the lingering scent of oil and of fire along with the remains of a smashed lantern.

"This, this is an abomination, the work of evil. How could this be here without our majesty knowing?" one of the guards murmured.

"What if just by being here we've put our souls in danger? We should leave and ask for help or..."

"Don't be ridiculous!" Nicky snapped, "If this shit was real, don't you think His Majesty would have been affected by it? He prospers, as does the city. No, this is the work of some fiend to frighten us; you're playing right into their hands. Keep moving; we need to capture anyone lurking here to cause harm."

"Of course, your lordship," the now-shamed men muttered, and tightening their grips on their swords and the torches, moved to the other doorways, making sure all was empty.

None of the traps in what Nicky thought of as his calling circle had been triggered. He was about to warn the men not to cross the line carved in the stone when they did exactly that, triggering the wards. He watched as the men died, angry he had no back-up. Whoever had been there would pay for their arrogance.

Beyond was his main workspace, and he could see his stuff had been searched there as well. It wasn't until he got to his storage space that his rage really started to boil over.

"How fucking dare they!" he screamed as he surveyed the wreckage.

All his supplies of botanicals, minerals and animal-based materials for spells lay shattered and crushed on the floor. Expensive and rare ingredients, all gone, beyond all hope of recovery. The entire room was scored black, showing his traps had all been tripped; several people had to have either deliberately or unintentionally given their lives to breach his space.

Nicky's eyes fell on a charred mess of wood and his eyes opened even wider in shock. "My chests!" he yelped, "I will see you all dead! NO, not just dead, but first writhing in pain!" How good it would feel to make them scream and beg for his mercy. Mercy he had no intention of giving them.

Those chests held the few objects which he had treasured from the long years of his life. He could see the remains of one, which some foolish person had tried to open; only the thought of how much agony they had to be in from the attempt kept him from going into a frenzy. Right now, he had other matters to deal with. Nicky retraced his steps to the circular chamber that was a gateway to all the other chambers in this underground space of his and turned to the entranceway in the west wall.

The thick iron-banded wooden door was unlocked, further confirming Rablias or another aware of the space had come this way, though it was odd the door remained unlocked. Rablias might be a devious, grasping traitor, but he was not careless. Had he not had a chance to relock it? Blood drips on the floor let him know a wounded person had been this way; Nicky hoped it was Rablias, hoped he had been horribly injured from the backlash of what he tried to set off, and therefore less dangerous.

I wouldn't have to worry about Rablias too if he hadn't tried to betray me with my own demon, just those two men of his. They're strong enough to overpower me, hurt me, even in this form.

As the door opened, he saw a rich golden glow ahead, giving him pause. The hallway shouldn't be lit. *Do they expect to ambush me in there? Can they be that stupid?*

Nicky edged forward, pausing again to listen, but heard nothing.

Where is everyone? Surely not with the king? Why would they set an ambush this far down? It's stupid, they have to know I can trap them down there and block them in to rot.

The space between his shoulder blades itched, had been itching for quite a while, Nicky realized.

Someone down there is doing magic! Those traitorous assholes! How dare they try to use him to learn my secrets! I will kill them! All of them!

Rablias must be desperate, and that meant he would be unpredictable. The young man felt the building pressure of magic sweep over him; it wasn't Rablias, but his demon. When did he escape control? That's what his acolyte and his demon burned his thigh for, to disable the tattoo which kept the boy safe from the demon. They would rue their attempt. Nicky's eyes turned cold as dirty ice chips as he hurried toward the chanting from Mica's cell. Enraging chanting. Driving him to new heights of fury.

The voice cut off as he kicked the door wider. The advisor stood in the hallway, mouth open in shock, rage momentarily forgotten. The duchess was in a far corner of the cell holding his traitorous acolyte at sword point. Her slave was standing next to her, while huddled across from Her Grace was a much mangled Mica and another man standing near him with both arms up in the air to show he was no threat.

"You will all hang!" the young man screamed just as that damn woman shouted,

"Eron! Grab him!"

Her voice echoed in the small room, as with a howl, Rablias tossed handfuls of round objects at both his captors and Nicky, one of which flew past the advisor; before he could react, they went off.

Chapter Sixteen

"Goddamn, son-of-a-bitch..." Eron let loose with more expletives as he staggered against a wall. Whatever the man had tossed at them burned like acid. He clawed the stuff off his face.

The immortal could feel his blood and skin pouring down in rivulets, and his hand smoked and bubbled as skin came off in runny strips. The pain was nauseating but he forced himself to remain conscious. He could barely make out Illyria dragging the unconscious advisor inside the room and chaining him up with the manacles previously used on Mica.

"Colin? Mica?" He tried to walk to them, his eyes tearing from the pain.

There was brief moans from the two men; at least they were alive. For now.

"You have no idea of what you have done with this farce," Rablias hissed from the floor. "Or of who the true traitor is."

"Then enlighten me, and perhaps we will all get what we want." Her Grace's voice was quite reasonable.

The Head Questioner let out a raspy laugh ending in a fit of coughing; a rivulet of blood and drool snaked out the corner of his mouth down his chin as he lapsed into semi-consciousness. Eron joined Colin and Illyria in looking down at the man before them.

"He's still damaged from what he tossed at us the night of the harvest ball. He must hate someone really bad to still cling to life," Eron said in a mixture of disgust and weariness.

"I... but that's not Nicky!" Colin stammered in shock at his friend. "This has to be the person he's paid to impersonate him."

"Do you trust me, Colin? I will vouch for the identity of the person before me: Nicky, and no mortal," Eron gritted out as he got the last of the burning, sticky stuff off.

"I..," his friend faltered, gaze shifting between his brother and the young man. "I'm sorry, but, I...not this time. I can't. I can't take it on faith. Not after all our talks of magic. What if the little boy used his talents to make the man before us his duplicate? We have to be sure. Mica needs to be sure."

"Fine, very well. Take this as proof," Illyria replied as she walked over to the chained man.

He was stirring to full consciousness and Eron knew what she was about to do and was amazed she would let her knowledge be exposed. She stabbed the young man in the heart. Colin yelled in outrage and scrambled up to grab her sword, but was too late. The young man gurgled once and died before them.

"How could you? You know we needed him alive!" He had his sword out, threatening her. He stumbled back at the casual way she knocked it aside as she moved back toward the head questioner who was moaning in pain as he came back to full awareness.

"Colin, please, trust me, trust us," Eron pleaded and moved up beside his friend, gesturing at the advisor.

The stab wound was already healing; Colin watched dumbfounded as the man woke, thrashing and screaming invectives at them as he found he was captured.

"You're dead, you fucking bastards, all of you! Dead, you hear me? And you, you traitorous whore! You'll fucking wish you were dead when I get done with you."

"Perhaps it would be best if you took Colin outside to the hall for a moment and explained to him. I doubt we have much time before Nicky's slave arrives to free him. I would not care to be here when that happens," Her Grace replied calmly.

Colin watched something pass between his friend and the duchess, then Eron sighed and gave a barely perceptible nod. "Come on, let me explain outside a moment. Please."

"No, I won't," Colin said mulishly. "Why she is not surprised by all this? What have you done, Eron? This, this betrayal, has Mica been right not to trust you anymore?"

Eron let out a weary sigh. "This needs to end. I had to put things on hold for this, things I can't put off much longer."

"I can see you have integrity, not like these others. Don't let them kill me; I'm the king's advisor, not whoever they think I am."

Colin wavered, his eyes skittering from the young man to his brother, the duchess, then back to his friend. "He's right, he's the king's advisor. We can't do this without knowing for sure he wasn't an innocent in all this."

"Your kindness shall be rewarded greatly if you free me. You are in here illegally, helping a traitor, think what the king will say."

"The head questioner does seem to be..."

"I can't believe I'm hearing this! If you don't shut him up, I will," Eron said to the duchess. "Colin, he kidnapped your brother! What about that says he's innocent?"

"I can't do what you want without knowing the full extent of his involvement, and you know why. Mica would say the same thing, if he wasn't the way he is now. It's already out of control."

"We don't have time for this, Colin. Mica doesn't have time for it. Do you want his life and this quest of his to be in vain?"

"We still haven't determined the extent of his guilt or innocence. I won't be a party to such rash condemnations."

"I knew you weren't like the others, these traitors and liars. Free me and I'll see to it the king rewards you well."

Suddenly Her Grace spoke. "Did you not tell me, Mister Dugan, you'd take any opportunity to speak with the young man caught up in the lies and machinations of the one you came here for? Here's that opportunity. Ask of him what you will, and if his answers satisfy you, then we shall bring him before His Majesty."

"Are you insane? And give him the chance to escape?" Eron hissed to her, aggrieved, Colin had not indicated whether he'd retrieved what his brother hid.

Colin faltered but his mouth firmed and he stepped decisively toward the boy, who had a self-confident supercilious air.

"Who are you working with?"

The young man's eyes flared in rage for a moment, then he subdued it. *Act like a mortal, this asshole knows nothing, but the other asshole's might, and who knows what that bitch whore believes.* "I am the king's advisor, and his closest friend since we were children. He will not like this treatment you show me."

"Who were your parents? What happened to them?"

"I'm an orphan," his tone implying it was a subject he wished to have left alone. "How dare you question me as if I am some criminal when it is you who have committed the crimes?"

"Let me rephrase the question. Who made you what you are? Who gave you our gift?"

The advisor tried for scared, but ended up defiant instead. "What the hell do you know of it? I knew something was wrong, he said..." He clamped his lips together.

"He who?" Colin asked a shade too eagerly, missing the quick, gloating satisfaction which crossed the advisor's face.

"I... He never told me his name. How do you know of Those That Cannot Die?" Nicky demanded, laughing inside at how the fool before him believed what he was told.

"Those That Cannot Die?" Colin repeated, "Is that what he told you we are called?"

Eron snorted and whispered, "I call bullshit." But this earned him a hateful glare from the young man.

"I never learned his name. I saw the kid, person die and then live again. He said I was mistaken, but I know dead when I see it." The tone was bitter and contemptuous at the same time.

"And for that alone he changed you?" Colin asked skeptically.

Nicky noted the doubt rethought what he was going to say. "No, you idiot; it was a reward for helping."

"Helping how?"

"Helping escape. He said some evil men were chasing him, had been for longer than he cared to remember. He said they did it made him Undying so he could be their slave. But he got free."

"I find it hard to believe a man with the intelligence required of a king's advisor would not investigate such claims."

"Of course I did, you fool!" Nicky snapped arrogantly, "My guards saved him from a passel of rogues who wanted to kill him and take his gift away."

"It could have all been a ploy..."

"I was there, you moron! You dare to question my word? The word of a nobleman?" He thought the outrage a nice touch, and was pleased to see the bow the man before him gave.

"But how is it the boy knew how to create those he called Undying if he was meant to be a slave? Would the men not keep that from him?"

"In the battle, those men lost some of their possessions, including a locked box. It took months to figure out how to open it, months I protected the poor, frightened kid as he fretted those who pursued him would come with an army. The secret was within."

"I still call bullshit," Eron muttered off to the side but no one paid him any mind, not even the duchess; surely she of all people would disbelieve this tale?

"How did you recognize the secret?" Colin asked.

Rage contorted the young man's face for a moment, then he sneered, "The kid recognized enough of it to identify it. He kept the paper, but made me what I am in return for help escaping those men. Aid was cheap in exchange for a gift like that." He rattled the chains. "Now let me go, you assholes, before the royal guard finds you and makes you suffer for what you have done to me." *Where the hell is my demon?*

The young man tried to call again, mumbling the words under his breath and making it seem like he was complaining about them to himself. He still didn't feel the sensation which let him know his summons was being answered, and his rage grew. They would all pay for this! Including his damn demon.

"Check his leg." The unexpected voice was raspy, as if it still hurt to talk. "He..." the man stopped to cough and continued in a much diminished tone, "bears a mark..."

"I, but, of course." Colin said dubiously and knelt before the young man. "Your pardon, my lord, but I must see your leg, for the truth of your tale."

"Denied!" Nicky hissed, but what was supposed to be menace came out more like fear as he tucked his legs underneath him. "How dare you question my word over that of a known traitor? The king shall hear of this..." Then he yelped as his legs were suddenly pulled straight by Her Grace's slave.

"You'll regret this! I'll kill you! I AM THE KING'S ADVISOR!"

"Let's get this over with." Eron struggled to keep his hold as the man howled and screamed and kicked and thrashed.

Colin wrested their prisoner's boots off and raised his left pant leg. Above his ankle was the mark. Colin let out a low whistle.

"You bastards! I will see you dead! No one lays a hand on me and treats me this way! Every undying has a mark there, they had better or they shouldn't live! I will see you dead!"

"Did the kid have a mark like this? Colin!" Eron demanded.

"I, yes. He did, same place. But, that, that doesn't mean. It could be a trap, meant to mislead us, I mean, not every Undying...Immortal has them." Colin replied, still shaken. "It's, it's possible the kid convinced the advisor to have the same mark tattooed there, just in case, you know, to throw us off. I think...perhaps...perhaps you should tell me what Her Grace wishes me to know."

Eron and Illyria flicked a glance at each other. Nicky's eyes narrowed speculatively; that was clearly not a master-slave relationship. The slave released his leg and stepped away out of kicking range.

"Your Grace..." the voice was thin and reedy, "I beg of you...a dying man's wishes..."

Nicky watched as the duchess paced toward Rablias and crouched down near his head, so she could keep an eye on both him and the advisor.

"Speak, if you have anything that isn't lies, otherwise, remain silent and take them to your grave. There is nothing I nor anyone can do for you now."

It seemed the man would not talk again, and Nicky glared at him, willing him to die. The Head Questioner coughed once and his mouth moved; they all leaned in close to hear what he said.

"The advisor is more than what he seems. Knows things. Fantastic things. I...have...seen them...with my own eyes. He...he is a child of but twelve...he can make himself...into the man...you see... before you now."

Rablias went into another coughing fit. Nicky fumed as Eron walked out of hearing range to have a heated though low-voiced discussion. He couldn't understand why his demon wasn't answering his summons, Rablias had to be behind the betrayal; perhaps his demon had taught the traitor something to prevent or block Nicky from summoning his pet. The young man looked toward his acolyte fighting for breath on the floor. The man would be dead soon, and with his passing, any magic he may have worked.

"There is... one more... thing...Your Grace..." the man whispered and feebly motioned for her to come closer.

She bent near him, as his lips moved. He spoke for several minutes before expiring with a gasp. The duchess regarded Rablias for a moment before turning her evaluation to the two men still arguing in hushed tones just inside the door.

"Duchess," Nicky hissed, straining at the chains and manacles preventing him from being able to do more than kneel upright. "This is treason, you think the king won't find out? I'm the only one who can save you from being condemned to torture and death. Let me free, take my side, and I will reward you. I don't know what shit those men told you, but I thought you too intelligent than to believe their lies." Her faint smile only further enraged him.

"You fucking bitch-whore! You will regret this if you don't! You can't kill me—I'm Undying! I always remember my enemies. For the rest of your life, you'll wonder when I'll strike. Think you can keep this secret? What I am? What you're doing?" He screamed vilest invective until he lost his voice, and could only wheeze scatology.

She continued to regard him calmly, as he was finally reduced to hanging in his chains, bowed over his knees in exhaustion. He barely had any magic left, and he still didn't know how to make the form he was in permanent. The last thing he needed to do was waste it on the slime before him; but if he didn't get free, he would revert to original form, giving the brothers the proof they needed to back up Rablias' claims. He had to escape, had to find a way out, a way to make them all pay for this.

Nicky refused to beg, he wouldn't, he wouldn't, and he wouldn't! He was sick of begging: of the king's forgiveness, of bowing and scraping and pretending to be less than royalty. He was Immortal! He was a god to mortals! They should fear him, they should beg him for favors, beg just to be allowed the privilege of continuing their miserable lives. He was no one's toy, no one's pet! It had taken him so long to make his demon his slave, rather than vice versa. The young man sucked in a breath perilously close to a sob.

"Duchess, duchess, forgive me, for cursing you, but you know this is a mistake to keep me prisoner. You know the only way to keep your life, title, and wealth once this is discovered is with my cooperation; persuade me to give it to you? Else you suffer as they."

"I'll take that chance. And you?"

"You could have had it all; my favor and friendship, my protection. Side with them and I'll see you hang. Free me and live as my wife. All I ask is obedience."

She flicked a glance at his chains, the abrasions on his wrists. What the hell was wrong with her? Any woman in her right mind would jump at the chance he was offering them.

"One more chance, my lady. Speak now or lose my hand of friendship and you will die as painfully as these men." He didn't want to call in the favor she owed him, not while other means to freedom existed.

She glanced at his nemesis, dead on the floor and he softly chanted the words to call his pet. Whatever Rablias had done to block him had died with the man.

As he finished his chant, the duchess knelt beside him.

"Too late..." he started to taunt her but he was astounded to realize she'd sliced his pant leg with a dagger he hadn't seen her draw, exposing his right thigh and what was tattooed thereon. "You can't, you don't... NnnnooOOOEEEEEAAARRGH!!!!!" The keen blade sliced deep and the blood welled up, smelling of cinnamon, ambrosia and sulfur as the words devolved to shrieks.

Colin and Eron were startled out of their argument when they realized what she was doing, but halted their approach as the duchess held up a chunk of flesh. There was so much blood pouring off the advisor's thigh, she couldn't tell whether the tattoo was coming back.

The men stopped speaking as the temperature plunged, breaths pluming white in the sudden cold; a feathery whiteness grew up the walls, across the floor and ceiling, coating the dead man in a glittering sheet.

"What, what's going on?" Colin asked.

Mica's eyes opened. "Something's wrong," he rasped. "What did you do?" he accused the still-screaming advisor.

The coldness intensified, the metal chains frosting over as Nicky writhed and twisted frantically, babbling to anyone who would listen to free him.

"What did you do?" Mica screamed at Her Grace as his brother came over to help him sit up.

Eron didn't want to get caught in whatever was about to go down, but he also couldn't leave his friends. He'd barely made it to Illyria's side when the torches were snuffed out as if by a sudden wind. A growling echoed in the chamber and the darkness lit red.

"You bitch! Someone get me free! I'll give you whatever you want! Please! Hurry!" Nicky's face contorted in terror as he stared at the redness. Blood flowed from his wrists where the manacles had abraded them in his struggles.

"Illyria, what did you do?" Eron cried out, staring in fascinated horror at the advisor.

The chains restricting the young man's movements shattered with a sharp retort as a vast darkness coalesced before him, two pinpricks of red centered in the cloud.

The boy seemed frozen in place; staring eyes white-ringed in a rictus of fear as his terrified breath whistled, high-pitched.

"What the hell is that?" Mica screamed as the oppression permeated them all; he stood, leaning heavily on his brother's arm to the side and slightly behind the darkness.

"Take him and go!" she yelled, "and never return."

"Oh, shit." Eron had his own sword out, unsure who or what he was supposed to use it on.

There was another growl, and a slithering sound, as Nicky's body was sucked swiftly into the darkness, the young man's cries incomprehensible to those left behind.

And the darkness reached for Mica. He screamed.

Colin cried out, as he made to grab his brother. "Help us!" he shouted at the other two.

Eron and the duchess could only stare at the train wreck unfolding before them as he said sotto voice, "Perhaps an exorcism is in order?"

Mica grabbed his brother's sword and plunged it into the darkness. The duchess had only enough time to step aside as the darkness flung Mica and Colin away. Colin's flying body slammed into Eron and they smashed into the wall, Mica falling to the floor. She felt a brief pain across her throat and wetness as a silver blur flashed past her vision and her hands flew up to clutch at the wound. The scrap of the boy's skin fell from her hands and disappeared in a lick of incandescent flame. Tendrils of darkness plunged into all Mica's orifices, muffling his screams as his outstretched fists and heels drummed the floor.

Eron and Colin staggered to their feet, swords in hand, but attacking the cloud again seemed rather a poor idea.

"Suck it up, buttercup," Eron spat at Illyria, who seemed to have a death grip on her neck, fingers red with blood welling out and over to drip upon the floor. Eron wrapped an arm around her waist and attempted to drag her toward the doorway, as Colin screamed his brother's name.

Mica was now being dragged closer to the main bulk of the demon. Colin followed, fishing a bit of metal and gemstone out of a pouch at his waist, yelling in Latin. The duchess broke free from Eron's grip and dived for Mica. She managed to grab his forearms and tried to brace herself but they were both now heading toward the darkness.

"Damn it!" Eron brought the sword down as if he could hack the blackness apart and sever it; when that didn't work, he made a grab for Illyria with his free hand.

An actinic flare blazed before them. The polar cold suddenly became tropical, volcanic, solar as the ice ran in rivulets of water to flood the floor boot-high.

"Down! Get down!" The shout rang out, Eron and Illyria dropped to their knees with the other man as something streamed where their heads had been.

The tendrils oozed out of the passed-out Mica with a nauseating sucking, whipping wildly as their bright white counterparts smashed into the inky blackness.

"Colin! It's forbidden!" Eron screamed at his friend, realizing the source of the whiteness.

"I'm not losing my brother!" he shouted back and dropped what he had been holding as it glowed white-hot.

The black and white tendrils shot out and grabbed the piece, merged into a formless gray. The darkness growled again, but its reverberation was counteracted by a high-pitched tone of chiming crystal. The soul gem glowed, the metal melted and the setting turned to ash as the gem itself shattered in a spray of shards. The white cloud boomed, hurtling inside Mica.

The immortal's body rose and slammed down as the inky coils, wrapped with the white, snapped back into the bulk of the darkness with a sucking sound. The ground shivered as both black and white condensed into tiny balls, exploded outward towards the walls, washing over the body of Nicky in a river. In a moment, black and white and the body of the boy were gone, only the normal darkness of underground remaining. The temperature stabilized to its previous chill. The sudden silence left ears ringing.

"Anyone got a light?" Eron asked of no one in particular.

Chapter Seventeen

"How's he doing?" Eron came into the room.

"Not so good, I'm afraid. I don't understand why he won't wake up. What did that thing do to him?" Colin looked sadly at his brother. "What if he never wakes up? What will I do then?" The man was slumped next to his brother's bed, dejection in every line of his body.

"I don't know what to tell you."

Colin continued like he hadn't heard, "He's my best friend. Did you know we had a large family? Six brothers besides us, and two sisters. I was the youngest, Mica the seventh kid. Our father was a moderately successful farmer. Our sisters married well, and our brothers had large prosperous farms of their own. Nobody but me saw the need to learn reading and writing. Mica, he defied my father and older brothers, apprenticed himself out and learned a trade; he sent for tutors for me. I was the first scholar of our family. Mica was so proud of me."

He stopped to straighten the already ruler-perfect edge of the blanket covering his brother.

"We'll find something to help him, Colin. The Duchess has pledged to put her considerable resources at our disposal." What he didn't add what he'd said to her to get her to agree.

Colin nodded. "Will you thank her for me? Let her know I shall do so in person later, just I don't want to leave him now."

"Of course." Eron stood a few moments more but his friend seemed to have sunk into a reverie so he left.

Illyria was waiting outside the door. "No change," she flatly stated, her nose flaring as she took in the scent of the man inside.

"What are you sniffing for? A bite to eat? Someone to steal

daylight from?" His anger bubbled up and over.

She didn't seem to notice his tone. "No," she muttered distractedly, sniffing again. "Can you get Colin out of the room? Just for a few moments or so? I can't tell with him in there; his scent is clouding Mica's."

"I'm not letting you alone in the room with him!"

She gave him a look full of scorn and impatience. "I don't want to eat him, Eron. Despite our differences of opinions, and the debacle with his protégé, I do want to help. The demon did something to him, as it did to Nicky, I can't quite tell what."

He hesitated; she sounded sincere, but she always did, even when lying to your face. Illyria never called it that, she called it sharing strategic bits of information, and she always claimed there was a grain of truth in all she said.

"You can stand in the damn room if you wish, be his protector."

The immortal glanced at the room, back at her, "That is one more item in a very long list of things we need to talk about. But if I see fang headed for his flesh, I swear I'll lop your head off."

It took him a few minutes to convince his friend to take a break, and not long after he had left, she came in. Eron stood near his friend's head. Illyria stopped next to him, took in a big breath of air, and her eyes narrowed in concentration. She picked up one of Mica's hands and brought it to her nose. Eron's hand tightened on his sword handle, expecting her to sink fangs into a vein. Instead, she took another big sniff, and looked more puzzled. Mica's hand was replaced on top of the blanket, puncture free.

"Well?" he asked.

"Curiouser and curiouser," her voice compounded of exasperation and disbelief.

"I think the demon did something which, from all accounts of what you've told me, should be impossible. His scent is conveying two conflicting messages. It would help if I could taste of his blood, blood does not lie."

He exploded, "You do just want to steal daylight!"

She gave him a vexed look. "I don't have to bite him, I can simply make a cut with my nails. The blood which wells forth will be sufficient."

"Fine, a taste and no more," he said, ostentatiously drawing his sword.

The vampire ignored his colossal rudeness and turned back to Mica. She spent long moments savoring the blood which welled from the scratch she inflicted on his arm. When she let his arm drop, the wound was gone. She had a look on her face he had seen on wine connoisseurs when they rolled the liquid about their mouth before swallowing. "He doesn't taste Immortal anymore."

"What the hell does that mean? Of course he's Immortal! The wound healed on him, and he'd be dead if he wasn't."

"I healed him; we do that so the marks do not show. I am telling you, Eron, I know blood. When I drank of the boy, I could taste the corruption inside him. You and Colin smell pure immortal; Mica, not so much."

"So you're telling me we taste, or should taste, the way we smell?" he asked incredulously.

"Yes. However, I have not tasted of an Immortal who wasn't demon-tainted since our time together so long ago, so there is a slim, however improbable, chance I am wrong."

The second part of what she said finally penetrated. "Wait, so you want to bite me as comparison?"

"Since Colin does not know what I am, it would have to be you. But I need a comparison, a control, just the same amount I took from him."

They stared at each other, he unmindful he had lowered his sword and was no longer in a protective stance. Didn't he owe it to the brothers to make sure she was right? To help find a cure, a way to wake him up if possible? But the last time she had drunk from him—no, he would not go there. He took a deep breath in, and sheathed his sword.

"Do it." He thrust his arm out, fist clenched so the tendons and veins stood out.

Her touch was icy cold, and the swift slice of her nail made the wound itch more than hurt. Her frosted lips pressed firmly to his hot skin.

Just the feel of her lips on his skin made him flush hotter, stirring his libido. *Don't think about it, think of something else, don't give her a hold over you,* he told himself and kept his face neutral, glad she couldn't read his thoughts.

Eron concentrated on controlling his breathing, but his heart speed up all the same and he hoped she attributed it to being nervous, as she concentrated on his flavor as she had Mica's. He peeked at his wound, and it was healing by itself. He wanted to make some cheeky comment, or a flirtatious one; something along the lines of: "So, do I taste as good as you expected? Want another sip?" but refrained.

"It is as I thought. He is no longer fully immortal, nor truly mortal, yet."

"What do you mean, yet?" His voice rising. "Is it possible for you to be clearer than mud?"

"I get the, how do you say, fading notes of immortality, and the stronger base of rich iron, mortal blood."

"But, but," Eron stuttered, "becoming Un-Immortal, it's impossible! We die if we do, just like your kind."

"Don't ask me how the demon accomplished what he did. I can only tell you Mica is no longer fully immortal, and as time goes by, his mortal scent grows stronger. If he wakes up, he will have a chance to live a mortal life; perhaps have children, grow old, and die."

"Somehow, I don't think it will be a comfort to him, not when he learns how he lost his Immortality."

She merely shrugged and turned to go. "If and when he wakes, I will offer him the same opportunity I gave you."

He scowled at her as she left the room.

Chapter Eighteen

"Hello, darling! It's been years!" the smoky velvet voice purred in his ear.

Mica jumped and jerked away, almost bumping into a patron behind him as merry laughter rang out over the pulsing music. He swore as his drink spilled onto the already sticky floor. The man looked over his shoulder to see his personal pain-in-the-ass posing before him.

"Damn it, Illyria! Must you do that?" he inquired as he slammed his glass down onto the bar top.

The woman signaled to the bartender to refill it, and slapped a bill down in payment. "I like knowing I can sneak up on a warrior such as yourself," she laughed.

The drink came faster than it would have for anyone else. "How 'bout you? Can I get you anything? A drink, water, my number?" The bartender smiled at the model-gorgeous woman in a swingy, glittery, sexy red dress and killer strappy heels, as high as the skirt was short.

"Maybe later, darling." She blew him an air kiss, slid an outrageous tip across the bar, and turned back to the man before her. "Don't tell me you're here all alone? At a dance club?"

"I like the music," Mica deadpanned.

She looked out over the floor, crowded with couples all showing off their moves, the flashing lights, the live salsa band; "Come dance with me, show these mortals what perfection looks like." She leaned in close so she didn't have to shout.

He caught a whiff of her perfume, spicy and expensive, and his glimpse of her perfect cleavage let him understand Eron's obsession with her, though he knew his friend swore he'd die before letting her know.

"Has it occurred to you I may be here with someone? And you could be disrespecting her?"

"I've been watching you. You dance with any single female who will consent, and there's only one glass before you—no partner out on the dance floor with someone else. Please?" She pouted. "Pretty please with a cherry on top?"

He rolled his eyes and finished his drink, setting the glass on the bar. Sometimes consenting was the quickest way to get rid of her, and occasionally she did have useful information. She may have been an unprincipled blood-sucking fiend, but she loved to dance and it had been a while since he danced with anyone of a professional caliber.

They immediately swung into the dancing crowd, adding their own little spins, and twists. Soon a space had cleared for them in the center, and the lead singer of the live band was crooning lyrics to them.

"¡Tiene calor! ¡Mover como un fuego, le quema con deseo! Tenga cuidado, tome cuidado, señorita atractiva"

She's hot! Moving like a fire, burn you with desire! Beware, take care, sexy lady!

"What's so important you had to go stalking me? I'm not one of your prey!" He spoke normally, knowing her superior hearing.

She waited until they came together again to speak. "I have heard disturbing rumors that something called the Great Hunt is taking place."

Her long, rich brown hair fanned out as she twirled, the large silver hoops she wore in her ears catching the light, as did the stacked bracelets on her wrists. Her outfit glittered, making her appear like a flame. He couldn't believe she had worn it out in public, a professional-grade performance costume. What material it did have was covered in sequins, fringe, and rhinestones.

"Someone is always screaming the end of the world is nigh."

"No dear friend, this is only slightly less worse,"

"Oh well then. No worries there." He was sarcastic as she shimmied her body to wolf-whistles, applause, and cheers of an appreciative audience.

"This is different!" Illyria persisted as only an undead could.

"Some group is rumored to have started exterminating your kind, along with large percentages of the population in out-of-the-way countries."

"I don't believe you. We would have heard about it by now if humans were being killed off in such a manner," Mica insisted. "And how can you have learned rumors about my kind that I have not heard?"

"It has been spoken of, only no one in the mainstream press is taking it seriously. Only the fringe element will report it; besides, this country has such a tumultuous history with those areas only certain groups seem to care what really happens over there."

He spun her again, wondering why she cared about the state of the world, or his kind, and said as much when they came together again.

"Do you know how hard it is to feed when most of your food source is dead?" The indignation in her voice would have had him laughing if she hadn't been referencing humans. "Allika told me that she narrowly escaped some of them. They call themselves The Immortal Wolves."

"Maybe it's a good thing; it will finally force your kind into extinction," he temporized.

"And expose those of your kind left alive as well." she spat back. "If the humans don't discover how to kill you, they may enslave you for eternity. Is that what you want?"

He had been a slave for over a hundred years, an experience he didn't plan to repeat any time soon. He got a chill at her words. He asked a few more questions, and her answers sounded convincing. He promised to keep his ears and eyes open, and to make plans to keep himself and those he cared about safe in case the rumors were true.

* * *

I curse you! Illyria Sasha Nicolette Caladonea Maison du Corbeau! I curse you and everyone with you! You will not remember them, nor they you! I curse you!

* * *

The siren shrieked relentlessly, and the driver laid on the horn as he approached intersections, cursing traffic which couldn't or wouldn't move out of his way fast enough. The men inside the cab and body of the truck hung on and swayed from side to side with the movement, tense and on edge. The first reports coming in sounded bad. The crackle of the radio as police and other emergency personal reporting the situation had the anxiety ratcheting up a notch. Finally the sleek red truck pulled up, its big diesel engine rumbling as the men spilled out and got their first look at the building before them.

"Holy Mother of God!" one of the men swore and someone else whistled.

Their team leader was barking out orders as they finished suiting up. "Listen up! We've got to get any survivors out before the next inbound strike in four hours! We're gonna concentrate on this segment of the building."

A cop had run up to them, along with a few of the medical staff.

"We got out patients as long as we could before it became too dangerous."

"There's still a lot of people trapped inside!"

A dizzying profusion of numbers followed, but the men, looking like astronauts, strode into what remained of the lobby.

Cries, screams, and moans from the wounded and trapped echoed in the twisted wreckage. Mica's breath sounded harsh in his sealed helmet, foreign even after ten years as a professional firefighter. Fragmented bodies had to be ignored, shut out as they made their way deeper into the building in pursuit of the living. Up the men climbed to the next floor. Lights hung from the ceiling, some dead and dark, others flickering, a few bravely shining. The screams and cries were louder now.

"Mommy! Mommy!" was a repetitious refrain.

Doors blocked needed to be cleared, the team leader cracked out orders, and the men split into units and got to work. They had been told this section of the hospital was filled with children. The men and women worked steadily, headsets and mikes crackling.

"Out, out, everybody out! We've got inbound in forty minutes!"

Mica ignored the cries over his headset; he was almost through one more door. He crashed through, the room in darkness. His powerful beam stabbed the darkness, illuminating cheerful animals painted on the walls.

"Hello! I'm a fireman! My name's Mica! Is anyone here?" he called out over his external speaker.

He systematically searched the room, still talking in a soothing tone, describing what he was wearing, trying to entice the child to come out. All the while his captain was screaming in his ear to leave. Mica found the girl, huddled under the bed, coaxed her out, and once he had hold, he moved as fast as the suit would allow him through the door to the corridor beyond. The immortal had just cleared the second floor when the whole building rumbled. The child's scream was lost in the sound of the missiles hitting the building. The man did his best to shield the girl as they were hurtled through the air, debris whipping past them. He felt chunks of stuff hit him, and a wrench and pulling in his arms, before he was knocked out by the collapsing building.

* * *

I curse you and everyone with you! You will not remember them, nor they you! I curse you!

* * *

Mica dragged the scrap of cloth higher across his face, so only his eyes were uncovered. Ash and other charred matter still drifted on the air from the recent fires which swept parts of the old city. The cracked pavement had disappeared under the reclaiming vegetation. He knew what had once been there by the almost straight swathes of meadow, interrupted here and there by mounds of covered debris. He had to be careful. Everyone did nowadays; strangers were regarded with suspicion and in some cases barely concealed hostility.

He had stayed in the crumbling cities, gathering supplies as the world broke down. He was good at scavenging, and having lived as long as he had, he had many skills he could rely on. His only concern was getting to the meeting spot prearranged with his brother. Every twenty-five years they met, no matter what.

Mica was behind on his promise; he hadn't taken the attacks seriously at first, thinking it just another war. When he realized it predicted the end of civilization, he had started making his way to the coast. It took a combination of bribing and working to make his way across the Atlantic.

He would need to find a safe spot to rest soon; preferably one by a small stream, and easily defendable. The next morning, refreshed, fed, and watered, the man got underway. Mica wanted to be away from even the outskirts of what had once been thriving city centers. Too many times he had encountered small bands of survivors with less than honest intentions.

Mica continued his hike, stripping down a nice-sized branch to provide a handy walking stick, thick enough to serve as a make-shift staff to back up his sword. He continued his hike at a swift, steady pace he had learned from his days in the military. So many miles per day, with quick rest and refuel breaks, before he would stop for the night. He had calculated a journey which should take him another six months to reach the meeting spot.

The man crested a hill and saw his ancestral family home, or at least where it had once stood centuries before. Whatever remained of the sleepy little village was long gone, buried under the land. There was no inhabitants now, either having left long ago, or been killed in the post-cataclysm wars. Mica made his way down the hill and through what had once been the center of the village, each step a bittersweet memory.

There was where he'd stolen a kiss from lithe Else. That small rise was the site of the blacksmith with whom he had apprenticed before the fever of war had swept the village. This little stream had supplied water to his cottage before his wife and the babe had died in childbirth. That meadow had been a field his father and siblings had tilled. He continued to the spot at which he and his brother always met.

* * *

"Hey, doesn't he look like Eron to you?" Colin nodded in the direction of a group of men sitting around a table drinking.

Mica looked, and saw in the firelight the sharp profile of their friend. “I believe so. What’s he doing here?” He wanted to go over, but wasn’t sure what identity the man was using.

The two brothers made their way over to the bar, and standing at its edge, ordered mugs of ale. After some time had passed, most of the men at their friend’s table had left. The man himself stood, and carried his mug over to the bar. He leaned against the edge a few paces down from the brothers, and waited until the bartender had noticed him.

“How’s it going, Erik? One more?” he was greeted.

The immortal nodded his thanks and idly glanced up and down the bar. He noted the brothers, but made no greeting until he had his filled mug in hand.

He took a sip, remarking, “Lotta new people coming in. How’s your business been, Rolf?”

Rolf shrugged as he wiped a mug out. “Not bad. How’s Evony doing after her scare with the kid?”

“She has her family taking care of her.”

“Lucky her. If I see the little brat again?” The man made a wringing motion with his hands and went to check on the brothers. “That little Nicklos, he is a very evil little boy. I hope you and your men ran him out of town proper.”

“Yes, Rolf, he won’t be back.” Erik finished his drink and left his mug as he wished the bartender a good night.

Mica took another sip, when what he really wanted to do was run out after the man; how many kids still bore the name Nicky? How many of them could be called evil? His brother glanced at him, as if knowing what he thought.

The night wind felt like knives cutting through even the fur of the men’s coats. Their breath came out in puffs as they spoke.

“Come on. Eron!”

“Erik!” the man hissed.

Mica ignored his friend’s groan, “I know it’s the kid! What’d he do to the girl?”

“Mica, it’s not your nemesis. Look, the kid’s probably dead by now. The wars of our kind decimated us. Why can’t you move on? Forget about him and whatever he’s done to you. Settle down!”

"I've tried telling him for years now, good luck with it." Colin chimed in.

"What did he look like? What story did he tell to account for why he was alone?" Mica persisted, blocking his friend's path when the man tried to leave.

"I don't advise that, not with my men watching." Eron/Erik warned him.

"Then just tell me what I want to know!"

"Fine. But you're wasting your time and energy. The kid called himself Nichlos, said he was an orphan. His parents had been killed by raiders. They were farmers or something, living in the outer reaches. He managed to escape and hide and was trying to get to his relatives."

"That matches what he always says!" Mica exclaimed.

"What did he look like?" Colin inquired.

"I dunno, twelve? Thirteen? A teenager. Reddish-blond hair, gray eyes, about this high." Eron/Erik held his hand up to demonstrate.

"That's him! That's Nicky! I can't believe you just ran him out instead of capturing him and going for his gem," Mica ranted.

"I have no beef with the kid, that's your deal. Look, we put him on the Austrian Road, told him not to come back."

"You have to come with us," Mica said, "I need your tracking skills. You know the region better than I do now civilization's ended."

"Mica..." Eron/Erik began.

"You owe me, remember?" Mica said meaningfully

"Dammit!" he swore, glancing at his men, who were paying the three of them an unhealthy amount of attention.

"Either you come with me, or the next time I find an Immortal Wolf, I may just forget myself enough to drop your name to them," Mica hissed.

"Just think about it. We'll be here as long as it takes to complete some repairs and stock up again."

* * *

"Worm!" The guttural voice sent icy shivers through his body.

“You dare cheat me out of what is rightfully mine. I will have the boy and his soul! I take your immortality, so the boy will be mine, so I shall have my revenge.”

Mica felt pain lance through him, would it never stop? He was suspended in darkness. Below unseen things roiled, laughed, and gibbered; above, a gentle yet bright clear light shone. He would be OK if he could reach it. Where was his brother? Where was Colin? He would help, he always did.

* * *

The strains of a waltz drifted through the crowded rooms, barely heard over the tumult of voices. Mica whirled around the floor with a beauty in his arms. When the music stopped, he bowed and she curtsied.

“You dance divinely, Sir. What other talents do you possess?” she inquired.

“I’m considered a fair hand with a sword,” Mica replied.

“But what good is that to a woman?” she asked.

He winked while giving a roguish smile.

Something is not right. She should be an innocent blonde, with blue eyes, and plump. Yet here she has dark brown hair, yellow-green, brown eyes, a sultry, knowing look.

She smiled back and tapped his arm with her fan. “Naughty man.”

Another man hailed them. He bowed to both the lady and Mica, “Pardon my intrusion, my lady. I wonder if I might have a word with my brother?”

She gave Colin a coquettish smile. “Only if you promise me a dance, Sir.”

He smiled back at her and raising her hand, planted a kiss on the back of it, “Done, my lady.”

Colin and Mica bowed to her and took their leave. Colin steered Mica through an open pair of French doors and out onto the darkened terrace.

“What’s this all about, brother? I had thought to dance with the lady again,” Mica asked impatiently.

Colin turned a sad, serious face to Mica. “Time grows short, brother. Disaster looms. Do not delay in petty pleasures and inconsequential matters."

"What? You mean the battle with the milksop Earl? Have no fear. I shall win,"

"Not that, brother, you have been asleep too long, The Duchess Illyria and Eron are more concerned than they let on."

"Who? Are you daft? There's no one here by such a name." Mica made as if to go back in and a vision flashed before his eyes. A beautiful woman, the one he had been dancing with, but in slick, form-fitting black leather

Colin grabbed his arm, stopped his brother. "Look into your heart, brother. You are not as you were. You have changed. The demon spoke truth. You are not immortal anymore. You need to wake up now."

Mica was growing uneasy, "Fain, I know not of whom you speak. You talk as if something supernatural was in the air. I think you need another drink, and a dance with the fair Earl's daughter. Come. She's waiting for you inside, no doubt."

Mica led Colin back inside but his brother had vanished. Mica looked around in bewilderment. The ballroom had faded, only the Earl's blonde haired, blue-eyed daughter remained. As he watched, she morphed into a woman who started to climb what looked like a never-ending staircase. He ran after her; somehow she had betrayed him and he wanted answers.

Just as he started up after her, she and the stairs vanished and he was surrounded by darkness. Lightning flashed and Mica closed his eyes, hoping it would go away. He felt himself drifting and suddenly he was awake, staring at a carved ceiling.

Mica groaned in pain. His brain felt as if acid had been poured over it. A peculiar rumbling started in his stomach and he felt bile rise in his throat. Mica had time to roll over before he vomited onto the floor. A thin liquid trickled out, as he had not eaten for several days. His eyes felt on the verge of rolling out of his head, and he groaned again. Dimly he was aware of people entering the room

* * *

The next time Mica woke, it was dark, and oil lamps burned.

He had been aware of a whispering going on, but was unable to tell to whom the voices belonged. He heard a woman say, "He is awake again," and that voice he did know.

"What...what did you do to me you, bitch?" Mica gasped. "Crack my skull open and dose my brain in acid?"

"Not I, what do you remember?" she calmly replied.

He felt his bones melt to jelly and his blood turn to ice. "I swear...first Devon, then Donny and now Nicky."

"Mica!" Colin spoke up, shocked.

He swallowed another rising wave of bile and struggled to sit up in the bed. "Colin," his voice came out harsher than he intended, "you are my brother, but I need you to leave now. For five minutes, no more. NOW!" he shouted.

Mica hated the look of confusion and hurt which crossed his brother's face, and promised himself he would make it up to him. Once Colin had left, the former immortal turned to the striking woman who stood silent, and the man who had been his friend standing next to her.

"What the hell happened in that cell?" he demanded of them, adding, "And none of your fucking lies. You did something, just like you always do, and like always, it fucks everyone over."

"A demon came and attacked you and the boy. Then something else came, as if to your rescue, and battled the demon, but the boy's soul gem shattered, and now you are mortal," Illyria flatly stated.

"Are you daft? I'm still immortal, you lying bitch! To think I thought I could trust a blood-sucking soulless fiend!"

"At least he has his memory back, all of it, and the curse is broken," Eron stated.

Mica glared at them both, wishing he had strength enough to stand up and kick their asses.

"I can prove it to you," Illyria said and snatched at his arm.

"Let go of me!" Mica tried to yank his arm back but her grip was cold iron. He couldn't believe Eron just stood there, but then again, the bastard had always been secretly in love with her.

"Do you not heal instantly if given a moderate cut?" Illyria demanded.

"Crazy bitch!" Mica shouted. He couldn't believe how

absolute her grip was and he tugged again but could not free his arm.

"You're going to pull my arm out of my socket!"

"Answer the question, please," she demanded.

"What was it again?" he asked. Mayhap he could still get away in one piece since she seemed to want to chat.

She sighed and repeated the question. "Of course!"

"Watch, please," Illyria sliced one of her nails across his arm.

A sharp pain blossomed and Mica watched the cut start to bleed. The blood oozed down his arm as the pain persisted. Several moments passed and still the blood flowed, running down his arm, dripping off his elbow to form a puddle on the floor and Mica was starting to feel lightheaded. He realized she had let go of his arm. The cut should have healed by now, leaving no trace.

"What...what the hell! Impossible! You did something to me! This is just one of your mind tricks!" Mica clamped his left hand around the cut and applied pressure. The blood was slippery between his fingers.

"Cut yourself again if you think it illusion. But don't waste the blood."

Mica shuddered in disgust and edged away from her. "You...you'd like that, wouldn't you?"

"I don't want to waste the life dripping on my floor and running down your arm," she replied and licked her lips lavishly.

An expression of horror spread on Mica's face.

"Stop it," Eron said, low-voiced, and stepped in front of her. He snatched a cloth laying on a table and applied pressure to his friend's arm

Mica took over, shaking his head. "You killed Donny, you let the kid escape, you cursed me..."

"Donny got himself killed by not leaving when he was told. Nicky did not escape, and it was the Fae who cursed us all. You are mortal now, however impossible that may seem. I will leave it up to you to decide what kind of a life you wish to live."

"I hate you," he said, "I knew you should have been destroyed the moment the myth became truth." He ripped off the cloth to see the wound had clotted over, but had not healed.

It should have been just a fading reminder by now, but its very existence mocked him. “No,” he whispered, “this can’t be. This is a disaster!” Mica moaned.

“If you insist. Of course, now you can live, take a wife, have children, grow old together, die.”

“Get out of here!” Mica yelled at her and tried to reach for the oil lamp to throw but he was so weak he merely toppled out of bed.

“You’re not helping,” Eron told her. “Let him calm down, it’s a shock to anyone’s system.”

She shrugged. “As you wish,” She left, Colin rushing into the room in her wake.

Chapter Nineteen

Mica stared down into the murky water, watching the bright flashes of the few fish swimming beneath. A cold wind blew on and off, chilling him, but he refused to go inside or get a cloak. There were slaves out working, marking off where new garden beds would be dug come spring. They gave him a wide berth.

Like I was a leper, Mica thought bitterly.

No one truly knew what had become of the little boy. The news left him numb. What was he to do now? The quest had consumed so much of his life he had never stopped to consider "afterwards", though he had never imagined he'd become mortal once more. He didn't think he could live a normal life. Flashes kept popping in his head, memories locked away; they said it would go away, in time.

If he could just feel something, anything, even if it was rage, he might be okay. The immortal heard a soft gasp, and looked up to see a figure frozen a few feet away from him.

The girl looked terrified and he struggled to remember her name. "Mary Elana. You look..." He trailed off.

She flinched, tears welling up in her eyes and she turned, perhaps to flee back to the house.

"No, I'm sorry, don't go. I didn't mean to be rude. I didn't..." He stopped and struggled a moment before going on, "I'm sorry."

She had stopped, shook her head as best as she was able, hurried away to another part of the garden.

Mica hissed to himself, feeling more like an outcast for having chased the girl away. She was covered in healing bruises, and he thought he saw the flash of a slave collar. He knew who had answers, but he just wanted to strangle her when he so much as thought of her.

There came the padding of feet again, and a solicitous inquiry, "Pardon me, sir, Her Grace sent me out to see if perhaps you needed anything? A cloak? Or a hot refreshment?"

So now I'm a child who doesn't know enough to look after himself? He wanted to send the man away, but the cloak did sound good. He let the man drape it around him.

He closed his eyes, the wool slowly warmed him up, and he dozed a bit.

* * *

The strings wailed, alternately sounding happy, sad, seductive. The dark-haired beauty in his arms gracefully arched backwards, then snapped forward and he took her hands. They moved fluidly through the dance, the last one of the night. When the last note had faded into silence, they stood facing each other in an embrace. He didn't really want to let go.

"You can't, I mean, would you, or even could you, I...

"Are you asking me to stay the night? To share more than your bed, knowing I must leave when the sun is about to rise?"

He couldn't help the blush suffusing his face, or the feeling of nerves; she was outside of his experience. "Yes."

"Very well, I accept."

* * *

"Bro! Where did you meet her? She is fine!" Donny enthused.

"She's taken," Mica warned him. He wasn't about to lose another potential protégé to her schemes.

"A guy can look, can't he?" Donny asked. "And man oh man is she some eye candy. I don't suppose there's any chance..."

"No," Mica flatly replied.

* * *

The ear piece crackled, "Crusader, Mica. Where you at, man? Come on, answer. Raptor wants to know where you at." The young man's voice sounded worried, trying to be cool.

How was he to answer when he wasn't sure himself? "Ducat, I'm fine. Just get out of the building. It's trapped, you don't need to be here." There was no reply, he kept looking for a way out, periodically trying to get the boy to respond.

The building shook and rumbled, metal screeching. "Donny! Donny! If you can hear me, say something! Please don't be inside, get out!" There was no response and Mica kept running, trying to keep his footing.

"Donny! Damn it, kid, the whole place is blowing up! Answer me! Are you safe?" Mica dodged falling concrete and metal, not sure if the earpieces even worked anymore. He had to try though.

Mica ran along the roof, making quick snatches of looks back over his shoulder. Section by section, the old building was sending clouds of dust and debris shooting out as each charge went off. He had just started down a rusting ladder when he was blown free.

He remembered running for the SUV, and finding bits of clothing and what could have been pieces of flesh. It looked like Donny's, and he almost collapsed there but Eron was urging him up and on. They would come back, the building was unstable and the mortal rescue personnel would be coming.

"I curse you!"

"No!" Mica howled, never sure if it was out loud or in his mind. "I have to find out what happened to the kid! His remains have to be properly laid to rest! Don't! You can't!"

* * *

He awoke with a wordless shout, and looked around, confused and bleary for a moment. The sun was setting and the wind had picked up. He was stiff from the cold. Painfully, the former immortal stood, huddling inside the cloak and made his way to the mansion. It was warm inside, with the bustle of slaves going about their business. For a moment he thought he was going to be sick, and he swayed, his vision going gray around the edges.

Mica stumbled to a small sitting parlor and collapsed on the nearest couch, where he waited for the sensation to go away. Did she remember the night they had spent together? He thought there had been more than one, over the intervening years. The rage bubbled up; she had gotten the kid killed. He had refused to leave the building; was it because he was in love with her? Because she had led him on?

"You bitch!" he hissed into the silence. He had to know, and now.

Mica hauled himself up, but before he could go and search for her, his brother came into the room. "The slaves said they saw you go in here. You're not getting sick from being out in the cold?"

"I'm fine!" he spat at his brother. "I'm not a child, stop treating me like one."

Colin held his hands up, "I'm not the enemy, bro, sorry. It's just it's been so long since we were, you know, mortal. They're a lot more fragile than us. I mean..." He stopped guiltily.

"You mean than you? Than immortals?" his brother snarled.

His younger brother had the grace to look embarrassed and uncomfortable. "Damn, I don't...Look, it's a big shock. I'm sorry." He was intent. "Just say the word, we'll get the materials, do the ritual. Anyway, I'm uh, going to eat. Supper is ready if you want it." And he left.

Mica stood, fists and teeth clenched. What did he want? He wanted answers, most of all. He was owed answers.

* * *

Mica paced back and forth, making Illyria's guards—Hah! What a laugh!—anxious he would try rushing the door to her office again as they stood blocking it. Behind the men, the plain door opened and the Earl appeared, looking less than satisfied. The very sight of the man made the former Immortal angrier than was rational; he attributed it to the rumors floating around about the Earl and the Duchess.

The nobleman made to ignore him and stalk off when Mica blocked his path and snarled, "Don't believe a word that lying bitch says. If you know what's good for you, you'll stay away from her, before she ruins you and your family with her machinations."

Sydney stiffened. "I shall excuse your rudeness as a by-product of having been illegally imprisoned and tortured, sir, and advise you not to speak of Her Grace in such a manner. Good day to you." He made to move around the man but was blocked.

"Here, now," her guards protested. "None of that."

"Tell me," Mica ignored them and spoke to the man before him, "how was your family before she came and seduced you?"

He watched the Earl's eyes darken in anger, and had a hollow satisfaction in seeing the worry lurking there before the guards each grabbed an arm.

"Stop it. I will not have guests treated with such discourtesy under my roof. I will speak with you, answer your questions, if it will calm your rage and stop you from attacking everyone in my home and those who visit." She stood in her doorway, eyes flaring slightly in rage.

Mica shook off the guards and stalked toward her office. The former immortal made no secret of his anger as he entered the room and she spoke a few words to the departing man and her guards before shutting the door.

He rounded on her before she could move away from the door, slapped his hands to either side of her shoulders and loomed over her. "I.want.answers."

She inclined her head regally. "Is that any reason not to be civilized? I thought you prized it above all else."

"What I prize is the truth, which seems to be in short supply for you."

"Correct me if I'm wrong, but I seem to recall you having trouble handling the truth when it doesn't fit into your world view."

"Is that what you call the lies you tell people that get them killed, bring ruination and destruction to all they love and hold dear?"

She merely regarded him, waiting for him to say something else. He had forgotten this aspect of her, and now she was giving him her full attention, waiting for him to finish ranting. He just didn't know what to bring up first.

What came out was, "Did you sleep with my protégé?"

She was startled enough to reply, "I have better taste than that, thank you very much!" After a beat, she added, "Why is it everyone seems so concerned with whom I choose for my lovers? Do I ask you who you sleep with?"

"Not Devon!" he roared at her, "Donny! Is that why he ignored orders to get out of the building? He was worried about you because you slept with him and you know damn well the effect you have on men. Is that why he's dead? You toyed with him and made him think there was more to your *friendship*," he spit, "than there really was."

"Donny was happy with our flirtation; he knew he had no chance with me. I think he stayed because he was concerned about you," she quietly replied. "You were the first male who took an interest in him as a person, the only one who let him make his mistakes and yet still stood by and helped. He looked up to you, you were a hero to him. You were more than a friend, you were a father figure."

He stood there, listening to her, and began to sag.

"I told him to get out, the same as you did. He mentioned his concern when you didn't answer. I told him you were okay, you knew how to take care of yourself. It was more important he get out, we were all leaving."

Mica's hands lowered and he staggered back and half-sat on the edge of her desk, facing her. "I never heard you say a word."

"The ear units' ability to transmit had been compromised. I liked Donny, I wished him the best. He was certainly better than the ex-convict you tried to mentor."

Her words, while logical, did nothing to take the edge off his rage; he didn't know anymore who was lying to him, and who wasn't. "Oh, you mean the one you murdered?"

"A simple 'thank you' would suffice. He was trying to blackmail you in the end, am I not remembering correctly?"

He didn't answer her; he was caught up in the past and what he had been told by his ex-friend. "Eron thinks Donny is still alive, suffering, buried under who knows how much dirt, rock, and rubble. He said he saw the explosion that took the kid out."

"If he was that close, he should have been trapped as well."

"He said he was in one of the control rooms, and saw it on a monitor before they were destroyed."

"I'm sorry about Donny, Mica, he was a good kid. I will help you lay him to rest if it is what you wish." She looked at him a moment, came over and stood behind one of the chairs near her desk. "Eron has already castigated me over those events, explained what you and he never had the chance to do because of the curse. I am sorrier about Donny's suffering then I can make you believe."

She paused, gently continuing, "What is really the problem? It's more than who I choose for my lovers; how I live." She waited, as she had always done when he felt a need to unburden himself.

He had to stop and take a breath as the memories of the past crowded in, wanting to smother him.

"I'm tired," he whispered. "I don't know who to believe anymore, who to trust." He struggled for air. "Tired of all the games, all the lies, the need to hide who and what I am...was. I... I don't know if I can live like this."

"Colin loves you, always has, always will. He will support you, but none of us can truly help you with your decision."

"I can't...This place... I don't..." Why could he not get air? Why was it hard to just say what he needed to? Why was he feeling so damn emotional all of a sudden?

"I will see you are furnished with whatever you feel is needed for your life and whatever direction you feel you want to take. I hope you will be comfortable staying here until then? Or perhaps you would prefer a room at the Silver Thorn?"

The now-mortal felt he couldn't breathe. Her words didn't want to make any sense to him, but he understood what she said.

He could only make a few ridiculous sounds of disbelief. "You really think that's going to make up for everything? I'm not one of your minions to be paid off to keep quiet."

"I am sorry this quest of yours didn't turn out the way you planned, but don't take it out on me. We're all hurting from being cursed."

"Oh, I see how much you're hurting."

She stopped, took a moment to control her rising temper. "I only lost memories of friends and lovers. You lost more than I. I repeat, I regret, bitterly, I didn't understand the hell your protégé has been in all this time."

He snorted in contempt.

"We were more than friends, for a night or two. I don't know if you still want to be friends, but I will do this for you: give you what you need, because of what we once had, and because I do still care."

He just stared at her; his world had been shattered, he found upon awaking, and now it was shattering again. He felt each and every one of his several thousand years of life. Mica staggered to a chair and fell into it, sprawled in misery. The silence stretched out between them. He remembered the time they had spent in some Spanish-speaking country. He had been happy, carefree for once, not dreading the empty, long centuries before him. The man didn't know who he despised the most at that moment: himself, or her. It was an effort to stand, an even greater one to walk to the door and open it. He paused in the doorway, wanting to say more, but decided against it and left, shutting it behind him.

Chapter Twenty

Mica found himself wandering aimlessly about the mansion, questions rattling around inside his head. *What do I want? I have a chance to be mortal again, marry and raise a family, die with them. I can leave this all behind. But do I want to?*

Once more he found himself outside and wandering aimlessly around the gardens. It was full dark out, and the temperature had dropped significantly. A few flakes of snow drifted down and melted. Soon they would pile up, and the people would be huddled in what shelter they could find. Many would starve; he might even be one of them. Mica realized with shock, *I'd be dead, no coming back.* This disturbed him; he wasn't sure if it was because he was so used to the advantages he had enjoyed being immortal, or if he had become that afraid of living since he could truly die now.

He needed someone to talk to, but there was no one he felt he could trust, not even his brother. The man walked around the garden, toward the stables, and training grounds for the female army, out through the paddocks, up to the start of the mountains. He found a handy boulder, sat on it, thinking. He was oblivious to the cold, to the biting wind, to the fact he was shivering. Mica tucked his hands under his armpits and continued walking.

He followed the line of rock until it dropped away to his left and a sheer wall of rock blocked his forward momentum. Below the river swirled, black and undoubtedly cold. He stood there, staring at it, almost hypnotized.

What do I really want? he kept asking himself as he stared at the shadows. *Do I want to live, grow old and die? Do I want to be immortal again?*

Mica turned to the mountain beside him. It was hard to see the path, if there was one. *Not that way, That way is nothing.*

The man started the opposite direction, walking along the edge of the cliff which sloped down to the roadway and the bridge. The guards challenged him, and let him pass as he muttered some answer, his mind swirling. Mica walked, ignoring the chill which seeped into every pore.

The ruined town was silent. Large areas had been cleared, a few new buildings had gone up, but for the most part the place was still a mess. Mica found himself heading toward the river, where a few ramshackle buildings, mostly ale houses, and a few places for the sailors to sleep had managed to escape the fire.

He wasn't even sure if he had coin on his person as he made his way into the press of men and half-clothed women. He groped in his money pouch and found a few lower-denomination coins. He sat on a rickety stool at the end of the bar, in the dark, and drank.

The former immortal forgot humans could get drunk so quickly. He had been too used to his body throwing off the effects, so he had had to drink several bottles of the hard stuff to even begin to feel what was commonly called a buzz. Now, after only three mugs of the potent brew, he no longer cared about where he was, who he was, or the danger swirling around him. A muzzy smile tugged the corners of his lips up.

"Hey sweetie, you lookin' fer some companionship?" An arm draped around his shoulder, and strong B.O. assailed his nose.

Mica turned his head to see a fairly clean woman by his side. In his hazy state, he thought she looked good. "Not really," he said as polite as he could.

She pouted, and rubbed a shoulder. "You look like you could use something, take the sadness outta your eyes," the woman persisted.

Mica gave a tight smile; he didn't have enough coin, and wasn't about to say so. Instead he lifted his mug. "I'm fine. Got my medicine right here." He took another mouthful.

The prostitute gave one last pout and let her arm slip off, "You change your mind, baby, you just ask for Mazie." She turned to the man beside Mica and was already chatting him up as Mica sipped again..

* * *

His head hurt, as did various other parts of him, and he was fast clueing in to the fact he was cold and wet. Mica forced his eyes open, groaned and immediately shut them again. After the nausea subsided, he tried again. Daylight was harsh and pitiless. The sky overhead more white than blue, the clouds a steel gray. He couldn't quite remember all of last night. Mica knew he had been drinking in some waterfront tavern, he had been propositioned... Then, nothing.

He forced himself upright, and immediately wished he hadn't as the world spun and his stomach heaved and he spewed up the contents. Mica felt a little better. Through streaming eyes, he saw he had been dumped in a stinking, filthy alley way. He was missing boots, shirt, pants, cloak, and money belt. The wind was like a knife against his naked body. He staggered up, wincing as his feet squished in the mud and who knew what else.

Mica's head still pounded, and he had a hard time breathing. When he swallowed, his throat burned and he was unsure if it was from the force of his vomiting or because he had caught cold from being dumped outside in the wet mud, naked.

"Damn it!" he swore to himself. "I know better."

He picked his way out of the alley, headed toward the stone bridge and Illyria's residence. He ignored the stares, laughter, and insults hurled after him. Mica was exhausted when he finally stumbled into the mansion, shivering violently. The first person he ran into was Colin.

His brother gaped in shock, and blanched at the ripe smell emanating from his brother. "Are you..." he began but was ignored as Mica stumbled for his room.

Colin wondered if his brother would answer any questions, but didn't think so. He went in search of Eron, and found him in meetings with Her Grace's men of business. His friend made a few moments of time for him.

"Look, you know as well as I my brother doesn't just go out and get drunk for no reason. At least, not since we had been mortal and young. He's way past that stage."

"He's had a big shock, Colin. I'd be drinking too much as

well, if I was him."

"No, you wouldn't. You'd probably plot how to get revenge, or what you planned on doing with your life.

"Me, yes, your brother, no. Give him time. He'll come around."

* * *

Mica stood swaying in the doorway to his room. He couldn't seem to stop the violent shivers wracking his body.

"Pardon me, sir," a male voice spoke. "Would you like the tub brought round so you may bathe?"

The man half-turned to see the slave assigned to his room standing outside the door. The slave's words barely penetrated the haze inside his head, and he stared idly around the room. Mica didn't know how long he stood, lost in thought. The next thing he knew, slaves had entered his space. They set up the cured leather tub and filled it with hot water. Another slave had started a fire in the fireplace. He was gently led to the tub and helped in.

The room was in darkness when next Mica floated up out of his stupor. His head ached and felt full of wool. His throat was on fire, and he kept alternating between being unbearably hot then cold. There was a cup of cool liquid next to him, and he picked it up in a shaking hand and tried to drink the contents. It soothed his throat somewhat, and he lay back down, drifting into sleep again.

Thank you for reading!
If you enjoyed the series so far, please spread the word.

Send Me Feedback:

If you have questions about the series, want to point out errors and typos, want to know how to become one of my beta readers or just embarrass me with totally undeserved adulation, I urge you to send me an email at

slfiguhr@gmail.com

I love to hear from readers and try to answer every email.

Share your Opinion:

If you enjoy the Immortalibus Bella series, please let others know, either by twitter, Facebook,wordpress, blogger, or your social media of choice and recommend to your friends.

Write reviews:

Most of the sites where you can buy ebooks or paperback copies have a way for you to post a review, so you can share with other readers whether a book or story merits their attention. The importance of reviews should not be underestimated. With 350,000 new books published, it's difficult for writers to get exposure for their novels.

Connect With Me Online:

http://slfiguhr.com/

Twitter: https://twitter.com/SLFiguhr

Facebook: http://facebook.com/SLFiguhr.Author

Look for Book 3 of Immortalibus Bella
Coming Summer 2014

www.ingramcontent.com/pod-product-compliance
Lightning Source LLC
LaVergne TN
LVHW020712110826
845149LV00012B/2223

* 9 7 8 0 9 9 1 1 4 9 8 3 4 *